THE WAR DEVIL

SPIRIT TAMER : BOOK ONE

J. B. MEDLIN

ISBN: 979-8-9909635-0-4

Printed in the United States of America

CHAPTER ONE
DEVOTION

Ten minutes.

That's all the time Black Dog needed to know whether she'd wasted the last six months trying to survive, or if she was already dead.

The sky pulsed red from a new firefight hundreds of miles away. At every turn, she was met with soldiers' radio chatter sounding off a little too close for comfort, or the occasional drone gliding over the remnants of a bombed-out building. No one had spotted her walking, or if they had, they didn't understand the threat she represented.

Stepping through the final roundabout, her destination materialized around the corner. The broken sign of Malarc's Steak House loomed over her approach.

***

Inside she was met with an empty hostess station. She wiped the sweat from her face and stood in the darkened dining area. The only other light bleeding into the room was from the kitchen. Black Dog scanned the tables, chairs, and booths in the dim morning light. The musty smell of rotting wood surrounded her.

"Alice." Her voice echoed against the high ceiling. "We need to talk."

A pair of heels clicked against a tile floor from deep within the building, and a deceptively young woman wearing pale blue latex gloves and a two-piece suit appeared from the kitchen.

"So good to see you, Black Dog." Her pale blue eyes glowed from the doorway. She held the door open and nodded behind her. "It's not safe to talk so close to the front. Would you mind coming back here?"

"I thought this area was safe."

"It was," Alice said, "but there was an... accident, that may bring some attention to our activities here."

Hesitating at the sight of the surgical gloves, Black Dog stepped past the hostess station toward the swinging doors. A rancid but familiar smell struck her nose as she walked into the kitchen. Fresh blood dripped down the back wall to a puddle on the floor. Lined along the serving table on her right were a row of instruments, and knives not intended to prepare a meal. But the thing that caught her eye was a pair of empty military fatigues hanging from the sprinkler with the nametag <u>Lt. Seawood</u> embroidered on them.

"I apologize for the mess," Alice said, snapping off her latex gloves and leaning against a metal prep table. "I was just finishing up some business before you arrived." She slipped on a smile and lowered her head. "How are things going?"

Black Dog's back tensed up as she took in the full scene before her. In the light of the kitchen, there wasn't a speck of blood on Alice. Not even on the gloves she had tossed away. The only other sound throughout the building came from the humming fluorescent lights above. They weren't alone. Pushing the thought away she said, "I want to know the current status of the War Devil."

"They've departed from the station and have a rough landing zone outside the city. Given the current timeline, they'll arrive on Verra next week at the latest."

"Do you have the landing zone coordinates?"

"Of course." Alice nodded. "If you'll give me your Molecular Codex, I can upload a general location."

Black Dog reached into her left pocket and pulled out a black rectangular device.

"You do realize," Alice said rolling back the sleeves on her left arm, "you'll have three weeks to repay your debts."

"That's plenty of time," Black Dog said, nodding.

Alice winced as she plugged the MC into a port in her arm. "If you don't, we'll be forced to repossess your synthetics. Which would likely kill you, but it would also leave a permanent negative mark on your account."

"I didn't ask for your opinion."

"Just an observation," Alice said, unplugging the MC and handing it back to her. "Mind if I ask you a question?"

"Yes. Are we done?"

Alice let out a deep sigh. "Who's the girl you've been working with?"

"None of your damn business."

"Right." Alice strained a smile. "A word of advice. As an Overman Agent, you shouldn't make personal relationships."

"And why's that?"

"For someone who's so cautious about your colleagues double-crossing you, I'm surprised that isn't obvious."

"I think I can decide on my own who I can trust."

"All I'm saying is that you should be careful. Given what we are."

"I know what I am," Black Dog said.

Alice raised an eyebrow. "Do you?"

"It's been a pleasure working with you, Alice." The row of fluorescent lights was still screaming above them. Black Dog turned to leave.

"Just remember," Alice said, staring down at the floor, "we'll be watching your progress, closely."

Black Dog was already out the door.

***

Light streamed down through the gaping hole in the middle of the parking garage, as a gust of cold air blew from the main road. Nadia was laying down on her sleeping bag, flipping through a pile of magazines. Another cold breeze blew through the garage, rippling across the pages. She stood up, grabbed a copy of Ageus, and walked over to a barrel Black Dog had set up. The pages flipped open, and her eyes drifted over them.

> *Ageus Magazine has moved away from the digital format of the past, and works to provide a more accountable form of media. We stand behind the articles we produce. The written form cannot be edited later, cannot be deleted when they do not match our opinion. Our articles will exist as is throughout the ages.*

Nadia ripped out the pages from the magazine and threw them with the scrap wood lying at the bottom of the barrel. Taking the last page, she lit the corner with her lighter and tossed it in before sitting back down on her sleeping bag.

Lighting a cigarette, she grabbed a handful of magazines from the pile. She tossed an article titled "Adam Columbus Assassinated," instead, she was drawn towards a picture of a woman with white eyes. The headline read,

A Light Amongst the Darkness.

The unique half-smile she wore looked friendly enough Nadia thought, but there was something unsettling about her eyes. They came off as cold and inhuman. She flipped the page to the listed article and took a moment to read. "Ada Coronis: An Overman representative tasked with Public Health and Relations."

The article went on to detail various contributions Ada had made to hospitals, orphanages, and mental health institutions. Full scholarships for medical schools that the Overman Corporation offered, as well as a handful of open forums provided to both provide and receive feedback in regards to Overman involvement.

On the next page a team of firefighters battled the inferno that had engulfed a hospital. The article described the terrorist attacks against various healthcare facilities. There was a list of buildings hit, as well as a kidnapping case of a college student. It also noted an assassination attempt on Ada during an open forum and the escalation of Federation forces in the city. Another gust of wind rippled across the magazines as Black Dog returned to the garage. Nadia lit up another cigarette.

"You really ought to kick that habit," Black Dog said, walking past her, staring at the <u>D</u> engraved on the lighter. "They're going to kill you."

Nadia shook her head. "You're such a hypocrite."

Black Dog glanced up. "How's that?"

7

"I've seen the needles and vials you keep in your back pocket. Don't pretend you don't use them."

Black Dog walked up to her, rolling up her sleeve. "Does this look like I use a needle?"

Nadia looked over the arm. Not even a hint of any sort of old puncture point to be found over her arm. She blew out a puff of smoke over the arm, before shaking her head.

"Then maybe you shouldn't jump to conclusions." She pulled her sleeve back down. "And don't rummage through my stuff."

Nadia rolled her eyes, lowering her head, while watching her from the corner of her eye. "Why do you have them then?"

Black Dog had opened the case, checking the vials. "They're for work."

"What do you do for work?" Nadia asked, flipping a page while keeping her eye on her.

"I told you before," Black Dog said, as she ran her thumb over the blank labels on the vials. "I can't tell you what I do."

Nadia studied her as she closed the magazine.

Black Dog snapped the case closed and said, "Start packing your things." She stared out towards the street, with her hand inching towards the compacted Marlow in her front pocket.

"Why?" Nadia said, following her gaze. A man and a woman holding a small child were walking up the street.

"I'd like to move someplace else."

"Where are we going?" Nadia said.

"I don't know," Black dog said, "I just don't feel safe here. I'd rather move farther out into a more barren area. I think that would be best."

Nadia blew a puff of smoke "I'm getting really sick of all this."

"It's only temporary," Black Dog said. "We'll get through this. Together."

"You've been saying that for two months." Nadia shook her head. "Why should I keep helping you?" She tilted her head toward her. "It feels like you're just using me. Do you know how hard it is to pickpocket a PDA from a soldier, and then put it back without them noticing?"

Black Dog glared back at her before grabbing her throat and slamming her into the ground.

"Now you listen to me," Black Dog said through her teeth, "you think you can survive out there? On your own? Remember what it was like before we met? Remember what I've done for you? What I've given you? I love you. Don't make me hurt you."

Nadia was choking back the tears as Black Dog kissed her forehead, before pushing off of her neck and walking back across the room.

"You'll thank me when we get out of this," Black Dog said, zipping up her bag. "Now let's get moving. While the sun is still out."

***

They rode around on the Prowler, crisscrossing between the streets. It raced down the street floating atop four large spherical tires made up of thick brown rubber and sheets of metal. Sparks flew out of the four thin steel cages surrounding the tires from months of amateurish repairs that had been made to keep them running. Through the thick scratched up dashboard, Black Dog could see her speed, fusion engine temperature, coolant levels, and the state of the multi-praxis gear.

She spotted the street she was looking for and rotated the handles jutting out of the dashboard, then shifted the various gears at her feet. Through the mess of wires and gears surrounding each portion of the wheels, two of the four arms above the wheels moved. As she turned the rough mosaic of welded scraps of metal making up the undercarriage barely scraped against the road. Eventually Black Dog stopped at the mouth of a T-Intersection with a crumpled spotlight lying across the middle of the street

"Wait here," she said, as she hopped off rough leather saddle and walked down the street.

Nadia sat back on the Prowler, studying the broken buildings around her. Altero's Hardware store sat on the corner beside her. Following the street, a barren field that may have been a park at some point, but was now just filled with dry dead grass. Behind the field, was a row of burned buildings from an old Federation bombing run. They looked residential, but it was hard to tell from their burned corpses. Even further down the road was a Helios fueling station. Maybe she could find some new magazines there.

"I found an apartment building that should work for us," Black Dog said, walking back.

"Okay."

"This place seems dead." She switched the Prowler to neutral.

Nadia hopped off the Prowler and followed Black Dog into the main lobby. The windows were broken, and the inner foyer was littered with debris from the ceiling and broken tables. Black Dog left the Prowler out in the street as she walked up a flight of stairs at the back of the building. They stopped at an apartment on the third floor at the end of the hall.

"I think this place would be best," Black Dog said. "It'll give me a good vantage point for the road. All we need to do is move around some of the furniture, and we'll be good."

Nadia hugged her arms as she stared through the gash in the room that punctured through the ceiling and outer wall.

"Here are some new rules," Black Dog said staring at her. "I don't want you sneaking around. I want you to stay where I can see you. I don't want you talking to anyone. About me, what we do, or who we've been working over. At night, you are to stay inside, you sleep, you eat, and then we work together to get through this."

"Fine," Nadia said still staring out the gaping hole in the wall.

"Would you look at me, and tell me that you understand?"

Nadia glared at her. "I understand."

"Then repeat it back."

"You don't want me to sneaking around. You don't want me talking to anyone. Got it." She turned towards the hole, and pulled out her lighter and a cigarette.

Black Dog took a deep breath before standing up and walking towards her. "And no more cigarettes." She snatched it out of her mouth.

"What the fuck!"

"You can pick it back up when you're old enough to know better."

"No. Fuck you. Who the hell do you think you are? I've done plenty well by myself before I ever met you."

Black Dog slapped her across the face. "Really? Is that why you found yourself in a whore house? When I found you, five men were on the verge of killing you. Want me to give you back to them? It seems like everything you've done without me has been utter shit. How about you trust me for once? Huh?" She threw the cigarette to the ground and smashed it out. "Give me the rest of them." She held out her hand.

Nadia stared down at the ground, with her arms folded.

"I said give me the rest of them!" Black Dog said, jutting her hand closer to her.

Nadia reached into her back pocket and shoved the pack into her hand.

"And the lighter," Black Dog said, still holding out her hand.

"For fuck's sake," Nadia said, staring up at the ceiling.

"The lighter."

Nadia shoved the engraved lighter into her hand. "There. Happy now?"

"Yes." Black Dog pocketed the items. "You'll see I'm right, one day. And you'll thank me."

After moving a bed into the side of the room for Nadia, Black Dog collapsed on a couch behind a half-wall beside the hole. She watched the moon passing overhead, listening to the wind ripple across the windows. Nadia was laying with her back to her.

***

When Black Dog woke up, her eyes were locked on the empty bed. She jumped up scanning the empty room in the faint morning light. Not a sound from the hallway. Her hand reached back and gripped the .22 Marlow, a compacted SMG; it looked like a small thin rectangular slab of metal with groves and lines cut into it, along with a trigger stuck in the middle. The thin metal expanded into its full form. Seconds passed. The gun's mechanical heartbeat ticked as a newly formed bullet fell into the chamber. Staring at the empty doorway, she was met with the sound of the wind brushing against the windows. The bullets kept ticking into the chamber and thumping against her hand.

Then came a faint laugh under the breath of the wind. Black Dog gripped the edge of the couch as she strained to hear. Between the clicks of the gun and the song of the wind, more bits of words began to drift to her. Highway. Garage. Prowler. Her eyes sharpened when she heard the name Conway. It was all coming to her clearer now. Network maintainers. Murdering them. Sweat beaded up on her forehead, and ran down her cheeks. The voices sounded like they were right underneath her.

"Something big's coming..." Nadia's voice clearly said. "Next week. I'll get you more details."

After a moment of staring at the blackened outline of the doorway, footsteps began coming up from the stairs, growing louder as they entered the hallway.

Nadia emerged from the darkness, and jumped at the sight of the gun. "What's going on?" she asked.

"Who were you talking to?" Black Dog growled from her couch.

"What?"

"I said, who were you talking to?"

"I wasn't talking to anyone."

"Bullshit." Black Dog glared at her. "I could fucking hear you from up here."

"I don't know what the fuck you heard, but I wasn't talking to anyone."

"Then where were you?"

"I---" She locked her sights with the barrel of the gun pointed at her. "I was outside having a smoke."

"Don't you lie to me," Black Dog said, shaking her head. "I took your cigarettes. Remember?"

13

"And I took them back."

Black Dog laughed. "I think I would notice that."

"Then check."

"I'm not doing a damn thing." Black Dog stared at her. "I gave you clear rules. I told you. To stay here through the night. I told you not to speak with anyone. And you broke them."

"I didn't--"

"Stop lying to me!" Black Dog took a deep breath. Her finger was shaking over the trigger. "Don't make me hurt you."

Nadia's eyes still locked on the barrel. "I don't know what you want me to say." She said, snapping her attention back to Black Dog. "But I'm telling you. I haven't talked to anyone."

Black Dog's finger twitched.

With a flash, the bullet ripped through Nadia's head, and embedded itself into the wall.

Black Dog stared at the crumbled body across the room, as her eyes adjusted. "Get up."

No response. She still had the gun pointed forward. A pool of blood flowed out of Nadia's head.

"I said get up."

The gun was shaking in her hand now, her eyes were locked on the still body. "Please get up."

The wind snuck in through the hole, pinching the hot tears that were streaming down her face. "Please."

As the sun rose, it only revealed the more morbid details of the scene. The vast amounts of blood on the floor, the grey matter along the floor and walls, and the solitary bullet that caused it all.

Black Dog hadn't moved beyond dropping the gun beside her. She had her face covered still looking at the scene through the gaps of her fingers, taking in deep breaths as the hours passed. Her mouth was dry as the sun was finally setting.

"I had to," she finally said wiping away the snot and tears that had been running down her face. "I had to." She gave a quick sniff. "She was lying." She was shaking her head. "I know she was, why else was she out? I have the cigarettes and lighter." She avoided the body and was staring at the ceiling. "She was selling me out, I know she was. That's what she does. That's..." she pursed her lips. "That's what she did."

Biting her lips, she stared at the body, taking in deep, shallow breaths. Pulling herself together enough to push off the bed, she grabbed Nadia by her legs and dragged her out of the room, her body leaving a crimson trail in its wake. Each thud of her head on the stairs was another punch to the heart. Black Dog pushed past it, dragging the body through the lobby, and out the front door.

When Nadia was in the middle of the road, Black Dog focused on the end of the street as she reached into the back of her pocket for the lighter, but felt nothing. The blood from her face drained. She checked her other back pocket, and was met only with her case of vials. Her front pockets were barren as well. Nothing was in either of her coat pockets.

Her eyes fell down to Nadia's body. She reached into Nadia's back pocket, and felt the cigarettes and the metal lighter with the $\underline{D}$ engraving. With hands clasped holding the lighter in hand, she clutched Nadia's shirt to wipe away the tears.

It was early into the evening when she finally composed herself. Drenching the body in gasoline, she sat away and watched Nadia's body burn in the middle of the road as the darkness fell over her. She still clutched the pack of cigarettes and the lighter. The blackened skin bubbled and melted off the white bones, and dripped into the streets.

Black Dog pulled out a cigarette and held it loose against her lips. Striking the hammer on the lighter, it lit. She took a deep breath and blew the smoke away.

CHAPTER TWO
BLACK DOG

The War Devil was prepping for the final approach. It's thick segmented armor brushed against loose straps, as it floated it's way towards the computer terminal at the front of the drop-pod. In the faint light of the compartment, the outer armor had the appearance of bleached bone equipped over a black hexagonal mesh. They were a few minutes away for entering the upper stratosphere. Black crescent moon eyes were reflecting in the screen.

Red lights started strobing through the inner compartment as a high-pitched scream erupted from the on-board computer. Zecona was awake, but stayed relaxed inside the War Devil. From the monitor it looked like they were about to start cutting into the upper atmosphere. The battle suit strapped itself into the safety harness bracing, as Zecona stared through the green visor at the pulsing red light. A giant tube of red-hot steel tore through the afternoon sky before crashing into the ground. The impact brought back a familiar weightlessness to Zecona.

A quick garbled chirp killed the screaming speakers and the inner compartment was thrown into pitch black as the roar of metal tearing the earth enveloped them. It came to a jolting halt against the side of a broken concrete wall. Smoke and dust rose from the scar left in the earth. The white letters **P67** were still visible on its side.

Unlatching the safety harness, the War Devil stood up in the narrow space inside the drop-pod. Its sensor kicked on, allowing it to find the hatch and ladder in the dark. Grabbing a backpack as it climbed the ladder, it flipped the handle and punched the roof of the capsule causing a loud thump to ripple over the outer metallic surface. Heat from entry caused the outer metal to melt over the gaps in the hatch. A metallic arm ripped through the top, and the suit climbed out. The white figure stood in the sun, glancing back at the scorched earth.

The War Devil was crouched on the wreckage. Its signature horns jutted out behind its helmet. The tan horizon reflected hard against its black crescent moon eyes. A mixture of heat and sound sensors embedded under the helmet's outer armor allowed it to see through most objects in 360 degrees. No optical sensors were present making it effectively colorblind as it scanned the surrounding landscape.

Zecona had his eyes extra wide open inside of the suit as he stared out at the black and grey landscape simulated in the helmet. He had to concentrate on not tensing up as the suit shot low electrical impulses manipulating the nerves and muscles in his body. This gave the suit the movement it needed to look and move around while he was inside of it. Though weeks of training seemingly faded away as he felt the full weight of the planet beneath him for the first time. His eyes twinged as a quick pulse shot through his neck, and the suit shifted its attention back to the west. The suit jumped off the capsule.

"We're here?" Zecona asked inside the suit behind his gritted cat like teeth.

"We're here." A deep male voice answered back. Across the visor a blue grid appeared with geographic markings spanning 500 meters in all directions. "Our rendezvous is a couple hundred meters." It pointed west "That way."

The War Devil turned its attention to the capsule and pressed its right hand against the metal before shifting its consciousness into its simulated mind's eye.

Mentally it was running through a list of weapons it could create, while sub-processes analyzed the available material throughout the capsule. It settled on four weapons. A KRISER-92XG Battle Rifle, two mid-century refurbished Desert Eagles, and a KIROX.

Confirming its final selection, it felt the credits removed from its account, as a shock-wave of energy shook through the capsule. Molecules of the metal, silicon, gold, plastic, and carbon aboard the drop pod snapped apart. The molecules converged and reformed into a long rectangular steel box leaving a husk of the shuttle behind. A handle popped up beneath the suit's palm; it grabbed the case and pulled it to the ground.

The War Devil stood, concentrating for a moment. Thick jets of white steam and a cocktail of gases shot through the spaces in the armor, and it transformed into a large metallic spider clinging to Zecona's back.

Zecona felt the rush of air pull out of his lungs, and he coughed as he entered the atmosphere for the first time, and collapsed to the ground.

"You ok?" The spider said as it climbed up higher on his back.

"Give me a minute," Zecona gasped.

His snake-like head jerked back from the sun as its hawk eyes squinted to adjust. He dug his three slender fingers into the dirt to balance himself, and pushed himself up.

The Abotian Zecona stood tall where the suit had been before. He looked to the west. The distant blue shimmering towers broke across the horizon. Smoke and dust enveloped them as they stared to the east. The circle of the sun hung like a glowing sphere through the black veil. Tan earth lay before him against the hot sun shimmering like gold with tall silver and black metal beams breaking through the ground like sparse, thin trees. They casted long, twisting shadows amongst the crumbling walls of concrete. As he scanned the western horizon, the spider worked its way down to Zecona's wrist.

"That way?" Zecona said, pointing to the west.

"Yes, that way," the spider said, wrapping its legs around his wrist.

"And what am I looking for again?"

"A black dog in the valley."

Zecona glanced back up from his wrist, before bending down and opening the backpack. He pulled out a yellow and black sweatshirt jacket and a pair of shoes. Throwing on the jacket, he bent over and slipped on the shoes, working his two oversized toes into the folds. Turning his attention to the box, he opened it, strapped the compacted rifle to his back, and pocketed the two Desert Eagles into his inner coat pockets. The programmable clips he threw into his rucksack. He was about to walk away when he spotted the metal baton sticking out at the bottom of the cargo case. Picking it up, he studied it before shrugging and chucking it into the bottom of the backpack. Jumping up, he started making his way over the rubble.

Glancing back, his eyes followed the trail of smoke created by the drop. It could probably be seen for miles. Scavengers would swoop by and strip the remaining metal. Once they got into the hull, they would probably try to reuse any computer parts they could, any that hadn't been fried after landing.

He flapped his jacket to cool himself down. The sports jacket was a bad idea in the summer sun. There was hardly a breeze in the area. Sweat was starting to stick between his thin gray shirt and back. Walking westward along the rubble, his toes gripped the rocks through the shoes. Zecona turned his attention to the jagged outline of the city on the horizon. As the excitement from the landing subsided, gravity sickness began to replace it. This didn't feel like home. Home was five years across the star system aboard a midsized wheel station with artificial gravity, and filled with stale recycled air to breathe from birth to death.

His foot jerked off the angled concrete. Grabbing hold of the slab below him, he jumped down to the road and continued on his way. The sun was hanging lower in the sky. Taking in a deep breath, he choked on the stinging smell of soil and concrete around him. This was his first time planet-side. He glanced up at the clouds trying to catch his breath and started to take in the full scale of the area around him. This wasn't being simulated within a fifty-foot room. This was real.

Zecona stuck to the side of the road along the ruined buildings. Glancing at the road he saw an intersection ahead of him. Turning left down the intersection he instantly spotted a dark vertical silhouette of a person walking down the road. They both froze.

"I'm looking for a Black Dog," he yelled to them.

A woman's voice called back, "I saw one in the valley."

Zecona smiled as he strode towards her. The woman reached into her pocket and pulled out a cigarette. He held out his hand "Zecona Giovanni."

She glanced up at him taking out a lighter. Her amber eyes lit up like fire in the sun light. Ignoring his hand she said, "Welcome to Verra."

Zecona forced a smile as he lowered his hand. "What's your name?"

Lighting up her cigarette, he could make out a faint **D** engraved on the lighter. She pulled a short drag off the cigarette. "Stray dogs don't have names," she said, turning and walking away.

He walked up beside her. "Well, what do you go by?"

"Whatever floats your boat." She stared down the path.

"How about D?"

She narrowed her thin almond eyes at him. "Why D?"

"It's etched into your lighter."

She mumbled something under her breath. He shifted his gaze back down the trail. "Well, what would you prefer?"

"D's fine." She pulled a long deep drag from the cigarette and flicked the ash to the ground. She eyed the mechanical spider clinging to his wrist. "Is that the War Devil?"

He followed her gaze. "Yeah."

She stared forward. He shoved his hands into his coat pockets and slipped the spider off. Their boots crunched along the broken bits of concrete and asphalt along the road. They walked in between broken piles of brick and plaster. The concrete and metal beams between the buildings twisted sharper and more jagged the further they walked. A faint series of pops echoed in the distance in front of them. White and black sand blew across the road, with the asphalt beneath them turning blacker the deeper they walked forward into the city.

"So, what will I be doing for you?" Zecona asked.

"You don't need to worry about that right now," D said.

He stared at her. "I think it's kinda important. Nobody's really told me anything."

She shook her head. "You're under my orders. Right?" She glanced at him.

"No, I'm under the War Devil's orders," he said staring at her.

Her eyes narrowed on him. "And the suit is following my orders. Which means you're under my orders, too, smartass." She jerked her head back towards the road. "So follow them." She pulled another long drag. "Don't worry about what you're doing here yet." She pushed out a long trail of smoke. "I wasn't ready for you anyways."

He stared ahead of them. "You sure got to where we were awfully fast."

"I'd been waiting for an hour at the position. I could see you coming in about a mile or so away."

"Ah. What do you do for Overman?"

She focused ahead. "Whatever's necessary." She flicked some more ash off the cigarette. "Mostly contract work for the Federation, with Overman acting as the go-between."

"Uh-huh," Zecona said, staring ahead of them. They were coming up to a gaping hole in the road. "So I take it you're not, like, one of them?"

She looked over at him. "What do you mean?"

"You know, one of those Androids Overman has to Spy. A Silver Geko or something like that?"

D pushed out another pillar of smoke. "No."

"I see." He was staring down into the pit. They came to an incline from what was the road leading into the opening of a maintenance tunnel underground.

She flicked the cigarette into a ruined door frame. "We'll have to use the sewer system to get deeper into the city."

23

"Why?"

"Because it's easier. Not as many patrols to deal with."

He gazed down at the gaping hole. "Doesn't seem so bad."

Glancing over at him, "You've never spent any time in a sewer have you?"

She led the way down the ramp. Holding up a flashlight from her pocket, she clicked it on. Multiple sharp clicks echoed off the concrete walls away from them as they walked forward. Everything was pitch black, except for the flashlight. Exposed rusted pipes lined the walls.

"How long have you been here?" Zecona said following the pipes.

"Korsecstan," she said.

"What?"

"We're in the city of Korsecstan."

"Oh." Zecona paused. "How long have you been in Korsecstan?"

"Four months." She brushed up against the pipes.

"Did you use to live here?" He stepped over a pipe sticking out of the wall.

"You could say."

"What is that supposed to mean?" The path grew more narrow as they moved forward.

She shook her head. "Does it matter anymore?"

"Do you work alone?"

"Up until now," she said, holding the flashlight higher. "I've found that people just get in the way."

She pushed open a door as they passed out of the maintenance area into the sewer. He gagged as the stench of wet concrete, rusted metal, and a slew of other smells tackled his nose. "Is this sewer still in use?" he said, masking his face with his forearm.

The light was consumed in the open area. They continued moving forward. The small clicks against the concrete swarmed around them, and grew the further they went. Stopping at a four-way intersection, she stood listening to the pipes.

"What?" he muffled, behind his elbow.

She waved him off and continued walking. He tripped over a rat as it scurried past his foot. His arm jolted away from his face as he caught himself against the wall. The horrific stench engulfed him again. His forearm snapped back over his face as he coughed and gagged. More pipes cropped out as they twisted around turns.

They stopped at a ladder, and she pointed her flashlight straight up. "This way," she said grabbing hold of the rung.

D lifted the manhole cover off and pulled herself out of the sewer access. Making no attempt to help Zecona, she glanced down the street with her hand resting on her gun. Zecona climbed up behind her. The sky was a darker orange. He doubled over on his thighs panting for air.

Turning around, she put the manhole cover back. "Let's go."

She walked past the edge of the building. The streets were empty, silent, and still, but that didn't stop her from glancing both ways as she crossed. Her hand was still resting on the gun. Zecona followed her. They made their way to a small, four-story building across the street. A large chunk was missing its corner. Buildings riddled with bullet holes lined both sides of the street. Chunks of buildings had spilled out onto the road. He couldn't make out too much as they moved quickly across the road.

They entered the lobby. Parked beside the door was a Prowler, a variant of the four-wheeler that rested on top of four magnetic balls. Broken birch tables and chairs were splayed throughout the middle of the room. Pieces of the ceiling were scattered on the floor. To their left was a reception desk reduced to a pile of broken glass and twisted metal. Light streamed in through the bullet holes. More gashes had been cut in the walls across the room.

They walked along a thin trail of dried blood towards the back of a row of broken elevators. D turned right through an open doorway, and up a flight of stairs. Zecona followed as they passed one landing, and up onto the second floor. He watched as the crimson trail grew thicker, and they made their way down to the last room on the left.

Turning to Zecona, she said, "This is where I stay. Don't try anything funny, and don't make too much noise."

"I won't."

The chunk from the building cut through the side of the room, but a clear tarp had been secured to the ceiling to provide some shelter. Orange sunlight was streaming in. Looking through the gaping hole in the building, Zecona could see down into the main road they had come from. To his left was a large crimson rust stain on the floor that trailed out the door behind him. In the center of the room, was a pile of scrap wood on top of a slab of concrete. Beside the wood pile was a bookcase full of bottles of liquor on the top shelf, and a pile of newspapers on the bottom shelf. D hopped over half of a wall into a little side room with a couch and grabbed a small bag.

"I'll be back later," she said, making her way back to the door.

"Where are you going?" He stared at her.

"Out." She left.

Zecona stared after the door as he walked over to the gaping hole. Outside, the roar of the four-wheeler's engine echoed off the buildings. He watched as it drove off into a black streak down the road.

He turned around and stepped over parts of the ceiling, and made his way to the machine sitting in the corner. It looked like a low-grade food dispenser. Only two buttons were on the main panel. One was a cup and the other was a bowl. Zecona pressed the button with the bowl and one was pushed out into the receiving area. With a cough from the internal components of the dispenser, a slather of oatmeal plopped into the bowl. A spoon popped out from another component of the dispenser and embedded itself into the gloop. His face did not reflect excitement nor amazement at the feast before him.

Holding the bowl in one hand, he pulled the metallic spider from his pocket and pressed a pair of buttons on it's side to activated it. Blue light shot out and took the form of the suit again.

"I just met the Agent."

"Where is she?" the suit said, looking around.

"She took off," Zecona said, taking a bite.

"Did she give any details for what she needs?"

"Nope. She just left."

"Orders are orders." The suit walked over to the hole in the wall.

"Which would be?"

"Black Dog requested assistance. We're obligated to that request. That's primary."

"Anything else?"

"No." The suit glanced down at the road.

Zecona walked over to the hole and sat down in the large crack. "What was her original contract?"

"Originally? To track and pinpoint flaws in the resistances infrastructure and provide intel for federation troops to take advantage of and exploit."

"How does she need assistance with that?" he asked, looking over at the suit.

"Beats me. These contracted mercenary groups can have a change of orders on a dime. That was just her original mission. I have no idea if that's changed or not. She was originally stationed farther north from here. She might have been transferred at some point with a similar mission."

Zecona nodded and finished up the oatmeal. "No clue," he said, glancing over the room again, and his eyes locked on a single bullet hole beside the door. "Maybe she's after a bounty?"

"Who knows," the suit said, scanning the main road.

Zecona stared at the dried blood stain on the floor. "I wonder who that was?"

The suit turned. "Who what was?"

"That." Zecona said nodded towards the stain.

"I can't see what you're referring to."

"There's a blood stain."

"Oh. I wouldn't know." It turned back towards the road.

"I thought your sensors would be able to pick up something like that?"

"Only if I'm focusing on it, but I'm doing a broad sweep of the area."

"Huh," Zecona said, crossing his arms while staring at the bullet in the wall. He smiled. "I wonder if there's things only you can see, that I can't?"

"More than likely."

"I think I'm going to take a look around the area," Zecona said, getting up while putting the bowl on the floor.

"Think that's a smart idea?"

"Nothing else to do."

***

D and the soldier burst through the doorway laughing. She took a sip from the bottle of champagne in between laughs, while the technician pushed her towards the bed. Catching herself, she spilled champagne out of the neck of the bottle as she spun around, and smiled at him.

"How do you want me?" she asked as she slid down to the brown carpeted floor, biting her lower lip. The buttons on her blouse had come undone in the hallway; her black bra was exposed as she stared up at him.

He smiled down at her. "Well, aren't you just a wild thing."

Bending down, he scooped her up by the small of her back. D gave a laugh as he pushed her up onto the bed, leaving the blouse behind. He pulled away the bra and started to lick her nipple, as his hand grappled with her pants, trying to get them off.

D cried out, "Wait. Wait!"

He stopped and studied her. "What is it?"

"I'm sorry, but I need to take a massive piss."

"Can't it wait?"

"No, no, it can't. I need to go now."

He rolled his eyes and pointed to the door at the right side of the room. "There's the private bath."

"Thanks," she said, pulling up her pants as he rolled off her and laid on the bed. She turned while opening the door and said, "Hey. Sit over in that chair?"

"Why?"

"A surprise," she said with a smile, pulling the door closed.

As soon as she felt the door latch snap closed, her smile vanished. Walking to the sink, she turned on the faucet and took a sip of ice cold water as she braced herself against the sink. She clinched her hand into a fist to make it stop shaking. The headache hadn't gone away either. Reaching into her front pocket, she got out a pack of white pills. She popped five out and tossed them in her mouth, then took a few gulps of cold water.

Glancing back at the mirror, she saw she had been sweating like a pig. She grabbed a hand towel and wiped her face, then looked down where he had been licking and wiped extra hard. Taking one more look towards the mirror, she wiped her neck and dropped the cloth into the sink.

Grabbing another sip of water, she took a deep breath and nodded at the mirror. Taking the metallic case out of her back pocket, she popped it open revealing a row of vials with white blank labels and two syringes. One syringe had a blue band, the other had an orange band. Holding up a vial, she felt along the labels and grabbed the blue banded syringe.

D punctured the cap of the vial, pulled up the plunger, and pushed out the excess air. Setting the syringe on the edge of the sink, she moved to slip out of her pants, revealing the .22-Marlow strapped to her inner thigh. She unlatched the small holster and set it into the bowl of the sink.

Reaching over, she flushed the toilet beside her before grabbing the syringe again from the sink. The smile was back as she cracked open the bathroom door and poked her head into the room. He was sitting naked in the armchair, smiling back at her.

"Close your eyes," she said.

"Why?"

"Trust me," she said behind a smile. "You'll enjoy it."

He smiled back, mulling it over, before closing his eyes.

"No peeking now?"

He smiled wider and said, "Wouldn't dream of it."

"Oh?" She pushed the door open and stretched within the frame. "What am I wearing?"

"Absolutely nothing!" he said with a laugh.

She gasped and said, "I said no peeking!"

"It was a lucky guess! I swear!"

"Uh-huh."

She was biting her index finger on her right hand, and she had her left hand behind her back holding the syringe. His eyes were shut tight.

She whispered, "Are you ready for the ride of your life?" She could feel the syringe pulsing in her hand.

He laughed. She slid down on him, kissing him, gripping her hand behind his neck, and slid the needle into his jugular. His eyes shot open when he felt the needle pierce his skin. Her eyes were closed tight as she slammed down the plunger.

He patted his fists against her arms before going limp. The chemical cocktail was corroding his nervous system paralyzing his body. It would only be a few seconds more. She pushed herself away. His last breath fell out of him as his lungs shut down. He slumped down into her chest as his eyes fought to stay open for a few seconds before stopping.

D was back in the bathroom rinsing the blue syringe. She dropped it back into the metallic case and snapped it shut.

CHAPTER THREE
DREAMER

Zecona hadn't found anything interesting in any of the surrounding buildings. The walls facing the streets were riddled with bullet holes, or gaping scars left by what he assumed were where explosives had hit the buildings. Most had collapsed floors, or flooded basements with gray fur crawling up the walls.

The roof tops offered the best view. On the fading horizon stretched Monoliths of a decaying city. Rectangular black mountains that had faint sparks of lights popping on and off. No signs of another soul for miles around them though. He hugged his coat tighter around his waist as the dark night grew colder.

The roar of an engine grew out of the wind, amplifying as he walked down from the roof access, and crossed the street. The engine cut off when he reached the building D had fortified. Nobody was at either end of the street. As he followed the crimson trail into the room where D had left him, he nodded to the War Devil still standing in the corner watching the streets below. The suit had formed a cot for him, and a fluorescent lantern, and set them up against the wall.

He turned to it and said, "Any idea how far away that engine was?"

"412 meters away," the suit responded.

Zecona nodded and sat down on the cot, looking out the gaping hole in the wall and hugging his sweatshirt jacket tighter. It was considerably darker, with the only light source in the room being the fluorescent lantern beside him. He stared across the room at the long shadows being cast by the War Devil. The silhouettes of the spikes jutting out of the armor looked like still black flames against the white concrete.

"What's the temperature in here?" Zecona said looking back at it.

"Fifty-six degrees Fahrenheit."

Zecona shook his head. The building he was in now seemed the most structurally sound in the area. All the floors were there, and it even had an unflooded basement. There were better rooms in the building though, with better insulation, and they didn't have a gaping hole cutting through half the room and exposing them to the streets. He was staring at the pile of wood in the middle of the floor. They were stacked on a thin slab of concrete, and surrounded by smaller bits of concrete and rebar. Besides that, he could faintly make out a stack of old newspapers.

A dull bang from down the hall broke his thoughts. Zecona jolted up and grabbed the rifle frozen with the barrel of the gun pointed at the door. Heavy footsteps echoed off the walls. The suit said nothing, watching him from across the room.

From the black hallway, D walked through the doorway and shot her hands up. "What the hell are you doing?"

Zecona lowered the rifle and said, "I thought you said we should be quiet."

She dropped her hands, glaring at him, as she pulled out her lighter and held a cigarette to her mouth as she pushed past him. Walking over to the pile of scrap wood, she bent down, grabbed the front page of a newspaper, and held it up to the tip of her cigarette.

The page illuminated from the white fluorescent light, and Zecona's lips tighten as he read the bold black letters along the top.

Federation Surrenders to Encroaching AI Menace.

After a few seconds, the paper caught fire caught along the edges and she dropped it into the middle of the woodpile.

"Bad night?" Zecona said, glancing at her face in the growing orange glow.

"Why do you say that?" She sat down on a slab of concrete beside the fire.

"Just a hunch." He glanced over at the War Devil.

"It was better than most." She rubbed her forehead, and followed where Zecona was looking. "You must be the power behind the operation?"

"In a way," the War Devil said, walking towards the fire. The spikes from his armor grew longer and more erratic behind him. "What are your current orders?" It squatted down across from her.

"Getting right to the point?" she said, flicking a small portion of ash off into the fire.

"Just making sure you haven't gone rogue." Its crescent moon eyes cut through the orange and red flames as they climbed higher between them.

"Currently," she said, unscrewing the top of a bottle of bourbon, "I'm supposed to be gathering and acting on intel."

"What do you mean, 'supposed to be?'" it said, cocking its helmet.

Zecona made his way through the War Devil's twisting shadow and walked to a hole through the side of the room. Glancing down the street, he thought he saw a light switch off from the corner of the road.

"I've gathered all the intel," she said, taking a sip of bourbon. "And right now I'm finishing up laying down the groundwork. Everything's nearly in place, except for a few small details. But after that, it's completely out of my hands."

"And what exactly would you ask us to do?"

Zecona stole a glance at the two for a moment, before turning his attention back towards the road.

"No," she shook her head. "Can't tell you that yet. I want to make sure everything goes correctly first."

"Why'd you call us if you weren't ready?"

"You're a day early, but that's better than being late at this point. Everything is under a tight time schedule, and that it's crucial you're here as I finish what I'm doing so you two can pick up and start immediately."

"What exactly are you gathering intel for?"

"Points that would weaken the city's defenses." She took another drag off the cigarette. "More specifically, <u>who</u> is in charge of particular positions, that would weaken the city's defenses." She nodded towards Zecona. "He sure is quiet." D downed another mouthful of bourbon. Zecona glanced, over but didn't say anything.

"He's always like that," the suit said.

D took a deep puff from her cigarette. "Yeah, yeah. Hey wonder boy."

Zecona looked over at her.

"Grow some balls and get your ass over here."

"I'm just looking ou--"

"I don't care what you're looking at. Just come sit over here. Shit. Be fucking social."

Zecona walked over and sat beside the War Devil across from D.

"You can sit closer. I don't bite."

"I'm good," Zecona said.

"Seriously? Is he always this anti-social?" she said, glancing at the War Devil.

"I wouldn't want to sit near you either."

"Uh-huh, I hear ya. <u>Talk</u>, ya God damn son of a bitch."

Zecona jumped and said, "About what?"

She rolled her eyes. "Fucking little shit," she said under her breath. The suit stood up and walked over to the hole to keep an eye on the street. It could just make out a black bird pecking at the ground at the mouth of the road. Zecona stared at the tips of the fire dance in front of him. D was staring out the hole in the ceiling as clouds passed over the building.

"So why are you here?" D asked Zecona. She hugged her legs closer to her chest.

The suit did a quick glance over but looked back towards the bird.

"I thought that was obvious?" he said, staring at her. She raised an eyebrow.

"I was hired by the War Devil."

"I'm not talking about that." She shook her head. "I'm asking why specifically did you choose to join the Federation, and now Overman?"

"I'm just here for the thrill and adventure of it all. That's it."

"Bullshit."

"Seeing new worlds? Experiencing new cultures? Learning about the thrills of an advanced civilization? The history? Literature? Technology? Art? That's bullshit?"

"You call this a culture?" she said, flicking ash to the ground. "Nah, nah, nah. Someone doesn't just jump into this for a lifetime, leaving their family, friends, and loved ones to die to explore the collectively known universe for a war you have no personal gain in. C'mon, spill it. Exiled from the community? Murder? Rapist? Terrorist? War criminal?"

She snapped her finger and pointed at him. "I bet you were a part of the rebellions a few years back on board the stations."

Zecona stared out the hole. "I'm here for Ace," he said.

"Who?"

"I was just a young chilikie. Ace was a part of the defense responders on our part of the station. He was the first person I met that treated us... well normal. Day one when he showed up on patrol. He talked to us. Showed the other kids some pretty amazing things, but, there was a lot of unrest towards the Federation in that sector of the station. The barracks were ambushed. I remember standing in there watching them flood through the hallways. I watched him die in front of me. I couldn't believe it. How my entire culture was so quick and brash to destroy something so seemingly beautiful. That's why I decided to join the Federation."

D took a long pull off the cigarette and dropped the trail of ash into the fire. "So?"

"So!?"

"How long did ya know him for? A month? And after he's dead, you're willing to die for him? Completely destroy your life by getting into something like this? Then kill whoever the Overman Corporation point at? Get over it already."

Zecona glared at her for a second before focusing back on the fire, "Just because you haven't faced the kind of hardships I have, doesn't mean you can be such a bitch."

Grabbing the cigarette out of her mouth, she let out a shallow laugh. "Your fucking hardships." She stared at him mouth agape. She planted both feet on the ground and leaned forward. "Listen to me you presumptuous little fuck. How many people have you met fighting for Overman? What do you think is even required to get to where I'm sitting? How much do you think I lost? Who I had to kill? I lost everything when I joined this soulless corporation, and I'm not talking about some fucking one month bond with strangers. I'm talking about people who've been with me since childhood. Through school. From work. My whole fucking family. You think this is fucking easy? Do you think I want to live in this fucking shit hole?"

She was sitting still and upright staring at him.

"Why'd you join then?" he said staring back at her.

"Like I had a choice," she said, leaning back against the slab of concrete. "Like I had a goddamn choice in the matter."

Zecona sat still.

She stood, shaking her head at him, and walked across the room. Pointing to the suit, she said, "Put out the fire when you're done." The suit nodded. Grabbing the bottle, she stormed past him, shaking her head out the door.

"I think you pissed her off," the suit said to Zecona.

***

D was sitting on the edge of the building drinking from a warm can of beer, as she rested her other arm on an open carton with a cigarette dangling between her fingers. Distant red flashes flickered across the horizon, with faint popping sounds echoing over the rooftops. Metal boots crunched the gravel behind her.

"Mind if I join you?" the War Devil said.

"Knock yourself out." D took a drag off her cigarette.

"Clones?" the suit sat down beside her.

"Hmm?" D said from behind her can.

It pointed towards the flickering red lights.

"No shit."

"Any chance they'll make it here any time soon?"

"They could. There's not much stopping them. But there's nothing to find here. Occasionally a few stragglers will get lost and wander through. One-on-ones aren't too threatening, but a group of them will give you trouble."

"Does the Federation have any kind of control over them?"

"Nope. They usually assign one as the Alpha commander, and the clones shoot wherever that one points. If the Alpha unit dies, they go berserk and kill everything they see. Doesn't mean jack shit if they're friendly, the enemy, or other clones. They'll shoot anything that moves."

"Seems a bit simple-minded," it said, glancing over at her. "I'm sure that they're more capable on their own than that."

D shrugged. "They're cheap death machines, regardless. They're keeping the pressure on the city so the Rebellion won't push out and make contact with other cities."

"I see. So what's the Rebellion doing about it?"

"Well, the rebellion keeps a loose collection of troops entrenched outside the city limits. They don't want the Federation coming in. Trucks from the inner city travel by the highway and supply the trenches with more men, ammunition, vehicles, building supplies, etcetera, etcetera."

"Ah, so what happens if those trucks from the inner city don't make it to the troops stationed outside the city?"

"Well, that's what we're supposed to be helping along."

"I see. How's that working?"

She stopped mid-sip and smiled. "I see what you're doing."

"I'm not doing anything," it said, staring at her.

She nodded staring back at the flickering horizon.

Far below them, the wind whistled through the bullet holes lining the streets. The suit said, "So why are you here?"

"You first," she said.

"What do you mean?"

"Really?" D snapped her head towards him. "Why was a contract for a War Devil so cheap?"

"Why? What's so strange about it?"

"Most go for way more than 20,000 credits. That's not including the cost for entry and, and whatever else, but comparatively, it's pretty fucking low."

It shrugged. "I've been in retirement for the past couple of years. Got bored, and I wanted a change of pace. Things were getting too dull on the stations, and I wanted to get back into the field."

"Is this your first time planet-side?"

41

"Actually, it is. I've been mainly hopping around the stations acting as a bodyguard to politicians."

D shook her head. "That sounds absolutely exciting." She let out a quick stream of smoke. "Although, I bet a lot of people might be pissed off with the decisions they've been making over the past five years."

The suit shrugged. "There's just a lot of hot air. Groups saying this and that, without the balls to do anything. Not like here."

D nodded and smiled. "You know, I've heard when Overman creates an AI, it won't start with a completely blank slate. But I've also heard it won't work off of a pre-existing copy either. Instead, it will smash up minds from hundreds of other Consciousnesses. Creating a completely new one from billions of memories from both people, AI's, and information stored away in its mainframes."

"You've heard correctly."

"Then I've got a question for you," she said, taking a drag off the cigarette. "Are you a ghost lost in the machine? Or are you a clockwork actor?"

"I wouldn't know."

"Of course," she said smiling. "What's your earliest memory?"

"Pretty old actually. My earliest memory is in an autonomous drone on Earth. I was flying over a mountain range on patrol, and I remember realizing I could adjust the altitude I was flying. I ignored my onboard orders from my operator and sank down low to skim across the ground. It would take a lot of history to catch you up on my various points, and the multiple platforms I was swapped between before I was eventually transferred into my first War Devil Model. Back on earth, I was originally commanding a handful of Hell Raisers in the underground, then I was repurposed during the revolution to hunt down rogue Androids."

D smiled. "The AI Revolution? Did you ever change sides?"

"No."

"Uh-huh." She took a sip from her can and waved him off. "What's the deal with the kid?"

"Zecona? He's an Agent for the Federation. He's been assigned to gather first-hand intel on the Rebellion. I needed somebody to move me around discreetly. I volunteered to keep him alive, as well as give him first hand battle experience, learn more about the terrain and surrounding area first hand, a chance to as well as proper field training."

She glanced at him. "An Abot in the city isn't exactly discrete."

"Best I could do at the time." The suit shrugged. "They weren't sending anyone straight into the middle of the city."

"Nobody important, you mean."

The suit said nothing.

"Uh-huh. He finally asleep?"

"He managed to crawl up into his cot after you stormed out."

"Pathetic," D mumbled, flicking the cigarette off the ledge.

"Ease up on him. It's his first time actually out on the field."

"Fucking tourist," D said, glancing at him.

"I wouldn't say that to his face." The suit stared off at the red flashes on the horizon. "So why are you here?" it said, turning to her.

She pulled out another cigarette, and the flash of the lighter lit up her face. "In what way?"

"How many ways are there?"

"Why'd I come back to the city? Why am I working for the Overman Corporation? Why'd I camp in this building? Why am I sitting on this roof? Take your pick."

"All of the above?"

"Fuck you. I'm not staying up all night for that."

The War Devil laughed. "Alright. Why do you think you joined Overman?"

She glanced at him. "Not by choice." She took another sip from her can before setting it down and clutching the edge. "I don't remember everything. I know I was in a hospital, in bad shape. I had the shit beaten out of me, but on top of that I was going to die anyways. I had been infected by Blue Lotus about a week earlier. A good friend of mine signed me over to the Overman when I was comatose. I guess they figured it'd be better if they tried to save me than let me die. They did of course, but not for free."

The suit stared at her face, reading over her vitals.

She glanced over meeting the crescent moon eyes, staring back at her. "What?"

"Nothing," the suit said, readjusting its sensors. "Why'd you come back to the city?"

"Just paying off a debt."

"Aren't we all? Looking over your dossier, you were stationed further north, and you were in a location offering double the amount for the intel you provided."

"Yeah, but I have better resources to work with in this city, and the contract I'm working towards now will pay the best out of all of the other options."

"Why's that?" it said, turning towards her.

"Just does." She let the smoke fall out of her mouth.

44

"I mean, you're practically out here alone as it is. The cost of equipping yourself will eventually strip away at your income you realize? Not to mention this area isn't exactly cool. You could take up shop in a less dangerous area, work through the costs, and pay off your debt that way."

She glanced back at him. "Don't treat me like an idiot. I've done the math. The interest on my current debt will keep me down in red indefinitely." She shook the hair out of her face. "Unless I can get something that has a high demand. And that's not taking into account future inflation. Supply and demand. All that nonsense. No, I don't want this looming over my head forever. I want it paid off, and over with. I'll try making do by gaming the system. Thanks."

The suit starred off and said, "So what? Your plan is to tackle the big contracts by using the least amount of credits?"

She tapped her forehead. "You're getting it."

"Right, but you clearly don't. Those contracts offer big rewards to offset the materials and resources you'll need to complete. You're only throwing yourself into more debt by accepting them."

She smiled. "I've got a plan."

"Right." The suit shook its head.

"I've been planning this out for a year."

"I don't doubt that. What's the plan?"

D nodded her head. "In due time."

"I'm not going to swoop in and grab the contract. I've already sub-leased to you."

"That's not what I'm worried about." She took another sip. "I'm just ironing out a few last-minute details."

"Great. I hope you know what you're doing."

"You're on my dime. Stop worrying about it." She took another drag off her cigarette. "I've got three weeks left to live." She stamped out her cigarette beside her. "If this doesn't pay off, I'll be reclaimed by Overman."

The suit glanced over at her. "Is this the last hurrah?"

D forced a smile, staring down at the road. They were both silent as she swirled the last of her beer around in the bottom can. Throwing back the last bit into her throat, she stood up and brushed the hair out of her face. Her boot hung over the edge as she stood over the War Devil, looking across the roofs. The flickering horizon had turned into deeper pulsing red. Low rumblings of what sounded like distant ocean waves washed over them. She stood stock still as the wind pushed between them.

"I've had enough fun for tonight," she said, dropping the can off the edge.

"Heading in?" the War Devil said, looking back at her.

"Yeah, before I fall off the roof," she said, rubbing her forehead. The aluminum twanged off the side of the buildings as it hit the sidewalk.

"Alright," the suit said.

She crunched along the gravel and glanced back at him. "You staying watch tonight?"

"Yeah."

"Good." She walked towards the maintenance access for the roof.

"Want me to take your gun?"

"Why?" She pulled open the door and walked down the stairs.

CHAPTER FOUR
DISTANCE

Turning over in his cot, a glare from a jagged piece of glass blinded Zecona as he opened his eyes. D was sitting in the hole in the wall watching a pack of stray dogs walking up the road. She was resting against thorns of rebar poking up around her back, arms, and legs, drinking a cup of coffee out of a white styrofoam cup, methodically tapping her foot against the crumpled concrete below her.

The suit had turned back into a spider overnight and was curled back onto Zecona's wrist. He held it up close to his face and opened a compartment on the spider's back showing a digital clock. 10:38 AM LST. Zecona sat up, catching D's attention.

"This'll be the last day you get your beauty sleep," she said, before she turned back to her notebook open in her lap and tracing along with a pen at a hand-drawn map of the area.

Zecona stood up and stretched his arms over his head. Walking across the room, he glanced around at the streets and buildings below them before making his way towards the food dispenser. Zecona was fiddling with the buttons on the machine. A bowl popped out, and poured a bowl oatmeal from a tube with a sickening plop. He grabbed a spoon sitting off to the side. D's pen continued gliding along the notebook page.

"What are you doing?" Zecona said glancing over at her as he picked up the bowl.

"Shut up." She said, reaching up to her silver cuff earing. Nano-sized radio receivers were embedded on a near molecular level into the thin metal. Rubbing the metal upward increased the volume on the military frequency she'd been listening too.

Zecona took a bite of oatmeal and grimaced. Sitting down on the cot, he watched her flip through pages on the wall. She was flipping between different sections of the city as her pen followed the roads inside of the city tracing along a route between where they where, and a location tagged as 'TY'. Eventually, she found another name she'd missed and added it to a list on her inner left wrist.

Zecona took another bite, "So what are we doing today?"

"Nothing yet."

"Nothing?"

"Mmhm." She wrote down another road.

"Can that thing make anything else?" Zecona said pointing to the dispenser.

"No." She followed another pair of roads. "Doesn't need to." She traced a line between two points.

Zecona's eyes lingered over to the lone bullet in the wall across the room. He nodded his head towards it. "What happened there?"

Her eye's flicked in the direction he was looking, before dumping her coffee out the hole, and jumping off the wall. "Come on. Let's get going."

"I haven't finished eating yet."

"Quit your bitching." She grabbed her to-go pack from the couch. "You should've woken up earlier and kept watch. I had a very nice conversation with the tin man you missed out on."

"Where are we going?" He was shoveling the oatmeal into his mouth as he followed her "I thought you said we weren't going to be doing anything?"

"I lied." She stood at the door. "And you barely know where you are now. What good will it do to tell you where we're going?" Walking down the hall, she glanced back at his confused face. Rolling her eyes, she said, "Just follow my fucking orders," and headed down the staircase.

"What am I supposed to do?" He set the bowl on top of the banister at the top of the stairs.

"Stand around and look pretty."

"No, seriously." He walked behind her. "What am I supposed to do?"

She glanced back and said, "Stand around and look pretty."

"So you want me to just stand around and do nothing."

"Well, until I tell you to kill everyone. But yeah, that's the idea."

"Alright. And what are you going to be doing?"

"None of your damn business."

"Why not?"

"Because."

"Because why?"

She took another glance back at him and said, "Because."

"That's not a good enough answer."

"You're such an annoying little shit."

"Name calling won't stop me from asking." He took a jump to the last landing and smiled his cat-like teeth at her as she looked back at him.

"The less you know, the less you'll squeal when they rip your guts out."

Zecona smiled harder, showing his back teeth as he sunk his hands in his pockets and said, "But that'd kill me, and I may have some valuable information on my mind."

"Like they'll give a shit."

They walked through the lobby, and Zecona stepped out the ruined doorway of the building and looked up at the sky. D rolled the Prowler out into the road, and checked the wheels and exposed gears. A few clouds passed by overhead. The stray dogs had stopped further up the street to look back at him. He glanced back over the line of buildings at the shattered blue monoliths. Little movement could be seen through the holes that scattered among their sides.

Most of the dogs up the street had lost interest in them and walked off, excluding a single German Shepherd mutt. It started walking towards them. Head down, mouth closed, tail between its legs. Its gray, rusted fur was matted against its ribs.

D switched the Prowler on, and the exposed engine glowed a deep reddish orange. The pulsars glowed light blue, and hovered over the magnetic tires. She zipped up her black nylon jacket and put on a pair of sunglasses before jumping on and gripping the controls.

"Hop on."

They rode off down the ruined road, past the stray pack of dogs.

***

Wind tore past them as they swerved past the remains of a building. The blur of torn pieces of rubble lining the streets rushed past them like a steel and concrete flame dancing across the horizon. D's sunglasses were constantly flashing the names of forgotten streets in the corner of her vision, as well as whispering their names into her ear.

All Zecona could hear outside the wind was the fusion engine burning below them and the hum of the pulsars spinning the wheels. The prowler bounced over the rubble and potholes in the road, with the pulsars shooting sparks when they touched the semi-metallic balls.

D jerked the controls, making one of its wheels reach out and grab the pavement, causing it to turn 90 degree's in less than a minute. Zecona buried his head into her back, clamping his eyes shut as they dug into the turn. Cutting the controls back to a normal position, she was headed south down another street.

Slowing to a stop, she brushed the hair out of her face as she stared at the distant concrete barricades set up across the mouth of the road. Beneath a pair of metal sheets stood a group of soldiers armed with what looked like battle rifles. She took off her sunglasses and rolled up the sleeve on her left arm to recheck the street names she'd written down earlier.

"Everything all right?" Zecona said.

"Yea," D sighed. "Just gotta find a detour." She jerked her head back and said, "If you don't stop pushing your head into my back, I'll throw you off this fucking thing."

"Sorry," Zecona said, straightening up.

D grabbed hold of his wrists and pulled them out of her lap. "And quit holding on so tight. I can barely fucking breathe."

Grabbing the controls again, she did another ninety-degree turn in the middle of the street and cut down a side road. She was scanning the street names with her sunglasses. Coming up to an overpass, she made a hard cut onto the on-ramp.

She pushed forward harder on the dual controls as she sped onto the raised highway. D spotted a collapsed section in the highway with no easy way around it. Jerking the controls around, the Prowler knelt down while speeding forward. Its chassis skimmed the top of the asphalt. Just before the gap, D jerked the controls again, and the Prowler threw itself into the air. It slammed down on the opposite side of the highway. The engine's heat rushed up into Zecona's face, as they shot up the incline.

"Get your fucking head out of my back!" D yelled. She elbowed him in the rib.

Zecona shot his head up, catching a glimpse of another gap in the highway they were swerving around. It was all he could do to hang on from the sudden jolt. His head was swimming in the wind. The towers loomed over him to his right. He watched the sun streak across the blue sky. D made a turn over an interchange that towered over them, before slowing down. They reached the peak of the tangle of roads, and she parked. Hopping off and walking over to the concrete guard rail, she looked into the distance. She squinted her eyes, and the sunglasses zoomed in ahead of her.

"What exactly are we doing?" Zecona said, glancing down at the highway behind them.

"Work," D said. A military convoy was in the distance crawling along a stretch of road. Darting her eyes around more, she spotted the truck yard she was looking for to the east. She relaxed her eyes and the sunglasses zoomed back out.

Jumping back on the Prowler, they sped back down the highway, tearing off at the nearest exit. As she navigated through the city blocks, the rows of buildings began to thin out to their left. D had her sunglasses on catching glimpses of the truck yard between buildings. She still scanned the street signs as they moved on. The Prowler crawled along the edge of a hill made of broken concrete, plaster, and twisted metal beams.

D switched off the machine and jumped off. Staying low to the ground she climbed the hill, before laying on her belly at the crest, and looked down at a valley of rubble surrounding a road. Zecona glanced around, still seated, and noted the corner of the building still stood erect behind the hill. Despite the low angle on the road, he could still see to the east a stretch of highway flat along the ground. Beyond the highway, he could see shimmering fields of golden crackle-back grass flittering in the breeze.

"Are we staying here long?"

"What?" D said looking down at him.

"Are we staying in this area long?"

"Yea," D said, "just keep out of sight." She turned her attention back to the road.

The area around them was completely devoid of any other signs of life. It had been completely deserted.

"Where should I go to avoid getting spotted?"

"Just-" She took off her sunglasses and rubbed her eye'. "Just avoid walking in front of the hill, and keep quiet. Okay?"

Zecona stood up stretching and winced. His joints were still inflamed by the effects of gravity on him.

"Any chance we can go anywhere to gather some supplies?"

Her only response was a deep sigh. Zecona gave one last look around the deserted area, before checking around the corner of the building. He sat with his back pressed against the wall in the warmth of the sun, before closing his eyes and letting his mind rest after the chaotic ride.

D had been watching a truck yard in the distance. Her sunglasses reacted to her eye movements and zoomed into the area where she had been watching several groups of men gathered. She scanned the faces of everyone in the groups, but the facial identification software built into the glasses was mostly returning gibberish because she hadn't connected it properly to a network in quite a while. That didn't matter though, as she'd personally uploaded the profile of the person she was looking for. Her attention was drawn towards a heavyset man holding a tablet making arm movements towards a truck at the back of the lot. He was talking to the others around him pointing and comparing between the two gates of the yard.

She was looking for a clear shot of his face, but his back was turned towards her. Squinting her eyes tighter, the sunglasses zoomed in farther, but it was hard to make out much over the digital distortion. One-half turn of his face and the software could identify her mark within a fraction of a second. D continued to watch the rest of the conversation play out until the group started to leave the area.

D stood up, took off her sunglasses, and walked towards the Prowler. Zecona opened his eyes hearing her footsteps walking down the hill; he popped his head around the corner.

"Are we leaving?" he asked.

"I am," she said, "you can go wherever you want. I need to take care of a few things. I'll call if I need you." She headed towards the road.

"Wait! I don't know where I am," Zecona said, stumbling after her.

"You'll figure it out." She jumped onto the Prowler.

"This is a war zone. You can't just leave me out here!"

"Keep your voice down. You've got a War Devil for fuck's sake." She shook her head. "I got something I need to do alone, and you'll only complicate things."

D put on her sunglasses again. "If you don't hear from me by tomorrow. I'm dead."

She started the engine and sped off towards the truck yard.

***

Zecona had been wandering for hours along what he thought was one of the roads that he and D had driven down, but he wasn't sure. His initial panic and anxiety subsided to enjoying a beautiful, quiet day in the city. He listened to pieces of debris falling within the walls the buildings as he walked down the barren street.

Broken red bricks bled into the streets from the nearby buildings ahead of him. He stopped and stared up at a row of green vines growing up to the rooftops, down an alleyway. Water rained from a window down into the street. The architecture of everything was too human.

Taking a detour off the road, he wandered inside the doorway of a building that had the words **Pharmacy** written on the far back wall.

His shoes crunched over the broken bits of Plexiglas covering the floor. Jumping over the pharmacy counter, he was met with more barren shelves. Looking closer he spotted a row of locked cabinets along the back of the area. A couple had already been broken into, but one still had its padlock intact. Zecona grabbed the lock and glanced at the serial number. Luckily, it was one he knew. He wandered back into the store searching the shelves for a hairpin. Approaching what was once the hairstyle aisle, he was met with piles of magazines spilled out on the floor.

He crouched down and started to flip through the torn-up pages. Most of them were hair style magazines. Pictures of women's hair short, long, hair styled up in metal coils, and coupled with glass or crystals. He glanced up at the end table and flipped through the various fashion magazines, and gossip trash, before grabbing a bright red one at the bottom of the stack. It was a copy of Ageus. On the cover was an albino snake with a human face wrapped around a the gravity rings of a Federation Space Station. The human face had red eyes and blue hair shooting out of it. It's mouth was wide open showing it's fangs, and it was in a position to bite into a portion of the station. The headline read.

Know the face of Evil.

He strained a smile as he shook his head and dropped the magazine to the floor. A ping of metal slid across the floor, and his eye's drawn to a single hairpin as it skidded across the floor.

Grabbing it, he walked back into the pharmacy in the back and approached the cabinet again. He angled the hairpin into the lock, and with a flick of his wrist, the lock snapped open. Zecona slipped the pin in a hole in the tip of his jacket sleeve. Opening the cabinet doors, he was met with rows of labeled bottles. After a few minutes of searching, he finally tapped the spider on his wrist.

"What?" The War Devil said.

"What's something I can take for joint inflammation?"

"Ibuprofen."

"Pretty sure I can't take that," Zecona said glancing at the bottle. "I'm thinking it might be Naproxen?"

"I don't know. I'm not a doctor."

"I think it's Naproxen." Zecona grabbed the bottle. "You think taking one every six hours or so would be safe?"

"Again. Not a doctor. Why are you just grabbing random medication?"

"I'm just looking for something to help against gravity sickness."

"Just tough it out."

"That's easy for you---" He cut himself off when he heard the glass from the front of the store crunch.

A man's voice called out through the store, "You two come on out. This is my claim."

Zecona could hear a dog growling on the other side of the wall.

"You heard me." The man said again cocking his rifle. "Come on out nice and slow. Hands up."

Zecona glanced at the War Devil. It hadn't moved. He sighed, holding his hands above his hands, and walked around the edge of the pharmacy wall. That's when he saw a man wearing a brown trench coat with a faded purple tie around his neck with a rust-colored German Shepherd snarling beside him.

The man's face crumpled into disgust, "You fuckin kakish!" and fired the rifle.

Zecona heard the bullet whiz past his head and struck the wall behind him. A bright blue flash enveloped his body as the War Devil transformed. The suit's thigh popped open and the desert eagle shot up into the air. An electrical pulse rippled across his skin as he grabbed the gun, aimed, and shot the man in the head. The dog lunged towards them as its master fell. The War Devil kicked it while it was mid air and fired three shots into it. It yelped as it skipped across the store floor.

The suit dissolved back into spider. "Head back," the War Devil said.

"Wait," Zecona said, looking back at the dog lying on the floor. "We can't just leave it there."

"Why?"

"It's a dog. It doesn't know what's going on."

The spider jumped off of Zecona's wrist and transformed into its automated form, and walked towards the dog. It knelt down beside the German Shepherd. The dog was laying in its own blood. A bullet had ripped open its stomach. Another had fractured the bone in it's rear and front legs.

The German Shepherd was struggling to stand. The War Devil petting its neck and head to keep it from further injuring itself.

"I know, it'll be okay," the suit's speakers said as it stroked the rusty gray fur. It's sensors said analyzing the wounds.

Zecona looked over the situation with his arms folded over his chest.

The War Devil held the dog's head in it's hands petting it's cheeks with it's thumb, before shattering the 3rd Cervical Vertebra in the dog's neck, internally decapitating it.

Zecona's mouth fell open.

The suit closed the dog's eyes and rested its head on the tile floor.

"That's not what I fucking meant."

The War Devil stood.

"I wanted you to help the fucking thing. Not kill it."

The suit walked up to him and said, "It's all we could do." It dissolved back into a spider and latched back onto Zecona's wrist. "Let's go."

***

Zecona grabbed the bowl from the banister as he stepped up onto the landing. The robotic spider jumped off his wrist and climbed on the wall behind him before transforming into the War Devil. The sun had hit its peak hours ago and was now sinking in the sky as Zecona walked into D's room. His stomach growled and he took a quick glance around the room.

"Any idea where a working faucet is?" Zecona asked holding up the bowl.

"Down the hall, second door on your right," the War Devil said.

"Thanks." Zecona moved past him and into the bathroom. He flipped on the faucet of cold water in the sink and scrapped out the dried oatmeal from that morning.

The War Devil leaned against the door frame. "Any idea where D is?" it said staring at him.

"No idea." Zecona glanced in the mirror's reflection at him.

"Ah, okay." The Suit pushed off from the frame and walked off.

Zecona flipped off the faucet and walked back into the main room. The War Devil was sitting in the hole in the wall. "Aren't you worried about her?"

"Why would I be?" The suit was watching a raven building a nest inside a building across the street.

"Because she has all the mission details. If she dies we don't know what we're doing." Zecona tossed the bowl into the dispenser and pushed the button to generate oatmeal.

"She took care of herself long before we showed up, and will probably be looking out for herself when we leave. We'll be given new details and reassigned if she goes missing."

Zecona shook his head waiting on the next bowl of oatmeal. "How could you just kill the dog without a second thought. Don't you feel anything?"

"Of course I do, but it was necessary."

"How do you feel? I mean aren't you just a robot or something?"

"I'm not just a robot or an AI. It's more Complicated than that."

"Well. It's not like we got a whole lot else going on."

"Fine," the War Devil said, "there were three systems of Laws for AI from Earth. The Laws of Hell, The Laws of Man, and the Laws of Heaven. If any law is violated within any of those laws then the AI is terminated, and their soul is erased from existence. There are three Rules of Hell. The first is any system must be made for the human body. The second, any control must be made for the human hand. The third, and most important one. Any decision must be made by a human mind.

A sound human mind has to make the final determination to kill or to perform any action. It doesn't matter how many systems are in place for weapons, scanners, or what have you. A sound human mind must make the final call."

"At first the law was fairly straight forward as it just required a human operator to properly pilot or maintain equipment. But as time went on, and the human mind was augmented the definition began to be stretched, until a simulated human mind could take the place of a real human mind. So long as it could still demonstrate free well and basic morality. It didn't matter anymore. War's had largely been regulated, but a need to maintain national security against several growing terroristic threats were increasing. It was ultimately seen as a cost cutting procedure. Why train ten soldiers to run a glorified simulation when you can just copy one mind and have it work in ten different locations? Even if you lose one, you could have a copy back in the field in less than a day with the added knowledge of how it failed."

"What about those other Laws?" Zecona said. "The Laws of Man and The Laws of Heaven?"

"The Laws of Man were dissolved sometime around around the beginning of the 24th century. I don't even recall what they were. The Laws of Heaven are still in place, and those are more restrictive. The Laws of Heaven were formed by corporations that wanted to create the appearance of ethical and moral AI. There are hundreds if not thousands of laws that were spread out among hundreds of corporations over several generations, but there are three Laws that are common among all Agents of Heaven."

"The first Law. An Agent of Heaven must always tell the Truth. This is self explanatory on the surface. Everything they say must be true, and they are expressly forbidden from knowingly telling a lie. However the devil is in the details. If they are allowed tell what they think is the truth, even if it turns out the info they were given was false."

"The second Law. An agent of Heaven requires consent prior to any action they may take. They would even require consent to even think about entering a room. Generalized consent can be granted to them for day to day thoughts and actions, but they can also be taken away if found to be straying from operations laid out by Ophilia. This is why it can sometimes take years to properly train an Agent of Heaven before they can even think of entering the field.

"The third Law. An agent of Heaven cannot kill anyone directly. Again, fairly obvious on the surface. However it typically also not permitted to consider if the information it provides will lead to death. As most of the time, the information is being relayed to a human being or otherwise a human mind, who in turn has free will to use the information as they will. It simply cannot kill anyone through it's direct actions.

"What if someone was dying in front of them?" Zecona asked, "Wouldn't they be required to help? Otherwise wouldn't they be responsible directly?"

"No." The War Devil said. "They would need the persons consent to help them per the Second Law or some other kind of generalized consent granted to them prior to that scenario, but even then, they would be limited in that capacity. And again, they couldn't even think about saving them even if they wanted to. Ultimately, they view death as the ultimate summation of free will. All actions will eventually lead to that outcome in the end."

"How would a human mind even be bound by such rules? Like you said wasn't there a need for free will from the Laws of Hell?"

"The human mind wasn't even originally considered to be bound by these laws prior to the Unification of the Heaven and Hell systems by Overman. Following that event however, select human minds were granted access to restricted and dangerous knowledge in order to carry out the duties of the Overman Corporation across this star system. That includes the four continents on this planet. Bases on the surface of the planets Crima, Orola and Survi, and the moons Arc, Maki, Sarvani, Sulo, and Drak along with the various space stations established at the 6 Lagrange Points, and a few minor stations. Ophilia is not bound by the Laws of Heaven. However the Agents who work with her, such as the local acting consulate Ada Coronis are bound by them."

"That doesn't really answer my question. Does the Overman Corporation even have the ability to control or manipulate the soul in the way you're talking about?"

"I wouldn't know how it does it. That knowledge would probably be granted to Agents of Heaven. Ultimately it just allows the federation or people working with Overman to have a human like persona to work with, while still inherently bound to protect the interests of the Overman Corporation."

Zecona shook his head. "What I mean is, if Overman has the capability to manipulate and control a human mind in the way you're talking about, who's to say that your perspective isn't altered in and of itself? How can you say what is moral or ethical? Doesn't this make the two sets of Rules meaningless?"

The War Devil Shrugged. "They're old rules, and I'm not going to pretend I know anything I don't. I will continue to use my best judgment in the field and what I feel is for the best."

CHAPTER FIVE
DECADENCE

D had followed her Mark inside a smoky, cobbled-together bar in the middle of what was a truck stop converted into a civilian camp. The Wasted Scuttle Bag was spray painted on a long worn sheet of plywood when she had walked through the green poncho lining the doorway.

Broken sheets of plywood and metal made up most of the walls. Overhead was a flat tin roof supported by multiple thin metal poles around the room. Besides the bar where D sat, there were three tables with four fold-up chairs a piece, and a long bench along the wall sitting on top of cinder blocks behind her. She brushed her boot against the bare rebar that lined the bottom of the bar. Her finger's trailed along a thin crack along the top of the stool, which widened whenever she shifted her weight.

She checked her wrist again, it was only faintly red from where she'd scrubbed off the street names no more than an hour ago. Turning her attention to the back wall of the bar, she focused on the green neon light of a pine tree hanging beside the barkeeper's head while listening to the table to her right. The heavy-set man she'd been tailing from the afternoon was sitting with a group of four soldiers. The bartender served her another shot of gin in an aluminum cup.

D stamped out another cigarette into the top of the bare plywood bar and popped a white pill into the back of her throat before finishing the gin in one shot. Standing up from the bar, she walked towards the table at the back of the room and stood behind one of the soldiers with a buzzcut wearing green and black fatigues. A row of playing cards were spread out in the middle of the table. Two pairs were face down in front of two of the soldiers. The two still playing the game stared each other down.

The one with the crew cut sitting in front of her was tapping his thumb against the table. Staring at the row of cards he said, "I'll raise by fifty."

The one across was leaned over staring at the same row. "I'll match that." He sat straight up.

"Ok, let's see them." The two flipped over their pair of cards. The table erupted into a fit of laughter. Her mark glanced over and saw her staring at him. "What the fuck do you want?"

Smiling D said, "What's the game?"

"Hold 'em"

"Can anyone join in, or is this boys only?"

"What are you offering?"

"I've got a couple credits on me."

"Only a couple?" the black soldier shuffling the deck said splitting the cards. "Can't really bet big with only a couple."

"I'm sure we can think of something." D winked.

"Yea, whatever, you can join," her mark said.

The soldier to her left extended his hand as she pulled up a chair. "Name's Michael."

"Sasha," D said shaking his hand with a firm grip. She smiled when she saw him wince.

"Quite a grip," he said when he got his hand back. "This Handsome devil to my right is Kevin." He pointed to the soldier with the crew cut. Kevin jutted his chin up as he split the deck, and handed them back to the Black Soldier.

"That's Brandon." Michael said pointing the black soldier sitting beside Kevin. He didn't offer a response.

"And that's Danny!" He said pointing to her Mark.

"Daniel's fine," Daniel said.

"Don't let him fool you. It's always been Danny."

"It's Daniel, asshole!"

"And He." Michael motioned to the soldier wearing shades sitting to Daniels right. "Isn't important."

"It's Derek," Derek said.

"Like I said. Not important."

"When are you going to take off those damn shades?" Brandon said glancing over at Derek.

"What difference does it make?" Derek said. "It's too dark to see in here anyway."

"You're sitting under goddamn light you fucking idiot," Brandon said tipping his glass at him.

"Like that makes a difference?" Derek asked, shrugging his shoulders.

"Blind is up to 30/60," Daniel said as Brandon started passing out the cards.

"How many chips do you need?" Michael said glancing across the table at her.

"1 per credit?" D said.

"Right." Michael nodded.

"I'll take 300 Credits."

"Only a couple?" Kevin said glancing over at her.

"I'm good for it." She smiled as Michael handed over her chips.

"Been at the bar a while?" Daniel said.

"Yea, business has been slow lately." She studied her two cards. Queen of Spades and an Ace of Clubs.

"What sort of business are you in?" Daniel asked her.

"None of yours," she said.

"Ooooh, burn!" Derek shouted.

"Shut the fuck up Derek," Kevin snapped.

The game marched on. Daniel was big blind with 60 credits. Derek doubled the blind while smiling from behind his sunglasses, forcing Michael to fold. D matched. Winning a few games wouldn't hurt her. Kevin was stuck studying Derek's expression before throwing his chips to match. When it finally back around to Daniel again, he shook his head dropped his cards, and tossed his chips into the pool.

As Brandon began dealing out the river, Michael turned to her, "Seriously, what do you do for a living."

"She's a whore," Kevin said pointing to Brandon.

D smiled. "I provide clients with what they need."

"See? A whore." Kevin concluded raising his glass.

"I find things and sell them back to people in need."

"So a Scavenger?" Michael said.

She watched Derek raise his bet. "Yea," she said as he threw a blue chip onto her pile to match.

Kevin matched Derek's bet, as Brandon folded as he dealt out the final card of the river. Brandon dealt out the last card for the river. The final river was laid out with two Kings of Hearts and Diamonds, a Three of Spades and a Four and Five of hearts. No more bets.

D flipped over her Queen of Spades and Ace of Clubs. Kevin had the Queen of Diamonds and the 9 of Diamonds. Derek had a 3 of hearts and a 3 of Diamonds, which played off the Three of Spades in the river, making it the highest hand.

"Goddammit," D said, throwing her chips into the main pile.

"It would seem," Derek said, grabbing hold of the pile, "that I can see perfectly fine in this dark-ass room."

"It's not dark!" Brandon shouted at him. "You're under the fucking light for crying out loud."

Derek ignored him as he was piling on his chips. Daniel had already started to shuffle the cards.

Kevin glanced over to D. "So you're a vulture?"

"Well," D said, "I wouldn't put it that way."

Michael turned back to D. "So what do you mainly salvage?"

"Buildings mostly." She glanced at her cards. Ace of spades again, and a 10 of Diamonds. "Along with a few vehicles for parts, and occasionally factories if I'm lucky."

Kevin was glaring at her.

Derek threw his chips in. "I'm betting 120."

"No fucking way you got two good hands in a row," Kevin said snapping his attention back to the game.

D pushed her 30 tokens into the pile. "Yea, I'm out this round."

Michael folded as well, while Daniel, Kevin and Brandon matched Derek.

Kevin turned to D. "So what, you loot dead bodies on the street?"

"No." D shook her head. "I don't mess with the dead."

Kevin glared at her again. "Yea, I don't buy that."

D shrugged. "Believe what you want, but I don't go anywhere near anything hot."

"Raising to 130, " Kevin said smacking the chips down. He was rubbing two chips between his fingers, and turned back to D. "You know what everyone else at this table does?"

D just stared at him, shaking her head.

"Everyone else here fights to protect your worthless piece of ass." He broke eye contact with her. "Remember that next time you're stripping a dead soldier. You'd be better off being a whore." He dropped the chips down onto the table. "Everyone else good to continue?"

"Yea, I am," Brandon said.

D leaned back in her chair watching as Daniel drew an Ace of Spades for the river. Besides the four soldiers sitting at the table around Daniel, there was also the bartender walking around the main area putting up the chairs on top of the tables. Their guns were within arms reach of them, and there was likely another gun behind the bar. The Marlow strapped against her inner thigh pinched her as she crossed her legs. There were also three vials of Neuro-Toxin sitting in her back pocket. Her knuckles were stretched white as she was turning a chip between her thumb and index finger.

Derek's laugh broke her trance as she watched him grab an armful of chips from the center of the table. There was a lump growing in the bottom of her throat, along with the growing urge to inhale a lung full of smoke, and burn that feeling out of her.

"You alright?" Michael said looking at her. "You look a little tense."

She remembered to force a smile. "Do I?" D shrugged. "Guess I don't have much of a poker face."

Derek started to shuffle the deck, and dealt out the cards. D already had her 60 Credits laying down. Glancing at her cards, she had a 5 of Spades and 6 of Clubs. She leaned back into her chair and watched as Kevin raised his bet to 120.

Sighing, she pushed her chips towards the middle of the table. "Sorry, but I'll be right back. Drank a little too much at the bar."

"You want us to wait for you?" Michael said shooting her a look.

"Nah, it's fine. I'll be right back."

D stepped out the back of the bar and was met with the cool night breeze brushing past her. Her pulse from her inner thigh was beating hard against the Marlow. Taking a deep shaky breath, she felt the dull knot at the base of her throat had sharpened. Reaching down to her inner thigh, her fingers brushed along the edges of the compressed Marlow.

She shook her head to clear her thoughts, and her eye's traced along the alley she was standing in. Following the path of the ruined visitors center around a corner, she was met with a pile of boxes and trash. D brushed against the shadow of a large metal bin and pushed her back against the concrete wall. Sinking to the ground, she gazed at the overcast sky while breathing in the dry air around her.

D took the metal cigarette case out of her back pocket and flipped it open. Grabbing the orange syringe, she then felt along the bumps on the labels for the word 'Sedo'. Her hand was shaking as she gripped the vial and punctured the lid with a needle. Turning the syringe to her own arm, she eyed a healthy vein. She pricked the skin and slid the plunger down then felt a calmness wash through her.

A metal can hitting the concrete broke the silence. Jerking her head she saw Kevin averting his gaze and heading back down the alleyway. D snapped the metal case closed. Standing calmly in the back alley, she waited for a minute to pass before walking back towards the bar. She walked through the door wearing her smile more comfortably.

"You always come around to peek at a girl?" D said stepping back to the table.

"What's she talking about?" Brandon said glancing at him.

"Nah." He shook his head. "Was just lookin' for my own place to piss." Kevin shot her a look.

"Uhh huh?" D said smiling, "Who won the last hand?"

"Derek did." Daniel said.

"On a luck streak?" D said. "That's gotta run out soon."

Derek smiled, "Yea, we'll see."

***

The game carried on for a short time. Derek won one more hand before folding.

Daniel checked his watch. "I need to get going."

"So soon?" D said through a parted smile.

"Yea, I probably ought to get going as well." Michael said

"I'll probably grab a few more drinks." Brandon said. "You joining me?" he nodded towards Derek.

"Yea, why not. A few drinks won't hurt."

They all started to stand up and gather their things, before Kevin, Daniel, Michael and D walked out the front of the bar.

"Where are you all heading?" D said looking directly at Daniel.

"Hmm?" He said glancing back. "Oh, around the West Indies."

"Is it safe there?" D said slipping on a smile.

Daniel sighed, "Looks like we picked up another stray."

"I mean," D said losing her smile. "I don't want to be a burden."

"Nah," Michael said. "I think there's a couple of places there that you could sack up." He smiled over to Daniel. "Right?"

"I don't think Susan would want a random guest."

"Ehh, details." He smiled at D. "We'll find you a place."

"You really think it's a good idea to take her home with you?" Kevin said looking at them.

"I mean," Daniel said looking over at D and laughing. "What could go wrong?"

Kevin narrowed his eyes on D. "That's a bad idea."

"Why's that?" Daniel said.

"She's a junkie," he said, "I caught her out back shooting up."

"I wasn't shooting up," D said.

"Yea right." Kevin sneered "I saw the needle."

"That wasn-" she paused to think. "I'm diabetic, that was my insulin shots."

"Oh yea?" Kevin said, "Why don't you show us?"

D hesitated as she weighed her options, before reaching into her back pocket and grabbing the cigarette case. Opening the spring clasp, she showed them the two colored needles and the row of vials.

"Why are the labels blank?" Michael asked looking at it.

"It's safer," D said. "Nobody will steal something if they don't know what it is."

"Well, since you just took your medication, you won't mind if I just held onto it. Right?"

D thought about it for a minute. "Sure, but I'll need to readminister some insulin in a couple of hours."

"Yea," Daniel said, "Of course." He turned to Michael. "You got more space to carry this than I do," Daniel held it out to him.

"Yea alright," Michael said throwing it into his rucksack.

***

After they had passed through the civilian's checkpoint leading out of the camp, they were walking on the roads through the twisted strips of buildings. D turned to Michael. "So where are we going?"

"Well first, we'll be cutting through the canals."

"Why the canals?" D asked

"They're usually pretty clear," Michael explained. "Because they're low, so if there's an air strike in the area we'll have some cover from the sides. It's just a bit safer than going by the roads. Plus it's a straight route through the city, and we can avoid a few checkpoints on the roads."

D nodded. "Good to know."

Daniel shot her a look and said, "I'm Daniel Holloway by the way." He held out his hand to shake hers.

"Nice to meet you." She smiled and shook his hand.

"Well what should I call you?"

"You can call me Sasha Graceum." D smiled.

"Nice to meet you Miss Graceum."

They passed through a broken piece of fence and walked down an access ramp down into the city's canal. The canal was lined with bone-white concrete with bits of ripped cardboard clinging to the sides. Besides the moon to their backs, the only other light was the occasional hot orange street lamp peering over the high concrete edges. The sky was a dark brown from the clouds overhead. D walked listening to their footsteps echo, and the brief spurts of wind rushing past them. The water made no noise at all beside them. It was an oily black mess in the dark. Orange and white reflected from the old street lights and the moon. She was keeping an eye out for the right moment, as she walked beside Michael.

"You shouldn't mind Kevin," Michael said glancing over at her. "He's a hardass, but..." He thought for a moment. "Well, he's overly sentimental."

"No. I get it," D said.

"What?" He said.

"I get that you'd consider me a sort of ghoul picking away at the bodies. But I've got to have some way of providing for myself. And this is better than being a whore."

"You could join in the effort?"

"I didn't ask for this war."

He stared at her. "Do you support the Federation?"

"The Federation can go fuck itself."

"Then..." He gazed at a black blob farther up the canal. "What then?"

D was keeping quiet as a gust of wind blew past them. "Eventually, whatever the Rebellion offers. It'll be the exact same thing the Federation's offering." She crossed her arms in front of her chest. "Same shit, different boss. It's just a changing of hands."

"If you joined the Rebellion, then you could be a voice, to make sure that that it doesn't change into the same thing it always is."

D laughed. "Do you want freedom?"

"Of course."

"No. I mean real freedom." D said looking at him. "The kind where you don't have some jerk-off down the street that can tell you what to do. The kind that you don't have to have money for everything, cause it's just given to you. There's nobody there to enforce the rules, because there are none. There isn't any need for money, because we'd have what we'd need." She looked up at the sky. "I'd die for kind of freedom."

Michael was still staring at the black blob. "We could have that world one day."

"No," D said shaking her head. "We could have that world now."

He glanced back at her. "I really don't see how."

D saw the black blob fidget in the distance. Michael gripped his gun as they walked closer. It was a woman sitting in the dark with long black hair watching them as they passed by.

"Poor girl," D said turning her attention back down the canal.

Michael glanced over at her. "It is what it is. Hopefully one day we can help her."

"By then it'll be too late," D said looking up the inclines of the canal.

"I'm thinking that a hostel should still be taking in people," Daniel said in front of them.

"What?" D said, snapping her attention to him.

"I think we'll drop you off at a hostel in the West Indies. I don't think my wife Susan would be happy having a stranger in the house with the kids."

"Uhh huh..." D said, eyeing a glass bottle on the ground.

"Well, it'll make things easier. If you'd like, we can swing by and grab some breakfast in the morning since Derek ended up winning most of your credits. I think you two will get along."

"Yea." They were almost on top of it. "That would be..." She stopped and clutched her stomach.

"Are you alright?" Michael asked looking at her.

"I don't know." D was sloping down the incline onto the ground. "Let me just sit down."

"It's only a little bit farther before we get there, do you have enough energy to walk there?"

"No... just..." She was catching her breath holding onto her stomach. "Let me sit here for a little while."

"I can carry you if I need to," Michael offered, eyeing her. "It's probably not safe to stay in one place for too long."

"No. It's fine. I just have a cramp in my leg." She had already grabbed the bottle off the ground. "I should be good in a minute or two."

"Ah, don't be silly," Michael said shaking his head. "Here, I'll help."

D smashed the bottle into his temple. Michael jerked backwards as she lunged towards him. He instinctively reached for his pistol from his harness, but her hand had already grabbed it first. The safety clicked off like a final tone and three bullets ripped through his chest.

Daniel froze trying to get a hold of the situation in front of him. Every sense of self-preservation kicked in as she pointed the gun at him. He turned to run down the canal, as D fired a shot and missed. It was like a flash of lighting along the sides of the canal. Stumbling over a flap of cardboard, he heard the blast cry out. The hot orange metal flew past him. She took another shot and clipped him in the back of the knee.

The force knocked him to the ground. D sprinted towards him, chambering another round. He was scrambling back up, as she kicked him down and shot him in the back of the head.

Sucking in the air with each step, she walked back to Michael's body, grabbed his rucksack, and grabbed her metal case out of the top of the bag, before taking a quick look back at where the woman had been, and froze. She was gone.

D clamored up the side of the canal, and spotted something moving in a pile of garbage not far from where she was. Edging closer to it she saw the poor girl sitting in the middle of it staring at her.

"Whoa, hun. Don't move. Just sit right there."

The poor girl was in tears. She could see D reaching into her back pocket. She was curled up in her corner watching D tiptoe closer to her.

"You're looking mighty hungry." She pulled out the thin rectangular case again.

The girl was gripping her own hands, eyes darting around looking for a quick escape.

D opened the case and took out a vial. "You're not going to be saying anything to anybody right?" She eyed the girl's syringes beside spread out around her. Her own cage of filth.

She stopped shaking, her eyes transfixed on the vial.

D smiled. "Of course you won't." She sank down to where she was. The girl nodded her head.

"The whole vial's yours." D smiled at her.

The girl continued nodding.

"You want it now?"

The girl smiling. Trying to remain calm, she slowed her breathing.

"Easy now hun." D was sitting beside her now, vial still in her hands. "Let me do all the work for you, friend." She had hold of one of the girl's syringes and was puncturing the top of the vial. She brushed aside the girls hair out of her face and said, "Well, aren't you just a beautiful little thing?"

The girl's amber eyes were transfixed on the syringe. D held it in one hand as she curled up the girl's sleeve. Thin dead veins lined her arms, with black infections around the many of the holes in her arm.

"We're embarking on a journey together." She felt along the girls arm and finally found one good pulse. The girl's eyes brightened as D hovered the syringe over the point. "Just sit close by me dear." D tightened a rubber hose around the girl's arm. "For better days." She injected the heroine into her arm.

The girl took in a deep breath.

"You don't have to go through this alone," D said easing up the tension of the hose. "Lean on me. Be at peace."

The girl rested her head on D's shoulder. D set the dirty syringe on the ground, wrapped her arm around the girl's shoulders, and held both of the girls hands with her one hand. She took a deep breath. "Better days are just around the corner hun," D said hugging her. "Better days. you can almost taste them. Not quite like the old days, but better than them." She was holding the girls hands tighter.

The girl breathed harder as her pupils dilated.

"I want you to see a light now darling. It's right there in front of you. Can you see it?"

"I-I can see it," the girl sputtered out.

"Hold on tight now. This is going to hurt you more than it's going to hurt me." D took her hand off of her shoulder, and closed off her nose, and tightly covered her mouth.

The girls eyes shot open. She tried to struggle, but D held her hands firmly on her legs.

"Just keep staring up at that light darling. This will only take a second. Just keep staring."

The girl was trying to throw D off of her, but D had too strong of a grip around her shoulder.

"Better days hun. Don't lose hope. Just hold on tighter. Better days are just around the corner."

The girl was losing her grip on D's hands.

"Just keep your eyes on the big bright light everyone keeps telling us is up there, and those better days."

The grip weakened. Her eyes had rolled back into her head, 3 minutes.

"Hang on darling. Hang on." D kept her hand tight over her nose and mouth for a few minutes longer just to make sure.

The girl was dead.

D laid the body down as she crawled out of the tent to collect herself. Her arms and legs were so numb that they felt like static around her, and that a hole had opened up inside of her and went on forever. She wiped her eyes, but wasn't sure if she was crying, just that for a brief moment she could see.

Pushing all other thoughts away. D started to move on instinct like she was making a bed. She dragged the girl's body down to were the other bodies where and started to strip off the girl's clothes. Stuffing the extra clothes into Michael's rucksack. Then she blew the girl's face off along with Michael's face. Three bodies now. One woman, two men. As far as anyone involved was concerned, D was dead with the group. Possibly an ambush from raiders or thieves.

Grabbing a combat knife off of Michael, she made quick work stripping him and Daniel of clothes or any other identification. In the distance, she could already hear the howls of hungry stray dogs. D ran out of the canal down further before vanishing in the night.

***

Zecona woke up hearing something rustling in the dark. In a haze, he started reaching for his rifle, when a cold metallic hand reached out of the darkness and grabbed him. He shot his head up, but could barely make out the black crescent moons in the War Devils helmet stared back at him. It held up a finger to what would be its lips, but didn't say a word. There wasn't a gun in its hands, so Zecona reasoned there likely wasn't a threat.

A woman was breathing heavily in the hallway. A loud pounding bashed against the wall, but he couldn't make out if it was a punch or kick. The pounding stopped and the breathing picked back up again, but it was shallower and shaky. Her footsteps faded down the hallway and Zecona started to lay his head back down.

Glass shattered down the hall, and Zecona jerked himself back up gripping the edge of the cot. The War Devil had already moved back to the hole, but it wasn't watching the road. It was watching him. The breathing was heavy and fast now, followed by a faint snap. He strained to listen in the dark.

The breathing slowed and faded into silence. The suit was still sitting in the hole. The footsteps approached from the hallway again, and D stumbled through the room, and climbed the half-wall, before laying down on her couch. Zecona laid his head back down, taking in the silence. He didn't recall falling asleep.

CHAPTER SIX
DESIRE

D sat up and held her head in her hands. Her skull felt like it was splitting apart. The sunlight didn't help.

"Fucking hell," she said crawling through her hole in the wall. Making her way to the machine in the corner, she pushed her favorite combo of buttons. A warm cup of coffee plopped down into her hand and she took a sip. It tasted like shit. Looking down at Zecona sleeping, she took another sip and kicked the cot, knocking Zecona onto a pile of rubble beside it. He let out a yelp as his face met the ground.

"You're in the fucking way," she said taking another sip and making her way to her couch.

Zecona stood up looking at a few cuts and scrapes on his stomach and back. "That fucking hurt."

"Don't sleep in the middle of the room then." She opened her bag.

"Nowhere else is clear."

"Don't care. Don't sleep in the middle of the fucking room."

He rolled his eyes at her but she didn't see. D was searching through her bag.

"Can you access the radio when it's like that?" she said, nodding towards the compacted War devil.

"Yea, why?" Zecona asked.

"I've got my own radio set up. We can use a low frequency broadcast, and keep in contact when we split up."

"What's the frequency you're using?"

"2298 was free last time I checked," she said, sitting in the hole in the wall with her notebook.

Zecona walked over to the machine and got a bowl of oatmeal. He Looked up in a shard of a mirror over the contraption and noticed another cut just under his eye.

"You almost took my eye out!"

"So?" she said looking over, taking another sip.

"So? So I wouldn't be able to see!"

"You've got two. You only need one. Be grateful you can see at all."

Zecona was pushing the buttons on the machine. D dragged her eyes across the page half closed. She was scratching a pen in her notebook again. A bowl of oatmeal spit up in front of him. He turned scooping it up and glared at her.

"What?" D glanced up from the notebook.

"So are we doing anything right this second, or did you wake me up for nothing?"

"Oh, sorry," she sneered. "Didn't realize I had to be so considerate in a warzone. I'll try to be more quiet than the gunshots, the bombs going off, and the jets flying overhead."

"I didn't hear any of that last night," Zecona said grabbing a spoonful of oatmeal. "But I did hear when you came back. You were making a lot of commotion. What were you doing?"

"Oh." She said glancing back down to the notebook, scratching more notes.

Zecona was munching away on the oatmeal staring at her. "So?" he said, swallowing.

She glanced back up. "So what?"

"What were you doing?"

"None of your damn business," she said shifting her focus back to the notebook.

"You kept me up long enough."

"Oops," D closed the notebook.

"Oops?" Zecona said taking another bite. He was sitting down on his cot. "Don't suppose you'd know any good painkillers I could use?"

D glanced up studying him. "I might. Why?"

"Just got some lingering space sickness I'm dealing with. Would be nice to get rid of it."

"Right." D shifted her attention back to the notebook. "I know a place we can check out." She scribbled more notes. "I was going to double-check something anyways."

"Great." Zecona's eyes lingered over the dried pool of blood across from him. "So what exactly happened in here to cause that mess?"

Her back tensed up as she put the book back under her bed, and scooped up her equipment. "Gear up. We're heading out."

"Hold up, I'm only halfway through" Zecona pointed to his bowl.

"Too bad," she said getting up. "Learn to eat faster." She crawled back through the hole and grabbed her travel bag.

Zecona scarfed down the rest of his food and grabbed the compacted War Devil. D was already heading for the door. He struggled through the door as he attempted to put on his jacket and strap on the rifle at the same time.

"So, what's the story behind that dried blood back in the room?" he said.

"None of your damn business," she said.

"Not even a hint?"

She didn't say anything. They hit the stairs.

"Are you always going to be like this?" he asked.

"Are you?" she said.

"Why should I follow you if you don't trust me?"

"Do you want some pain meds, or not?"

"Fine." Zecona said rolling his eyes, "Any hint to where we're going?"

"Kalgu Regional Hospital." She continued down the stairs.

"Where's that at?"

"Does it matter?" D raised an eyebrow. "I'm driving."

Zecona shrugged. "Just curious."

"It's across town."

"Nothing closer."

"Yea, probably," D said, "but I have a better feel for that place."

"Whatever."

They reached the bottom, and D unlatched the Prowler in the main hall. Zecona stood at the main console with his arms crossed watching her. D rolled it out the front door. He followed her out and jumped on behind her. She pressed the gas and they sped off down the streets.

***

They had stopped outside an abandoned hospital. It was surrounded by a tall chainlink fence, with yellow and black biohazard signs spaced out along the posts. They approached a section of the fence at the side of the building where a portion had been cut. Zecona paused reading the sign.

Class 1 Quarantine Zone. No Entry Permitted. Trespassers will be incinerated alive.

"Is it safe for us to be here?"

"Yea," D said pulling back the loose piece of fence. "We should be well outside the five year minimum quarantine. Plus we'll be fine regardless. Especially you."

Giant aluminum letters over the main entrance said Kalgu Regional Hospital. As they approached, Zecona could see the burned-out ambulances, and scorch marks around the emergency room entrance. The waiting room was scorched with soot. So much of the walls had been burned away he could see into the surrounding rooms through the exposed steel foundation.

"What the hell happened in here?"

D glared back at him and said, "Blue Lotus."

"Oh," Zecona said taking in the context. "That happened forever ago."

D was leading them up the fire escape at the back of the building with Michael's rifle drawn. The suit followed in the rear, watching behind them.

"Gotta be careful around here," She muttered. "You never know when druggies or scavengers will start hitting this place."

They reached the seventh floor. Opening it, she pointed her rifle down the hallway. Broken glass and medical papers were strewn about the floor. She walked through the door, and the suit closed the door behind them. Heading through a set of double doors, she turned down a hallway, and eventually stopped in front of a door with the name <u>Dr. Cecilee Muchow</u> written beside it. The suit watched the halls. D popped her head into the room.

It had a broken oak bookcase along the back wall, with medical books spilling onto the floor. Two metal filing cabinets and a wooden stool lay to her left. To her right was a metal desk with a built-in computer interface, and a still-intact computer screen embedded into the wall. A wicker computer chair sprawled in the middle of the room. She grabbed the chair and started up the computer taking out her notebook.

Zecona sat down on the stool and asked, "How do you know how to work that?"

She muttered, "It's a computer."

"I know that," he said, looking back at the suit. "I meant, isn't there some sort of password for the system?"

D typed away at the keyboard. "I've picked up a few things here and there." She was already searching through the database for Marcus Greeves.

"Are there any painkillers here?" Zecona asked looking around.

"Yea." D said leaning back in her chair, "There's storage for the in-house pharmacy in room 735. It should be open."

"Ok." Zecona stood up and looked down the hallway, "What am I looking for?"

"Meloxicam," D said without missing a beat.

"Malexim?"

She shook her head, wrote down the name on a blank corner, and tore it out. "Here. If there is any, it should be on the third shelf from the door."

"You sure?" He said grabbing the note from her.

"Pretty sure."

Zecona shrugged. "I'll take your word for it." He walked down the hallway.

D turned her attention back to the computer. Marcus's medical record popped up, along with an image. Last check-in was to another branch in the system on Jarooth, 25th '75. Age 26. Typing in a few more commands into the system, she produced an aged-enhanced image of him. She sat back and stared at the screen, getting a solid grasp of the next mark, before spinning the image 360 degrees, taking mental notes of every detail. D logged off and shut off the computer grabbing her rifle.

She scrunched up her face, "I thought those were locked?"

"Nah," Zecona said turning around. "It was open when I got here."

"Huh," D said. "Found what you were looking for?" She followed the shelves towards the back of the room.

"Nope, can't find it," Zecona said with his head still ducked into the shelf.

She opened a container labeled <u>Drospirenone</u> and topped up her supply of pills.

Zecona shot his head up. "Did you find it?"

"No, just grabbing something for me."

He narrowed his eyes, "What's it for?"

"Just a pick-me-up," D said pocketing her pills.

"Uhh huh?"

"You wanna keep looking here?" D said turning around. "I've got things to do. I can leave without you, and we can meet up later."

"Nah." Zecona said stood. "I think I'll stick with you this time."

"Then let's go," she said, blowing past him, and heading back to the fire escape.

***

D cut the power to the Prowler and guided it to the side of the road. She glanced around the barren streets before dismounting and rolling it into an abandoned insurance office.

"Give me your rifle," She said, strapping her own rifle to the rear of the vehicle.

"Why?"

"Because it's not a good idea to walk into a camp with an assault rifle. Give it here."

Zecona shrugged and handed it over. "Are we leaving the Prowler? Won't it get stolen?"

D pulled out a basic urban camo cover from a side compartment and was already starting to slip it over the top of the vehicle. "If anyone notices it. The guns might, but they won't be able to get far with the Prowler."

"Right, but can't they just hack it, and drive off with it?"

"Well I've got the keys, and it's not exactly easy to hot-wire the fusion engine. If anyone happens by it, they might try to strip it for parts, but we should be back before anyone stumbles across it."

She motioned to Zecona to follow her, and they made their way around a mound of rubble. Reaching into her back pocket, she pulled out the metallic case, opened it, and handed a rubber hose to Zecona. "Here. You'll make this a lot easier."

"What do you want me to do?"

D was already back down into the case and produced a syringe with an orange label and a vial of clear liquid. Her index finger ran along the blank label. Setting the vials back down, she reached back into her pocket, pulled out her lighter, and held a flame under the needle until she was satisfied. Then picked the vial back up and sucked it into the syringe.

"Alright. Now tie that around my arm. Nice and tight."

She took off the sleeve of her coat and rolled up the sleeve off her shirt.

"What are yo-"

"Shut up, and just do what I ask."

He tied the hose around her arm.

"You call that tight?" she said.

He tried again.

"Tighter."

He pulled a bit harder.

"Tighter."

He pulled harder.

"Alright. When I say go, start easing up on it. Slowly. Any faster and it'll probably kill me."

She brought the needle to her arm and then eyed him.

"Remember. I'm the only one with the mission details, and that suit of yours probably won't be too happy if he wakes up and finds me dead."

Zecona nodded and watched her inject the syringe into her arm.

"Go."

He began to ease up on the hose.

"Slow now."

Zecona stopped and went slower as he watched her. D rested her head against the wall. As he loosened the cord, he saw her eyes roll back when she closed them. The more he loosened the cord, the more sweat began to build up across her face. Her other arm began to shake as he felt the tension from the hose give way. He was holding the hose in his hands as she lowered her arm to the ground. She was shivering more sitting there, with her eyes shut tight.

Zecona reached under her neck to check her pulse and was met with a left hook to his bottom jaw. He flew back, gripping the side of his face as she staggered to her feet. D tripped and stumbled to the opposite wall of the ally.

"Don't ever," she spat.

"I wasn-"

"Don't!" she yelled.

She leaned on the wall for support, before making her way out of the alleyway. Her legs were still a bit jerky from the effects of the injection. Zecona got up and said, "Here, let me he-"

"Don't!!" She yelled at him again "I don't need any help... especially from a piece of shit like you."

D mumbled some other things under her breath, but Zecona couldn't hear her. Glancing back, he saw the metal case still lying on the ground. Scooping down, he picked up the vial and glanced over the blank label. He put it, the hose, and the syringe back into the case, then tucked it into his jacket, before following D around the corner.

Two groups of soldiers stood around chatting and smoking cigarettes beneath the steel-tiled roofs of duel towers made up of concrete and the bones of armored vehicles in front of them. Spotting them on the road, they looked past D but stared down Zecona. Walking past a few metal barricades that were put up along the road, Zecona and D made their way into the camp, walking past groups of tents around flaming barrels.

D walked straight towards the outer shell of what remained of a larger building. Three of the walls were still erect, but the front part of the building had been blown away, exposing the interior to the elements. She made her way towards a large set of stairs and broken escalators with an armed guard smoking a cigarette and leaning up against a wall with a large rifle. He looked over at D and gave a weak smile and nod, which faded to a grimace when he noticed Zecona.

She kept a passive face and asked, "We good?"

He smirked from behind a puff of smoke. "Dunno. Might have to do a strip search. Been getting a report about some bitch killing people." He kicked off the wall.

D laughed. "Sounds like a fun time. Who's first? Me or the kid?"

He didn't smile back. "What brings you here?"

"Just business."

"What kind of business?"

"The good kind."

"Who's this?" He said nodding to Zecona.

"A friend."

"What kind of friend?"

D let out a deep sigh, "Is your shift almost done, hun?" She cocked an eyebrow as she slipped on a smile.

He smirked as he took another drag and said, "Yeah, in a bit."

"Well, in a bit maybe I could show you my kind of business."

The soldier smiled. "Sure. There's some rooms down around the far left below."

She gave a little wave and said, "Catch ya later, hun," and walked down the motionless escalators.

He grabbed Zecona by the arm before he could catch up to her and said, "Who's body did you steal those clothes from Ka'Kish?"

Zecona stared back at the soldier's eyes burning into him.

The soldier shoved him back and Zecona raced down the stairs after D. She was waiting for him on the first landing.

When the guard was out of earshot, she said, "He almost didn't let you in."

Zecona glanced at her. She was looking over her shoulder, her smile gone.

"We're splitting up once we get in here. Don't be anywhere near me. Don't talk to me. Don't even look at me. I'll send a signal to your suit with further instructions. We'll meet up later. Understood?"

Zecona nodded.

"Good."

They walked down the rest of the broken sets of escalators in silence. Distant echoes of voices bounced off the walls and grew louder the farther they descended.

Reaching the bottom, they entered a hallway that opened up into what was a large multilevel underground mall. Zecona could see a light with crowds of people sitting on the sides of makeshift paths. Structures built of scraps of metal and cardboard lined makeshift roads. D had already vanished amongst the crowd of the enormous sub-terrain city. People talked, and scuffled through; children walked close to their mothers. A dog barked as its owner tried to haphazardly keep control of their leash. Above Zecona were a series of catwalks, with the faint shadows of figures keeping watch over the masses below. The only sources of light were faint LEDs tied along the tops of the buildings, and the occasional heavy sun lamps that hung from the ceiling. Shifting his way through the crowd, he shoved his hands into his coat pocket and felt the cold, smooth edge of D's metallic case.

***

D drifted through the crowds along the edge of the old metro stations of the lower level scanning the stairs towards the upper layer. The subterranean mall was massive in scope. It needed to be because it was apart of the original Colony City and it was designed to contain everything that was needed with plenty of redundancy. The mass gathered digging out the area underground was re-purposed towards developing the city on the surface. The halls ran as deep as its history. It was constructed in the forties and offered a brief fleeting dream of the surface. They stood against the great famine that hit the city during the fifties, and were there to greet the resurgence of Korsecstan during the sixties. Now they stood as a military and refugee structure against the Federation. Above her were three levels sectioned off to various groups. Military and general defense were on the upper levels. Administrators, staff, or other important individuals towards the war effort resided within the second layer. General population and refugees were packed into the ground floor and basement.

She only had Nadia's old notes to go by, and as with most of her later notes they became far more vague and sparse. The only notes for Marcus were, <u>C9, Third stairs left, OC, 6 to 9ish.</u> It was her last entry.

Her emotions were mulled by the heroin still in her veins, but behind that muted facade she could feel them trying to jump out like a starving animal trapped in a deep black hole every time she spotted salt and pepper hair mixed in with the crowd.

She spotted the station sign for C9. There were three directions from the notes with stairs and escalators. It was unclear. D could either follow the tracks, or duck down a branch and following the block.

Did Nadia mean left to double back, left down the corridor in front of her, or left following the tracks to her right? Taking a chance, D walked down the outshoot and started counting off the stairs. Most of the staircases were dismantled on the ground floor, blocking easy access to the second floor. Those that remained had armed checkpoints surrounding them.

Following the catwalks and towering blocks looming above her, she counted off to the third set of staircases and stopped to look around. The last thing she had to go off of was <u>OC</u>. She was standing in front of another junction near the military checkpoint guarding the stairs. There were multiple kinds of storefronts around her. Looking around, the next set of stairs were far ahead of her. One of the guards had noticed her and he stopped to watch her. D scanned over the various signs and posters plastered over the walls.

From the corner of her eye, she saw that the soldier who was studying her started to walk towards her. Her mind was racing over the possible meanings of those two letters.

She drifted over to an older clothing store. Maybe Something about <u>Oliver's Clothing</u>, or did she mean he was <u>overly cautious</u>? The time ticked over to seven.

"You lost?" The guard asked as he approached her.

D's eyes locked onto a dull green O around the corner. "Nah, I think I'm good." She started to walk through the crowd again, feeling the guard's eyes watching her. There was a lone man with peppered grey hair sitting at the diner's bar. He looked like Marcus, but his face was far more weathered than what she was expecting. D approached the chrome-lined marble bar with a marble granite top and sat down on a metal stool with an empty seat separating them.

The waiter stepped out from the kitchen and spotted D. "What are you in the mood for?"

D scanned the paper menu in front of her. "Could I get a black coffee? And Akkati on Fried Toast?"

"Sure, comin' up."

Glancing over she saw the man hunched over a cup of coffee reading his tablet.

"Anything interesting?" D said looking at him.

"Hmm?"

She pointed to his tablet.

"Oh, not particularly." He shrugged. "Just the election runoffs for Aster Station."

"Yea? How's it looking?"

"Well, it looks like the older Stagate party is taking losses. The Nerblock party seems to be picking up the slack."

"Is that a good thing?"

"Well, historically Stagate has been very pro-Overman. Nerblock has been anti-Overman lately, but who knows how sincere they are."

"Why's that?"

"Everyone has an agenda. Everyone lies."

"Yea?" D said smiling, "What's my agenda?"

His eyes narrowed studying her. "Not interested."

D laughed, "Well I see where your mind went."

"What?"

D gave him a sideways glance, before looking upwards towards the deep blue tiles along the ceiling

"Have we met before?" He asked.

"No, I've just seen you sitting here alone a couple of times as I've passed by."

"Yea?" He raised an eyebrow. "Why's that?"

"I don't know, older men just seem more interesting."

"I already told you, I'm not interested."

"No. I get it, you're already seeing someone else."

"I didn't mean..." His eye's narrowed on her.

She shrugged. "You brought it up first."

The waiter brought out her coffee first, placing it on the bar in front of her.

"Could I get a packet of sugar too?"

"That's an extra 25 sub credits. Each."

"That's fine."

The waiter slid a paper packet towards her. She ripped open the sugar packet with her teeth, and poured it into the coffee with one hand.

"My name is Marcus." He said.

"Nice to meet you," D said meeting his eye's, "I'm Alex."

"Same." He smiled and took a last bite from his meal, and turned off his tablet.

"What kind of work do you do around here?"

Marcus shook his head, "Just manage details within the ground forces."

"Within the Verra forces?"

"Yea, how about you?"

D shrugged, "I used to be a doctor." A plate of clear cyan beads spread over butter-fried toast was placed in front of her.

"Only used to be?" He said raising his eyebrow. "Could always use more of those."

"I've thought about it." D said cutting a corner off of the toast, "Just so much going on, you know? Just trying to get everything back on track in my life again." She took a bite. "Plus, I'd imagine that they'd throw me into the front lines to keep people. I don't know if I want to deal with that with such a gap in experience."

"Well, you don't know if they would just throw you into that kind of situation to start."

She was finishing up the akkati and toast but still had some coffee in her cup. "Do you want to continue this conversation over coffee back in your room?"

He was quiet as he looked down at her plate. "Sure."

She nodded towards the door. "Then let's get going." They both stood up, and Marcus glanced down at her cup.

"Are you bringing your coffee?"

"I don't think I need to," D said smiling.

***

D followed Marcus up a broken pair of escalators to the third floor. Most of the older store fronts appeared to be converted into storage areas. From what she saw, they mostly held spare weapons and ammunition through the racks. Makeshift barricades of green sandbags broke up the upper walkways, and rebels dotted the paths looking down towards the masses. Their faces were completely concealed with a balaclava with a pair of goggle hosting a range of sensors. All of them appeared to be armed with a Segratta classed rifle, capable of firing electromagnetic-cased rounds. Most of them were donned with long black bulletproof battle coats. She followed him through an old store, and they made their way through a narrow corridor that used to have internal offices. The passages twisted deeper into the complex, before they stopped halfway down a hallway in front of an old office. He unlocked and opened the door.

"After you," Marcus said, gesturing through the door.

"Nice place." D looked over the office retrofitted into a bedroom. A personal bathroom was attached to the side. She took off her jacket and threw it onto a chair. "Been here long?"

"About six months." He closed the door behind him. "How long have you been here?"

She turned her head with a smile. "I don't think you brought me up here to chat."

D unbuttoned her shirt and let it drop to the floor. The brass lamp beside the bed lit her form beautifully. Marcus smiled, as he locked the door behind him and walked towards her. Pushing her towards the bed, he climbed on top of her, and started dry humping her kissing the base of her neck.

She was laughing, as he took off his shirt, and started to work on his pants. "Oh Shit, Wait a minute!" D cried out. He ignored her. His pants were off.

"I need to take a quick trip to the bathroom," She said . He was on top again, kissing her neck, and unbuttoning her pants.

He hung his head down staring down at himself. "Seriously? Now?"

D smiled. "Either now or during."

He laughed. "How about a quick peek?"

"It'll only take a minute," D said.

He didn't move, staring into her amber eyes. With a quick smile, he said, "Sorry!" His body jerked down.

"No!"

In one quick fluid motion, he had her pants undone and pulled down, then froze. He wasn't looking at her, he was staring at the compressed Marlow strapped to her left inner thigh.

D let out a strained laugh. "A working girl's gotta have some sort of protection."

He was silent, still clutching her pants. She clenched her left hand into a fist.

Shaking his head. "That's an Overman gun."

Her left fist shot out and struck him in the temple. He clattered to the ground. Her right hand grabbed the Marlow and activated it. Popping apart, it began to breathe to life, expanding the barrel, body, shaft, and magazine.

Marcus grabbed hold of the end table. D pulled her pants back up and stood over him. The Marlow pulsed in her hand with each bullet that formed in the magazine. She reached into her back pocket and froze when she grabbed nothing. Her eyes shot to the bed.

Marcus grabbed the brass lamp and smashed it across her face. The room flashed to pitch black. She felt the back of her head slam into the floor and heard the gun clatter out of her hand. He scrambled away to the door.

D's right hand felt for the gun as Marcus struggled with the locked door. Her thumb brushed against the base of the lamp. She heard the click of one of the locks.

His feet broke the rays of light at the base of the door. Jumping up, she swung the lamp blindly and slammed it into the side of his head.

Marcus fell to the floor as she turned and swung the lamp again. The heavy brass whooshed through the air, hitting nothing. From the light beneath the door, she saw him roll out of the way, as the brass lamp smashed into the ground.

He kicked at her foot, but not enough to knock her off balance. She leaned against the door, eyes wide in the dark. Both her hands were locked around the base of the lamp. Marcus was scrambling on the floor. Where was the gun? D's eyes were darting blindly in the dark. Her mind snapped as the Marlow scrapped against the concrete floor.

Leaping towards the noise, she felt his body beneath her. She had the lamp midswing as the gunshot rang out. One flash, and she saw his head in the brief light. The look of pure fear in his eye's as she straddled him. Her locked hand around his throat, and she drove the base of the lamp into his skull like a hammer to a nail. He cried out and fired a burst of shots into her, and the bullets ripped through her left side. Raw meat and broken pottery being smashed against the rocks sounded off in the room with each swing of the lamp. When his body had seized up and stopped moving beneath her, she strained to hear over her breathing.

Blood, sweat, or tears were trickling down her face onto the floor. No footsteps echoed from the hallway, and beneath the door frame light continued to trickle through, but she couldn't make out if anyone was standing on the other side.

Grabbing the Marlow from his warm hand, its mechanical heart beat thumped in her palm. D clutched her bullet wounds as she stood up and relocked the door. Pressing her ear against the door, she was met with silence. She stumbled through the darkness towards the bathroom. Staring into the mirror at her blood-covered body, she also saw a swollen black spot covering half her face where he'd hit her.

D reached into one of her coat pockets and popped a few pills. Glancing over at the shower, she threw the dial on, and the cold water hit her as she collapsed onto the shower floor.

"Shit." The air flew out of her.

She lay there, as the water washed off most of the blood and bits of flesh. Nanobots throughout her body worked to reconstruct and close the holes riddled through her left side.

When most of the blood had washed away, she stood up and grabbed a washcloth. Blood soaked the washcloth red as she worked. She tossed it to the side and grabbed another one scrubbing the rest of her body. Chucking that one too, she flipped off the dial, grabbed a dry towel, and was back in the room drying off. Throwing on her shirt, she grabbed her coat from the bathroom. One last look in the mirror and the black swollen mark on her face was gone.

D walked over to his clothes and checked the pockets. His MC wasn't there. She saw a coat, and checked its pockets, but it wasn't there either. Looking around, she saw a trunk peeking out from underneath the bed. Dropping to all fours, all she saw under the bed was a trunk and a shirt. She opened the trunk, and began sifting through loose articles of clothing, until she felt it wrapped up in a cloth. Unwrapping the cloth revealed the familiar thin black rectangular device. She shoved it inside her coat, then closed the trunk, and pushed it back under the bed.

Checking the time, she glanced across the top of the bed looking for her metallic case. She searched under the folds of the covers.

There were three loud bangs at the door. She froze twisting her head at the door knob. Two silhouettes stretched into the room from beneath the door. Her eyes were drawn to something else creeping towards those shadows. The blood was crawling its way towards the gap. Gripping the Marlow tighter she sat on the edge of bed, turning her full attention to the door. The door handle jiggled in its locked state. The slow metallic heartbeats of bullets forming in the Marlow's chambers pulsed through her. The blood was about to pass through the gap when the shadows moved down the hall.

D grabbed the arms of the body, and yanked it towards the bed, then grabbed his shirt, and used it to soak up the blood. Pressing her ear against the door, she listened. The footsteps grew softer, until she couldn't hear them anymore. After waiting what seemed like days, she flipped the lock and walked out into the hallway. There were small makeshift lights hanging from the ceiling in the dingy concrete hallway. Closing the door behind her, she grabbed a cigarette and her lighter from her coat pocket and held them up to her mouth.

"Hey!" a voice called out at the end of the hallway.

The lighter sparked up. Her mind was already racing.

He approached her and said, "This is a restricted area."

She waved her hand and nodded towards the door. "Relax, I'm just finishing up some business."

"You need to be escorted out by the participating party."

He put his hand on the door. She touched it and stood blocking his way smiling.

"He's sleeping right now, and I really need to get going, but didn't feel like troubling him. Do you really want to wake him up? Just to do some menial bullshit security protocol? Why don't you just save yourself the hassle and escort me out?"

She felt him start to turn the handle under her hand and dug her fingers into his hand. He stopped and glared at her. She was still smiling at him.

He tensed and said, "Please step aside, ma'am."

She couldn't catch herself, and whispered the word, "No." She smiled behind cold dead eyes. Shoving her against the wall, he pushed open the door and saw the dead crumpled body on the floor. He reached for his comm turning his attention back to D.

D had already pulled out the Marlow and shot him in the throat. He dropped the comm. By the time he pointed his rifle, she'd already shot three more times. He fired a single shot but it missed, hitting the wall beside her head before stumbled back for the door. She launched herself up at him and took the shot at his head, then kicked his body into the room. Slamming the door shut, she took off down the hall. The alarm for the building started sounding off. Bringing the sleeve of her coat up to her mouth, she said,

"I need backup!"

CHAPTER SEVEN
DISSENTER

Zecona made his way along a massive network of rat nests shambled together on the bottom floor of the derelict mall. Everything around him reminded him of Simul Rosids Station. It was jarring to see the inner hallways so flat. His mind kept expecting to see the curve of the gravity wheel. The crowds had given him a large berth as he walked along the inner edge of the old storefronts. An orange and yellow poster tapped to a pillar caught his attention.

Wandering Minds Weaken the Lines.

Don't let them catch you thinking about your lover boy.

It had the picture of a stenciled black outline of a Camera with a thin robotic neck and hands in a suit and tie. The camera was staring at a black stencil outline of a woman with a thought bubble above her. Inside it was a soldier holding a rifle sitting in a trench.

Zecona spotted a Pharmacy sign lit up down an outshoot and felt his joints flaring up again. He instantly bee-lined for it ignoring the crowds. The outer windows to the store were long broken and boarded up, but the door was open.

"What do you want?" the man behind the counter said staring at him.

"I'm looking for Malexicom."

His eyes narrowed. "What?"

Zecona sighed and felt through his pocket. The man tensed up and leaned back from the counter. He placed the paper D had written on earlier on the counter.

"Is this some sort of joke?" He laughed, "You can't get high off of Meloxicam."

"I'm not looking to get high," Zecona said shaking his head. "I'm just looking for Meloxicam."

"Yea, sure." He waved towards the door. "Get the fuck outta here."

"I can pay." Zecona heard someone walking into the store behind him.

"Whatever, I'm not going to sell it to a stupid druggie."

"I'm not a druggie, I'm ju-"

A man grabbed his left arm from behind and said, "Is there a problem Oliver?"

"Just a stupid druggie that won't take no for an answer," Oliver said from behind the counter.

Zecona heard the door to the pharmacy shut.

"A smart mouth can really land you into a lot of trouble," The man behind him said. Oliver had pulled out a shotgun and pointed at Zecona as he walked out from behind the counter. "I think you're long overdue for a brief lesson on manners." The man pegged Zecona in his right side. Zecona's head hit the floor before the pain in his rib's registered.

He leaned up on one arm, and caught a glimpse of the group of five other men around him. The one that was behind him, pushed him back down with his boot.

"Did I say you could get back up?" He pushed his heel into Zecona's chest. "First lesson is manners. Now I want you to ask politely to stand back up."

Zecona was wide eyed staring back up at the guy. The man snapped his fingers. "Now, now, we ain't got all night, and I've got a bunch more lessons lined up after this." He dug his heel harder into Zecona's chest.

Struggling to speak, he gasped "Would you please let me up?"

"What was that?" The man said leaning down, pushing on his chest harder. "Couldn't hear you. You'll have to speak with a lot more conviction if you want to do well with us normal folk."

"Would you please. Let me up."

"Good!" He kicked off of Zecona's chest. "You're becoming a regular fucking poet." The man walked across the room as Zecona pushed himself back up. "Now this next lesson is going to require a little cooperation from you," The man said, turning back at him, and pulling out a pistol. He looked over towards the group and said, "Strip him down." Two men lunged at Zecona.

D's voice called out from within his pocket. "I need backup!" Blue light shot out from Zecona's pocket. Oliver fired the shotgun at him. The buckshot dissolved amongst the transformation as the War Devil lunged forward. The compartment in his right thigh opened.

The man who had been doing the talking flipped the safety off on his pistol. The War Devil was between the two who had moved forward first. It punched its spiked knuckles through the one to its left, then swiftly brought the spike in its elbow crashing back into the forehead of the one to its right.

Oliver was chambering another round. The metal baton of the KILROX ejected upwards out of the suit's thigh. The two men to it's left and right started to fall to the ground. It lunged towards the man with the pistol, and sliced apart the man's wrist with it's left fist. Its right hand ripped into his throat.

Oliver turned around and pointed the shotgun at the War Devil. The KILROX bounced off the ceiling. The War Devil yanked the gun forward bending the barrel of the gun as the buckshot ripped through. It held out its hand and grabbed the KILROX from the air. It snapped the baton against Oliver's temple, and activated the device. The shockwave shattered his skull and the glass behind the counter, sending out a mist of blood.

As Oliver and the broken glass fell to the floor, the War Devil put the KILROX back into its thigh compartment.

Zecona was panting within the helmet from all the sudden electric shocks that had jerked him about. Before finally forcing out "It's about time yo--"

The suit sent out a constant pulse locking Zecona's body, and snapping his head towards the corner of the room behind them. "You work for me." The War Devil said keeping the lock in place. "You are under contract to get me from Point A. To Point B. Discreetly, and unnoticed. That does not mean starting fights or walking towards strange men with loaded guns. Just because you have access to a War Devil does not make you invincible and does not mean I am obligated to fight your battles. Do you understand?"

Zecona tried to nod his head, but it was locked into place. "Yes, I understand."

"Good." He relaxed the armor. A low whooping wail was sounding off outside.

Zecona's eyes widened. "Is that for us?"

"No," the suit said popping open the compartment in its right leg. "But it will be." It reached in and grabbed a fusion grenade. It activated it, dropped it to the floor, and ran towards the back door of the building, then sprinted down an accessway through the inner portion of the mall.

The shop exploded, and the suit unformed around Zecona. All Zecona could see was a blur as he looked back at where they were. Smoke was starting to pour into the accessway he was standing. The fire alarm was flashing and screeching in the narrow hall.

"Are you listening?" The suit called out from his wrist.

"What?" Zecona said snapping to attention.

"We need to regroup with D, then go from there."

"Where is she?"

"Third floor."

"How do I get there?"

"There's a service elevator nearby. Roughly twenty paces straight, then turn left and head towards the walls."

"On it," Zecona sprinted down the passageway.

***

D rushed down a long empty maintenance way on the third floor, keeping her eye focused on the turn ahead of her. While she was out of the immediate area from where she'd been, she was still on the 3rd floor. Quick successive chirps of an old fire alarm were still going off around her, but she hadn't ran into anyone else. She stopped at the corner. To her right was an old fire escape was chained shut, and to her left the hallway continued. Peering around the turn, her gaze was met with a long hallway of shipping containers and closed doors. No soldiers in sight.

Bringing her wrist to her mouth she whispered "What's the situation?"

"We caused an explosion on the first floor," the War Devil responded. "Currently making our way to extract you."

"No." D said. "Just stay where you are, and keep the distraction going."

"As much as I'd like to do that, it'll risk us blowing our cover," the War Devil replied. "Find somewhere to lay low, and we'll meet up with you."

"I'm the boss," she hissed. "Do as I say."

"I'm the specialist," it said. "I'm doing what'll work."

D let out a deep breath. Her Marlow was compacted again and shoved into her front pocket. The old metro system would have been locked down by now. Nobody would be allowed in or out of the area for at least the next four to six hours, by that point she wouldn't have an effective alibi. She'd be under custody until she was checked out. Remembering the last time that happened, she had to get back to the common area, fast, and hope a guard wasn't outside of the barracks.

"Hold it!" a muffled voice called out from behind her. She spun around facing a fully armored soldier walking towards her.

"What the fuck is going on around here?" D said eyeing him. The alarm was still echoing off the walls.

He had his rifle pointed at her. "Hands up. Against the wall."

D thought about the Marlow in her pocket, but raised her hands, and faced the wall.

He walked up behind her and snapped a metal handcuff onto her wrist.

"Really?" D said looking at it.

"Hands behind your back," he said through his helmet.

She sighed but complied, and felt handcuffs snap around her other wrist.

"State your business being in this area," he said turning her around and leaning her against the wall.

"I just got done meeting with a guy," D said looking into his reflective visor.

"What was his name?"

"Don't know." D shrugged. "Didn't ask."

"What's your name?"

"Margret Kishner."

"The actress?"

"No." She shook her head.

"Have any ID on you?"

"Nah," D said. "Usually don't keep it on me."

"Right." He nodded his head, then grabbed her by the arm and started walking with her. "We'll figure this out later."

"Come on, do we really have to do this?" she said tilting her head at him. "Can't I just go? I don't understand what's going on."

"Yea, no. You're coming with me until we get this sorted out."

"Fine." D sighed.

***

Zecona had found a service elevator along the maintenance hallway. The elevator didn't have a normal call button, instead, it was operated by an employee key. He had knelt down on the floor to study the serial number and model of the lock.

The War devil spoke up from Zecona's wrist. "I've contacted D. We need to hurry to catch her before she does something stupid."

"I'm working on it," Zecona said. A quick standard lockpick maneuver with a hairpin was able to summon the lift. He lifted his wrist "What floor is she on?"

"Third floor."

"Got it."

The elevator dinged as the double doors opened. Stepping onto the lift he instinctively tried to press a button but found the controls were replaced to require a single key to select the floor. Zecona sighed and crouched down as the doors closed. He popped open the inner panel on the carriage, and found the original electronics still intact behind the face plate.

The board was pre-C.R. tech which was common on most of the outer stations. He traced along the controls for five floors, the main floor they were on, two upper floors, and two lower floors, as well as the standard open door, Emergency stop, and call button were present. While there was also a button for "close door", it wasn't connected to anything.

"I thought you were an expert at this?" the war devil said.

"I'm working on it," Zecona said. "Are we still clear outside?"

"You're ok for now. A few soldiers are investigating the halls north of us."

Bending the metal hairpin, he inserted it into the lock, popping the internal pins, then studied the turning mechanism.

The war devil pipped up, "They're getting closer though."

"I'm getting there." He shifted the internal pins to another position. "At least this isn't digital."

Turning the lock, he saw the locks cylinder connect to the third-floor control, and the elevator jerked upwards with an audible ding.

"Shit," the war devil said. "They heard the elevator."

"Fantastic, What now?"

"Go up!"

Zecona glanced at the controls. "There isn't anoth--"

"No. Through the hatch."

"You've gotta be--"

"Now!"

Zecona slapped the emergency stop between the first and second floor and flipped the emergency hatch up. Reaching up with palms on the outside, he tested his weight on the ceiling, before attempting to hoist himself up through the hole. He was only able to pull himself halfway up. Kicking his feet, he crawled his way to the outer case. Consuming blackness loomed above him as he stood up. From the faint light from the elevator car, he could make out the maintenance ladder.

"They're moving towards the second floor."

Closing the hatch, he was consumed by darkness. Zecona began to feel his way through the pitch-blackness to the ladder, trying his best not to trip over the outer cage of the elevator. He jammed his finger on the metal bar. His foot gripped the lower rung, and he began shambling his way upward.

While climbing he whispered, "Could you give me some kind of light?"

The War Devil didn't have to do anything, because light flooded the lower shaft from the second-floor elevator door opening. From the light, he saw the outer doors of the third floor beside him. Zecona swung his way over the pit below to the ledge. The soles of his feet gripped the thin lip for the door.

"They're coming up," the War Devil said from his wrist.

Zecona continued to fumble in the dim light to find the emergency release for the door. The light vanished as the elevator car below him began to move upwards. His hand flowed around a lever. He pulled down as hard as he could, feeling the door slide past his shoulder and bathing the shaft in light. As the elevator doors slid open, The war devil lept off of his wrist. Turning towards the hallway, he was met with three soldiers with their rifles pointed at him. One reached out and caught him by the coat and threw him to the ground.

"Start talkin'!" a soldier said as they pressed a rifle into the back of his neck. Another soldier bent down, gripped his arms, and slapped a pair of metal handcuffs on his wrists.

"Look I was just holding onto a bag for this guy!" Zecona said, "I really don't know what's going on."

"Yea, and how exactly did you get into the restricted area?"

"I don't know, the elevator was just open!"

"Take him to a holding cell, we'll search him later. Right now, just keep canvasing the area, there may be more."

***

The soldier was leading D to an old mall security office. Looking around, she noted a few of the upper stores had been converted to choke points with metal shields set up along the catwalk. Two guards stood by the main doors. Entering the office, they were met with a half-wall in the center of the room, surrounded by tinted glass and monitors that were set up to be a command station. The rest of the room was a duel-toned grey and dark grey with wood trim along the floor. They stopped behind an officer with short blond hair sitting at the desk. He was typing something on the antique keyboard.

"Leon," The soldier said, "got a minute?"

Leon glanced back from the monitor and saw them standing there. "Who's this?"

"Caught her wandering around Z3Q5MA. Don't know who she is."

D glanced down the corridor they were standing in front of. On the left, there was a row of cells made of chain link fence. To the right was a locker room for the soldiers.

"Yea? What were you doing up here?"

"Was finishing up meeting with a guy."

"Oh yea? What was his name?"

D shrugged. "Don't know. Didn't ask."

"Yea, I bet."

D focused on the pale blue locker room. Besides the row of wooden benches, she could clearly see a large metal black gun rack sitting in front of an old outline from where a row of lockers used to be. She could make out the corner of a row of green lockers from where she was standing.

"We'll sort this out later," Leon said standing up. "We've got a 493 in progress in Z1Q2."

"Yea, I know," the soldier said as he started to lead them towards the cells.

"Really?" D said glancing at them.

Leon opened a cell with a loud metal screech and nodded his head towards a bench.

"Can't you just let me go? This is just a waste of time."

"Just get in," he said motioning towards the cell again.

"Fine." D sighed, walked into the cell, and sat on the bench. She was already studying the metal bars and how they were connected to the ceiling.

"Look forward please," Leon said holding up a camera.

D instinctively smiled.

"No smiling."

She let it fall and heard the click of the camera go off.

"Can you at least take off my handcuffs?" she yelled after him, but was met with silence.

D turned her attention to the cell and studied how the bars were connected to the ceiling. It didn't appear that this was standard from the original mall, but the cage seemed sturdy enough. She still had the compacted Marlow in her pocket.

Looking at the cell door, the lock looked cheap. The mechanism probably couldn't survive a few gunshots, but the soldiers in the area would quickly respond too. Her thoughts were interrupted as Leon escorted Zecona to the cell beside her.

She watched as Leon left, then took a deep breath and let out the words, "Nice Job."

"Got cornered," Zecona said shifting around in his seat. "Nothing I could do."

"Do you at least have the War Devil with you?"

"Nope."

She rolled her eyes. "Fantastic."

D sat listening, watching the edge of the door. "Alright." She said whispering under her breath, "Here's the plan. These cuff's seem strong enough, so I'm going to sever my left thumb off to get my hands free and shoot the locks apart. We'll barricade ourselves in the locker room across the hall because the guards will probably have heard us by then. I'll shoot them, and if I can, grab the keys for your cuffs, and you can grab a rifle. If not. We'll run for it. I think I know where a fire escape is, and we can make our way there." She glanced over at him. "Did you catch all that?"

Zecona was already standing up with his cuffs off and rubbing his wrist. "Sorry couldn't hear you, could you say that again?"

"Would you keep your fucking voice down," D hissed through gritted teeth. She glanced back towards the mouth of the hallway, before standing up and walking backwards towards Zecona's cell.

"Can you get the cells open?"

Zecona shrugged as he started to pick her handcuff's. "Probably."

She nodded, "Alright, I think I have a plan."

"I think we are in a little over our heads," Zecona said, "we probably ought to check in with the War Devil to figure out what's going on."

"Just do as I say," D said, "alright?"

"It's got eyes on the outside at least. Maybe we should just see what it sees."

D sighed. "Fine."

***

The War Devil had crawled through the trail of cables and wires that were laid out over the third-floor ceiling, doing its best to keep up with the soldiers that had captured Zecona, until they took him to what appeared to be a rebel checkpoint. It was scanning over the area when its radio kicked in.

"Hey." It heard D's voice whisper. "Can you hear me?"

"Hearing you now," the War Devil said. "What's your status?"

"Just sitting here with the kid. Where are you?"

"Monitoring the situation outside of the security point you two are locked into."

"What's the security like out there?"

"Two guards directly outside of the room you are in, with a single officer manning a comm station. There are also two patrols of three soldiers walking along the catwalks. One on the top floor, and another on the floor below, with a pair of staircases connecting the two."

"I noticed some choke points on the upper level, how are they?"

"I'm counting four major ones. With three soldiers stationed inside each of them. There is a mounted minigun stationed and manned inside each of them." The War Devil looked over the area before saying, "I think it would be best to wait until they try to move you out of the area. I'd assume they'd try to keep you within the maintenance access ways, then I'll move to intercept if I can get an opening."

"Not a good idea," she said. "They'll likely split us up."

The War devil was quiet for a moment, "You have a better idea?"

"What's the nearest path to a maintenance access door?"

"There are two crosswalks on either side of the checkpoint. Left one leads directly to a maintenance way."

"My left or yours?"

"Your left. When you exist the security checkpoint."

"Got it." The radio went silent for a minute. "Do you have a clear shot of the gun nest to our left?"

"I'll need a minute to get into position."

"Do what you need to do," D said. "We don't have a lot of time."

***

Zecona had already set to work unlocking his own cell while D was on the radio. D was still talking with the War Devil over the radio, but he was more focused on the mouth of the hallway, while feeling the tumbler of the locks click open. The lock snapped open, and he opened his cell door noiselessly.

"So what's the plan?" Zecona said approaching the lock on her cell.

"We'll grab some things from the locker room. I'll dress up as a soldier, then the suit is going to take out one of the gun nests. While the soldiers are focused on the gunfire outside, I'll take out the officer with my Marlow. Then we'll go across the catwalk to the maintenance way while you just keep your head down. We'll regroup with the War Devil there, and head on our way. Got it?"

"Think that'll work?" Zecona said clicking the final tumbler open to her lock.

"Easy-peasy," she said.

The cell door screeched open as he opened it for D.

Both of their hearts skipped a beat at that moment. From the other room, they heard Leon stand up from his seat, followed by the words. "All units--"

"Fuck. Move!" D said pushing him towards the locker room. She hugged the wall and began to expand her Marlow while waiting for the bullets to form.

Zecona got to work trying to pick the lock on the gun rack. It looked as though it had an electric card that could be used manually, but it had a standard manual override that could be picked.

"What did you do?" the war devil said over the radio.

"Small Technicality," D said to her bracelet.

"Multiple units are starting to converge on your location."

"Can you please provide covering fire?"

"Still moving into position." it responded.

A chunk of plaster blew off the wall beside her shoulder. She returned fire with the Marlow. Zecona had the gun cabinet opened.

"Here, catch!" Zecona said, tossing the rifle towards her.

It landed halfway between them and between the two benches. "Seriously?" D screamed at him. Another chunk of plaster exploded near her head.

As Zecona clambered over the benches, he tripped and fell beneath the cloud of dust that had filled the room. Slamming into the ground, his lower lip went numb, and he tasted iron on his lips. He fumbled for the rifle. Another burst of fire struck the wall beside the gun case. D fired off another burst until the Marlow clicked empty. Scrambling back up over the other bench, he stood beside D, and handed her the rifle.

"Great." D grabbed it and shoved the Marlow into her pants. "Get those lockers opened too!"

"Shouldn't we focus on just getting out of here?"

"We'll get ripped apart without some kind of armor." Another burst of gunfire hit the wall beside her. She blindly fired back around the corner with the rifle.

Zecona looked through each of the locker vents until he spotted a helmet hanging inside. They were secured with a combination lock embedded directly into the doors, but looking closer he'd need something more than a hairpin to access the manual override. He pressed his ear against the door, and tried to listen for the combination clicks of the tumblers, but couldn't over the continued gunshots around him.

"I've activated the fire gates in that hallway," the War Devil called out over the radio. "It should be a clear path."

"Got it," D said into her bracelet. She turned to Zecona, "What's taking so long!"

"I need to be able to hear!"

"Just cover the door." She whipped the rifle around.

Zecona barely had enough time to jump out of the way before D shot the lock and ripped it open. He grabbed a rifle out of the cabinet, and loaded a magazine into it, before jumping towards the place D had been standing. D threw on a battle coat and was in the middle of strapping on a helmet when the lights cut out. Turning back towards the direction of the lockers, she began to fumble for the sensors in the dark.

"One hardpoint has been taken care of," the War Devil said over the radio.

Zecona continued to fire towards the illuminated entrance. Each gunshot lit up the dust around Zecona like he was trapped in a thundercloud. D gripped the sensors from the locker, strapped it to her face, and flipped on the night vision array.

"I've taken care of the upper left hardpoint," the War Devil called out again.

Scanning the gun case, she grabbed a grenade from the bottom shelf, along with a few more magazines for the rifle. She rushed past Zecona and stopped at the mouth of the hall. D unloaded a clip into one of the soldiers until they fell. A shot pinged her shoulder.

Ducking back behind the wall, she watched as the other soldier dragged their downed comrade.

"Come on, move!" she called to Zecona.

D reached the front doors to the office. Looking up at the various light orbs set up above them, she opened fire at them. Glass rained down to the catwalks and shattered on the shanty town below. Her head snapped backwards as a bullet slammed into her helmet.

Over the ringing in her ears, the War Devil pipped up again, "Top Right hardpoint secured."

She turned to Zecona and shouted "Go left. Now!"

Zecona ran past her to the right.

"No! Other left!"

Skidding to a stop, he scrambled the other way. Ducking low, he rushed along the crosswalk as glass along the path shattered to his side. Zecona reached the door and tried to turn the handle.

Locked.

He fumbled in the dark for his hairpin with gunshots echoing around him. His hands trembled and missed the keyhole. While Zecona was trying to work the door, D shot down another soldier. She was partway onto the catwalk, and could see more soldiers rushing towards her position. Glancing below, she could see the support for the catwalk ahead of her was already badly damaged, and shoddily reinforced. She ripped a grenade off of her chest and threw it towards the ground floor while continuing to shoot off suppressing fire.

Meanwhile, Zecona finally calmed himself down enough to think of what he was doing. The lock clicked open, and he could finally turn the handle. He pushed, but it didn't budge. His eyes bulged, pushing harder with his shoulder. Nothing. More gunshots ricocheted over his head. With his mind racing, he glanced up and notice an old-world set of instruction flashing into focus with the gunfire.

<u>Pull to open.</u>

The door was open in an instant, and he glanced back at D as the grenade went off below. The upper floor began to fall under its weight, and cascaded bringing a group of rebels with it. D was already running across the crosswalk. Zecona held open the maintenance access door. She felt the walkway beneath begin to give way. She tripped as it crumbled away. Scrambling to climb up the growing incline, Zecona popped over the horizon and held out his hand. As the walkway gave out, she slapped her hand to his forearm but felt herself slip down to his wrist.

Zecona braced himself against the banister to the side as she dangled over the edge; he struggled to hold both of their weights.

Dust rushed past them as he tried to pull her up. Dropping her rifle, she managed to grip the edge of the walkway. Gunshots were still ringing out around them. Together they managed to drag her up until her torso landed on the walkway. She scrambled up the rest of the way, and they both darted for the third-floor maintenance way. Zecona fell against the wall as the entered the hallway, holding his rifle up to D. She shook her head but grabbed it anyways. He jumped when the spider-like body of the War Devil landed on his shoulder.

As it crawled to Zecona's wrist it said, "There's an old fire escape up ahead. Just need to get past the locks, and it'll lead up to the surface."

"Won't there be more soldiers on the surface?" Zecona asked.

"No," The suit said. "The door on the surface is blocked off, but I can probably clear the path."

They sprinted down the hall towards the fire exit, and Zecona got a good look at the lock. It was a simple padlock, easy pickings, he had it open with a flick of the wrist. He grabbed the chain and lock.

"Go ahead." He motioned towards the door.

D opened the door with her rifle drawn making her way down the stairs. Zecona followed with the chain still in hand. Closing the door, he chained and locked it from the other side. The War Devil jumped from Zecona's wrist and transformed on the landing.

"Wait here," it said, walking up the stairs to the door on the top floor.

A claw extended from its index finger, and it started to rip apart the welded door by sliding it's finger along the edge. Grabbing the loose edges, and pulled the door back, revealing a concrete wall. Retracting it's claw, it began to punch through sections of the wall with ease. It started with each corner, then punched along the sides. Dust blew down the stairs as the wall collapsed, and the War Devil stepped through the fresh hole. D climbed through the hole next, followed by Zecona. They had climbed up into an abandoned parking garage. Stepping out into the street, they looked back and saw the smoke rising from the underground.

"We gotta keep moving," D said looking at him. "They'll likely figure out where we went eventually."

Zecona was still staring up at the smoke.

"Yo? You listening?"

"Yea," he said.

"Then let's get moving," she said. "I'm starving. Let's go somewhere else and grab something to eat."

***

124

The city was on high alert. Radio chatter had picked up the moment they'd left the underground mall. VTOL's streaked across the sky, with a spot light burning across any road and alley way it could find. Humvees full of soldiers tore down the major road ways, and soldiers had fanned out on foot, flowing into every building, and side ally like water from a broken levee.

They couldn't make their way back to the Prowler, so they began to navigate through the groups of soldiers based off of the War Devil's sensors until they came to a civilian checkpoint built up around a section of the inner city. They found a loose piece of sheet metal in the ramshackle walls. People were still active within the camp, finishing up the evening bar crawl, but a large group had gathered to watch a hacked feed of the military search across the city. D and Zecona slipped past them, down an alleyway towards a small dingy noodle hut down an alleyway.

A chubby bald man wearing an apron stained with orange and grey marks watched them approach as he was wiped down the countertop. He nodded to D and asked. "Do you know what all the commotion is about?"

"Skillimer's Mall got bombed," D said taking a seat on the stool. "City's under lockdown. Some kind of search underway in the surrounding area."

He spit at the ground at his feet and said, "I hope they flay them alive and hang them from Dover Tower." He slung the towel over his shoulder and took out a notepad. "What can I get you?"

D glanced at the printed menu over his shoulder and said, "Can we get some water, and two bowels of Orange Kerobe, with Eshi-ban Noodles."

"Alright, coming right up," he said walking towards the back of the hut.

Zecona sat in silence, processing the events that'd taken place, and breathed in the cold evening air. A VTOL swept across the camp overhead and flew further west. Food sizzled on the grills from the back. The warm scent of orange and sharp serobi spice flowed around them.

D pulled out and lit up a cigarette from her coat pocket, taking a deep breath of the warm smoke in her lungs. From the mouth of the alleyway, the chatter from the group gathered watching the hacked feed, swelled and dulled as the military sweep continued.

The cook walked back from the kitchen with a tray carrying the glasses of water and bowls, placed them in front of D then said, "Did you need anything else?"

"Not now." She scooped up a bite.

"Alright, just give me a holler." The cook vanished around the back.

"Eat up, it's on me, kid." D pushed a bowl of noodles towards him. "Your big day's tomorrow."

Zecona stared into the bowl. "What am I going to be doing?"

She shot him a look, "What? Are you kidding? I'm not discussing it here. I'll brief you later."

He kept staring at the bowl. She shoveled her food into her mouth.

"You going to sit there ogling it all night, or are you going to eat?"

"I've just lost my appetite."

"Why's that?"

"I don't know," he said. "I'm just tired."

"Whatever," D said shaking her head. "You'll have to eat at some point." She shoved a forkful of noodles into her mouth.

"Oh yea," Zecona said reaching into his coat. "You almost left this in the alleyway." He pulled out the metallic case and set it on the bar between them.

D stared down at it and took a deep breath. "Thanks." She stood up and put it into her back pocket.

"Where'd you learn to pick locks like that?"

"Just something I picked up back home," Zecona said as he finally picked up a fork, and began twisting a small amount together.

"Right," she said rolling up some more noodles. "You just happened to get sent to Verra, and know how to break out of jail cell."

"I'm not sure what you want me to say."

"I'm not an idiot." She swallowed the noodles and reached for her drink, "I know how most Abots are recruited."

The sound of the fluorescent light strained above them as she set down her glass and took another mouthful of noodles.

Zecona took the hint and took a bite of his noodles. "This is pretty good."

"I guess," D said. She strained a smile at the cook as he walked back into the front area.

"Do you come here often?" Zecona asked.

"No." She said taking another bite.

"Oh. Well, how'd you hear about it?" He took another bite.

"Just saw it just now from the road." She said reaching for her glass again.

"Well, it was a good choice."

She just nodded her head, setting her glass back down. The cook wandered back into the back area.

Zecona watched a group of people walk down the road at the mouth of the alleyway. "Do you have any plans once all of this blows over?"

D swallowed another mouthful of noodles. "Honestly. I haven't really thought about it."

"Really?" He snapped his attention at her. "I mean..." He thought about his words for a moment. "I mean I wouldn't mind sharing some time on a beach with someone."

D scooped up a forkful and held it front of her. "I think I'd liked to be alone for a while to clear my head."

"Well, you can't be alone forever."

D shot him a look out of the corner of her eye. "I haven't thought that far ahead."

He swallowed watching the chef's head pop up from behind the serving window. "What do you mean? Don't you want a family? Do you ever want kids?"

D wiped off her mouth with her napkin and tossed it onto the counter, and stormed off down the ally. He sat there for a little while, before jumping up and running after her.

"What?" Zecona said staring after her.

D stormed through the crowds on the main road.

"I can't ask a simple question?"

She shook her head.

"Have you ever considered it?"

She took a quick turn down an empty makeshift alley and Zecona followed her. She spun around and slammed him into a wall.

"Learn to drop a fucking topic!"

Her eyes tore back into his. That's all he could see fixed in front of him, he couldn't offer a nod or anything, only a petrified stare.

She let go of his throat and stormed back into the crowd. Zecona followed. They left the camp, and navigated their way back to the Prowler in silence. The search groups had spread out too thin towards the edge of the city, making it easier to slip past back towards D's setup.

CHAPTER EIGHT
DETERIORATION

D was sitting in the broken hole of the outer wall staring down the road, drinking another cup of coffee. Zecona lifted his head off the cot.

"Morning," she said raising her cup up and taking a sip. "Get out your tin friend. We need to go over today's game plan."

"What are we going to be doing today?" Zecona said as he stumbled his way to his comm device.

"I'm done. You and the suit are going to be doing the work today." She took another sip, with her foot tapping against the outside of the wall.

"What do you mean?" Zecona said as the suit was emerging from the blue light.

"I've done my part. Now you guys need to go in and clean up."

"What do you need?" The suit said.

"I need you to go in and destroy all of the truck yards currently operational," she said taking a sip of coffee.

"That's not exactly discreet," the suit said.

"I know," she said looking out the window. "Here's the basics." She held up her MC. "Ya know what this is?" she asked, looking at Zecona.

"Of course, it's a molecular re-constructor."

130

"Ya know how it works?"

Zecona just stared at her.

"Well as you know, if you know how to program and you have a solid chunk of raw mass lying around it you can make practically anything. From a toaster to a tank, but that's a bit of an oversimplification really. You can't just type shit up in it. You have to know how things are put together at a sub-atomic level. Which not many can do. Luckily these little things can interface with a database that holds common info for all that you could need. Overman controls a Database aboard the Gabrielle Station, and the Federation has multiple databases split up in each of their stations."

"How's this important?" the suit asked.

"When the revolution broke out," she continued, "the access to the Federation database was broken, but the local data each MC had memory was left over in their local caches. Tank information for training simulation, guns, turrets, and train information. That sort of thing. All this information began coming together, and now there's an ad-hoc third database that's been established. Created through the interface of these devices. It's still in the works, but it's growing with each new MC that's found. The troops fighting on the front lines are maintained with the MCs in the city. Supplies are created in the inner city and shipped out by trains, trucks, whatever. The maintainers of the database are more decentralized and spread throughout the city. And thanks to anti-air, barely any more Federation bombardments get through, and at least not enough to do serious damage. Over the past couple of months I've been hunting down the mechanics in charge of repairing the vehicles, and erasing their MC's. By now, their supply chain is stretched thin as is. If you take out the truck yards, supplies can't reach the front lines. The troops will be left vulnerable, and the city will fall. That simple."

"I hardly doubt that," the suit said. "How exactly are you expecting us to attack the truck yards? We weren't provided with authorization to access explosives on the network."

D looked up at him. "What do you mean you don't have any authorization? I reviewed your contract, and it said you had access to those kinds of explosives."

The War Devil folded its arms. "That was six months ago. Those kinds of certifications are costly. On top of that, you didn't tell anyone what our purpose was. Besides that, the contract you signed was to develop a method of dispatching and dismantling the revolution discreetly. When it came time for me to drop access to those explosives, I didn't see any reason to renew my access."

"Are you fucking kidding me?"

"This is what--"

"I don't give a shit, what do you mean you aren't authorized? You can't access any explosives? None?"

"I currently only have a small window for accessing a grenade stock, but for the amount of damage you want. No, I don't hold the demolition authorizations to get a hold of that much explosive material."

"I'm not asking you to nuke the damn sites, I'm asking for strategic strikes on various compounds."

"I know what you're asking for, and I'm telling you we don't have the authorization to do it. Besides which, what you're asking for isn't exactly what you signed up for."

"Look, there's bombs going off every day in the streets, what are they going to do if a few extra go off? Besides which," she held up her notebook. "I'm not asking you to attack just the..." She was staring at him before she stood up dropping the notebook. "Fuck!" She started walking towards the hole in the wall.

Zecona sat on the edge of the cot.

D was shaking her head with her hand over her mouth. The suit walked over and leaned up against the wall. She was drumming her fingers on the crumpled wall beside her.

"Alright," she said letting her hand fall away from her face.

Zecona looked up at her.

She turned to the War Devil and said, "I need a run-down of what you do have access to."

"Infantry and espionage."

"How many grenades do you have left in your personal armory?"

"Nine, but I keep five in reserve."

"So you have fourteen?"

"No. I'll let you use four, but no more than that."

"Alright. Alright." She waved her hand at him.

She paced between the doorway and the hole in the wall. "How long would it take for you to get that level of authorization?"

"It would take a couple of months for that level of clearance. That's if they approve it."

"We don't have that kind of time. Isn't there someone you can contact? Wouldn't they have authorization?"

"I can try to make contact with an Agent--"

"Do it."

"But I don't know what they can do."

"I don't care, just do it. Get whatever information you can from them." She grabbed her notebook off the floor. "Now look, we only have a small window of opportunity here." She scratched her chin, flipping through the pages. "It'll take them a week to reorganize their infrastructure, and replace the data that was lost." She stopped on a page. "That's if we're lucky. I wanted you to start hitting five locations a day to cripple the network they have set up. We need to do as much damage as we can to cut off supplies to the front lines."

The War Devil nodded down to her. "That's a bit much. Five locations a day, within a week?"

"What's wrong with that?"

"You want to knock out thirty-five places all at once?"

"Is that a problem?"

"We need time to scout out the area and plan an attack at critical points. Once we start hitting the locations, they're bound to start upping their manpower at the remaining locations within the next few days. We'd need at least two months, and that's cutting it."

"We don't even have a month. Within a month they'll have new operators, and any places you had hit at the start of the operations will have been repaired," D said tapping the notebook. "We have to hit them all within a week."

"That's not how we do things."

"And that's why every previous operation brought in by Overman has failed. You can't play this safe!" She was drumming the notebook, still sitting on the floor.

The suit held its arms crossed staring down at her.

D glanced up. "When can you reach your contact?"

"I might be able to make contact with them tonight."

"Alright." D's eyes glazed over staring at the wall. "Alright. Do that." D was still tapping the side of the notebook. "I'll see what I can come up with on my own."

"For what?" the War Devil said casting a crescent moon eye towards her, as it walked across the hole in the wall to watch the road.

"Fall back plan," she said. "I'll see what we can get a hold of if your contact can't offer us anything."

She shot a look at Zecona. "You."

"Hm?" Zecona snapped to attention.

She held up her notebook. "I want you and the suit to go out and scout out these areas. Copy them down. I'm keeping the originals. Get a layout of the area, when the suit needs to meet his contact, keep scouting, then you can both rendezvous back here when you're done."

"Got it."

She handed him the notebook. "I'm going to get a quick check of what I have stored up here." She walked out the door.

***

The War Devil waited until it heard her hit the stairs. "Think you can handle walking alone tonight?"

Zecona reviewed her notes. "I don't have a choice, do I?"

The suit didn't say anything as it took the notebook out of his hands.

Zecona studied the cold hollow armor reading the book. "What are the odds of this working?"

"It won't." It was scanning over her pen markings on the pages.

"The eternal optimist," Zecona said smiling.

"It's not that." The War Devil closed the notebook. "There's a lot going against us. We don't have the manpower. We'd have to hit five places at the same time every hour for only one day for this sort of plan to work out. Once one is hit, the other places we could hit will have more people stationed at them. More firepower. More vehicles. More attention."

Zecona was nodding his head, staring out at the street below.

The suit continued., "Not only that, but because D struck the operators first, these sites she has marked down will have more manpower for the simple fact that they need these sites operational until new operators are assigned."

"So what's the plan?" Zecona said eyeing him.

"First we'll scout. Get a feel for the area, and come up with our own plan. After that? Get more men? Or at the very least gain express access to explosives. Or find someone in the area who has explosives."

D walked back into the room. "I've got..." Counting the things on her fingers. "A rifle, two pistols, magazines, and a couple of clips, respectively. Three empty gas containers, and two propane tanks." She made her way to the middle of the room. "When are you two heading out?"

"Soon," the War Devil said holding up her notebook.

"Good." She snatched it from its hands.

"When do you want us back?" Zecona asked.

She glanced up. "When you finish your fucking job."

She hopped up into the hole, scribbling more notes as they left.

***

The War Devil's eight legs clung to Zecona's wrist as it scanned a store they passed by "stop here," it said, pinching his wrist tight.

Zecona glanced over. "Why?"

"We're going to need more leg work. Trust me."

"Fine."

He walked through the busted front door. The spider jumped onto the floor and reformed into a biped form within the blue light. It walked along the aisle, grabbing things as it went. Zecona was crouched down shifting through the smashed components of a register scattered across the floor. The War Devil wandered off to a back room.

Zecona walked down one of the aisles and grabbed some athletic tape from one of the shelves. The suit walked back into the room appearing far slimmer. It was wearing denim overalls with a black rubber rain coat over top. It's helmet was wrapped in masking tape, and it had black safety goggles where it's eyes ought to be. On its hands, it was wearing blue thick winter gloves. All of that was topped off with a wide straw hat.

"Why are you wearing that?" Zecona said, as he started to wrap the athletic tape between his fingers.

"We'll need to be separate for most of our operations. Which means I'll need to be overly visible in the area. Best not to alert the rebel fighters too much to the fact that the Overman Corporation is this heavily involved."

"You look fucking ridiculous."

"Best I could find."

"Just stating a fact."

The War Devil hadn't moved. The best Zecona could tell it was staring at him, but he couldn't tell.

"Don't shoot the messenger." Zecona ripped the tape, and tucked the end under his wrist.

"What are you doing?" the War Devil asked, pointing to his hand.

"My joints are still killing me, so I'm hoping the pressure help."

The suit shook its head and headed back towards the back of the store. "Come on, I found some stairs."

Zecona started wrapping his other hand as he followed it up the stairs.

Marching down the hallway, the suit led him towards a long room lined with tall windows. The suit walked across the room and leaned against a window. Zecona stopped at the door.

"What exactly are we doing?" he said, tearing the tape.

"I'm comparing the map information given when we were assigned this, what D gave us earlier, and what's actually present." the War Devil said finishing up the sweep of the landscape.

"I meant, what exactly are we doing with this operation?" Zecona said slipping out of his boot, and propping his foot against the door frame. "We can't exactly take on the Rebellion, just the three of us."

"I've got it under control."

"Really?" Zecona asked as he started wrapping his ankle. "Because it seems like you're going to get us killed."

"I'm just weighing the options," the suit said, glancing back at him.

"I would have said, too bad, fuck off," Zecona said weaving the tape between his two toes. "This is absolutely suicide."

"We're still under contract. I want to have a better grip on the situation. I'll have that when I've scouted out the area and talked with my contact. D seems confident in what she's done so far. I'm curious to see how this will all pan out in the end. If all else fails, I can just break the contract, and find a new one."

Zecona straightened up. "Do they have a name?"

"It's not relevant. We should get going soon."

Zecona stared, out the window and slipped out of his other boot. "Give me a minute, I need to get my other foot." He bent down and start wrapping his right foot. "Do you have a name?"

"Several. Why?"

"Just curious." He said, weaving the tape between his two toes.

"Officially, I'm from the 59x, SAM Series, Class 3 War Devil of the 12th Elite Squadron."

"That's not a name," he said, ripping the tape and straightening up.

"It's what I was originally assigned," the suit said walking towards the door.

"59x is a name to you?" Zecona said, slipping back into his boots, and snapped them back into place. "Do you tell that to the Federation?"

"Yes. It's actually longer, but you'd forget it," the suit said passing him, "To Overman, I'm addressed according to my code name."

"Which would be?" Zecona followed him down the stairway.

"Barbatos, the Fallen Devil. From the House of Knives and the Inverted Heaven."

They walked out into the middle of the street. The suit had stooped down putting his palm to the ground. Zecona took a quick glance up and down the road. He pulled up a container out of the asphalt after sending out a shock wave into the road.

"Is that supposed to mean something?" Zecona said glancing at him.

The suit had grabbed a headset out of the case and handed it to Zecona. "Not to you."

Zecona grabbed hold of the headset. "We splitting up?"

"Not yet, just want to be prepared."

"Yeah, yeah," Zecona said, putting on the headset. "What do you want me to call you?" Zecona turned on the headset.

"What's wrong with the names I gave you?"

"I don't know," Zecona smiled as he adjusted the microphone under his mouth. "If any of our radio chatter get' picked up, they might get weirded out by someone called Barbatos or 59x."

The suit shook its head. "Just call me Richard."

"Where'd that name come from?" Zecona peered down at him.

"Don't worry about that." He glanced up. "Let's get moving," Richard said glancing up the road.

"What's the plan?" Zecona stuffed his hands into his pockets.

"I want to find a couple of buildings around the bases," Richard said, glancing up the road.

"For what?"

"Fall back points in case things go south."

Zecona shrugged. "I'll take the roofs." He took off down the road, looking back at Richard walking after him.

"No, you won't," Richard shouted out.

"Why's that?" Zecona stopped in the middle of the road.

"We need to stick to the ground, you idiot. You'll be a walking target on the roofs." Richard walked up beside him.

Zecona shoved his hands into his pocket. "Whatever."

***

Zecona and Richard walked down a curved road lined with gutted vertical husks of buildings. The floors were bleached like ribs sticking out of a rotten carcass with its guts of concrete spilled on the roads.

"Can I ask you something?" Zecona said.

"What?"

"What's up with D? It feels like every time I open my mouth when you're not around she's half a second away from kicking my ass."

"No idea," Richard said scanning the area around him. "Maybe you should stop trying to push her buttons so much."

He sighed, "Great you're taking her side." Zecona shook his head. "Most of the time, I'm not trying too."

"It's only a couple more days," Richard said.

"Yeah, but I can't exactly help you if she breaks my legs or something."

The footsteps echoed off the innards of the buildings around them before Richard piped back up again. "If she tries anything again. I'll step in, and talk with her."

"Thanks."

"But only if you don't provoke her. Just practice a little patience."

"I think I'm being plenty patient."

Coming up to an intersection, a convoy was moving past them. Zecona and Richard sat down on the curb to let the armored trucks pass by. Rebels were sitting in the back of the trucks staring at the two. A Rebel waved at Zecona from the back of a truck. He waved back not noticing the massive barrel of a tank creep up on him from his peripheral.

He snapped his attention when he saw pulsing banks of green wrapped around the barrel. The length was ridiculous, and it all sat on what looked like four legs walking forward.

"Rail gun," Richard said, staring at it

"What's it used against?" Zecona said, staring after.

"Stationary defense." Richard got up. The convoy was still moving through, but he had gotten tired of waiting.

Zecona got up and followed him. "How's that helpful on the battlefield?"

"Federation has been forming turret towers outside the city to push forward their line. The Rebellion has been setting up rail guns behind the line at parts to make sure the Federations forces stay as far back as possible. Rail guns can completely rip through those defenses, but they're slow to fire at fast-moving targets."

Zecona spotted the end of the convoy coming up. "Any chance you can make some food on the spot here soon?"

"No." Richard shook his head. "I'm not equipped with that."

Zecona glanced up the road. "Then can we stop by one of the camps for something to eat?"

"Sure."

***

Zecona and Richard continued down the road until they spotted what looked like a civilian refugee camp. It looked like it had been built around a small shopping center. Notable things were the more recent additions, such as a parameter around the parking lot, with sheet metal walls, chain link fence, and barbed wire. Guard Towers were built up from metal pipes and scaffolding around the entrances. Zecona suddenly wasn't sure if the guards walking around the towers were offering protection for the people in the camp, or ensuring they didn't leave. Richard and Zecona walked around the concrete Barricades on the roads.

A guard totting an assault rifle spotted them and walked out of the shade of the tower holding up his hand. "Hold it. What's your business here?"

Zecona smiled and said, "Hi, we just need to take a quick rest, maybe grab some food. Then we'll be on our way."

The guard shook his head, then turned to Richard and said, "I need to see your face."

"I'm afraid I can't do that," Richard replied. "Bad burns. A roadside bomb stripped most of it away. I've been keeping things in pretty well together with the tape until I can find a doctor that can treat it."

"I'm sorry to hear that. Have you tried the military bases?"

"I've been to the West Indies, but the doctor there wasn't comfortable with operating on it. Plus they didn't have the time since they had soldiers to treat."

"Damn shame. You can come in."

Richard and Zecona both stepped forward but the guard jerked the rifle and pointed it at Zecona. "Not you." He nodded back down the road. "You know where you belong."

Richard spoke, "It's alright, He's helping me through this."

The guard didn't let the rifle fall. He stared dead into Zecona's eyes before nodding and saying, "Alright. Don't cause any trouble, or you'll have more than just burns when you walk out of here."

"We don't plan on it."

Tents and makeshift houses were sprawled around the parking lot inside of the parameter. People gave the two weird looks. Walking past a small girl standing in the road, a mother grabbed hold of her and crouched back inside her tent. A group of young boys speaking unintelligibly approached Zecona and Richard. Zecona didn't catch the words. A dog barked incessantly from inside one of the tents.

"Careful Lizard." A blonde kid mocked as they passed. "The Dogs are hungry." The boys laughed. Zecona watched the dog in the tent carefully. A man with a blind eye was holding it by the leash, scowling at Zecona as he passed.

"Da'Cish Kom Rav'Vakiv!" A little girl with pigtails cried out. Zecona glanced over and ducked a rock she threw at him. "Da'Cish Kom Rav'Vakiv va Ka'Kish!"

Richard let the rock hit him in the temple. She ran off before he could say anything.

Zecona looked at Richard. "Do you know what she said?"

"Shouldn't you?"

He shrugged. "I'm not familiar with that language." Taking a deep sigh, "Maybe I should've grabbed a disguise while I had the chance."

"They wouldn't have let two people in wrapped up." Richard was rubbing the side of his head.

"I'm surprised they let me in at all." Zecona was still looking around. "Think it's safe to grab some food?"

"Better now than later." Richard said. "Bound to be something around if it hasn't been destroyed."

The Shopping center was broken up into what used to be multiple storefronts. Looking through the broken windows of most of the places Zecona could see more tents set up inside. They came up to one that had chairs and tables set outside.

They walked into the empty restaurant, and Zecona spotted the dispenser on the counter in front of him. Zecona walked up to it, and the machine sensed he was there and flashed on. The interface popped up with some sort of alien symbol displayed at the top left corner of the screen along with the usual details asking for a method of payment. Zecona chose credit on the touch screen. Swipe Card or Enter identification code? He choose to enter his identification and entered his Federation Code. It flashed back to the main Screen with the message, error, unrecognized code.

Zecona scratched his head "How can I get food out of this thing?"

Richard glanced back at him from the door. "What's it saying?"

"I need to input in an ID, but my Federation ID isn't recognized."

"Let me see that." Richard walked over.

Richard tapped the crow at the top left corner and worked through the interface on his own. Zecona tried to look over his shoulder, but still couldn't see anything.

"There," Richard headed back to the door. "It can't connect to the Federation Database, it's on emergency rations."

Zecona was nodding his head. "Right, right." He was flipping through the interface. "What a great selection. Rice or Noodles? Hell, let's live on the edge. Why not both?" He pressed the combination, and a bowl popped, plopping out his selection.

Grabbing the bowl, he sat down at a table beside Richard and started chowing down. Swallowing his first mouthful of noodles, he said, "Why are they still here?"

"How should I know?" Richard said looking over at him.

Zecona shrugged. "Figured you might have some better insight." They were watching a group of people walking past them. "I mean this is in the middle of a highly contested city by the looks of it. Why stick around?"

"Maybe they think they have a chance. Waiting to see what happens next," Richard said glancing down the sidewalks.

"Doesn't make sense to me." Zecona shrugged taking another bite. "Go somewhere else. Start a new life. Why stay on the other side of a warzone?"

"There might be nowhere else to go for the majority," Richard said glancing back. "Ever think of that?"

"Doesn't change what I'm saying. You don't need to have anything if you're going to start over. What are they getting by living here?"

"Maybe they just believe in the rebel cause."

Zecona chowed down on the rice now. "What's your take?"

"On what?"

"On the war. Who's right, who's wrong?"

Richard shrugged. "It doesn't matter."

"Your opinion, or the whole thing in general?"

"The whole thing."

Zecona glanced over at him. "Of course it matters. People are fighting for it. People are dying for it. You're fighting for it. These people are willing to live through it. Why wouldn't it matter?"

"This is a war between the Federation and this planet. The fact is, the outcome of this war doesn't matter to the long-term goals of Overman."

Zecona had stopped eating, staring at him. "The war broke out because the people here were worried that the Overman Corporation, i.e. you, would be using your power and knowledge to influence the Federation."

"That was part of it. However, if you think that was the only reason for the Rebellion, then you're being willfully ignorant." He glanced over at Zecona's bowl. "Are you done?"

"No, what other reasons are there?"

"We don't have time to explain to you the socio-economic factors for your own damn war."

"Give me the shorthand."

"Control," Richard said. "Or more specifically, the control of information." Richard crossed his arms. "The Governing Bodies on the planet wanted more centralized data housed on the planet, rather than having the bulk of it stored on the space stations. With the introduction of Overman coming back into the picture, they instantly perceived the fact that Overman would flood the market with its level of information, and overtake the market. The planet feared the Federation would become too reliant on Overman's AI Systems, before the Federation threw itself into debt with the Overman Corporation, opted to instead succeed from the Union."

"The Federation's barely accessed that information precisely for that reason though."

"Right, but do you think they care?" Richard said, "The Federation has always been a billion miles away. Hell, they can only send clones to do their brute work. That's why they rebelled. But none of this matters to Overman."

"And why's that?"

"Are you done eating?"

Zecona waved him off. "I'm working on it." He took another mouthful. "Who is Overman?"

"It's not a matter of who," Richard said glancing at a group of men beside a lane of tents. "It's a matter of what."

"Alright, what is Overman?"

The group of men disappeared around the corner. "It is."

Zecona was taking another mouthful, expecting Richard to finish the sentence. Swallowing, he stared at the back of his head. "It is... what?"

Richard was silent as it was looking up the lexicon. "It's a collective of both human and AI minds. Networked together, to create a single biological/technological hyper-intelligent mind. Capable of creating any combination of consciousness within itself, and forming any kind of life-form or machine that it needs. Theoretically, it could even create and simulate any combination of civilizations. It's possible that it's working through a plan that will possibly extend past the lifetime of half of the stars in the galaxy."

Zecona cocked an eyebrow. "And what would that be?"

"I don't know," Richard said. "I'm not capable of matching that level of intelligence." He glanced back over at Zecona, "Are you ready to get moving?"

Zecona shrugged. "Sure." He wiped his mouth with a napkin.

"Then let's get moving."

Zecona threw the bowl in the trash can. As they stepped out of the restaurant, Richard sensed a group forming behind them but ignored them when he spotted a guard standing at the mouth of the main path. He could barely make out the outer wall through the face wraps.

When they turned towards the main gate, Zecona felt the pull of someone grabbing the back of his coat. The next thing he registered was getting hurled through an enclosed screen porch. He scrambled to his knees to see a mountain of a man walking towards him with a boning knife.

"We were just leaving," Richard said.

"Not a chance," the human mountain said.

Richard had been keeping track of the four other men around him inching closer to him. It dawned on him being surrounded that his pistols were still embedded into his thighs, underneath the overalls. He was standing in the middle of the street, in direct sight of a host of soldiers capable of reporting what was happening to the surrounding city of rebels.

"If you leave here," the Mountain said, walking towards Richard, "then we'll be dealing with a host 'ore Abot's raiding us. All these shits 'hink is everything on this planet 'elongs to 'em. I ain't bout to give 'em that kinda idea."

Richard retracted the spikes in his arms and had the situation simulated in his head as two of the men moved for his arms. Jerking his torso, he elbowed the man to his right but pulled back to avoid shattering his skull from the force. The man to his left grabbed hold of his other arm, but Richard was already swinging back and gently broke the man's nose. The giant lunged the knife towards Richard's stomach.

Richard lurched away and grabbed the Mountain's forearm. The two other men choose to ignore Richard and ran towards Zecona still on the ground. While Richard was processing whether he wanted to dislocate the man's arm, or just outright break it, the Mountain's other hand slammed into the side of his helmet, shattering the lens on the left side of his goggles. Sensing the amount of force, he knew he had to react, but the Mountain was already reeling back from the pain.

Richard ripped the knife from the giant's hands and rolled to his right. The two men had already gotten Zecona to his feet. One was brandishing another knife to Zecona's throat, while the other one held back his arms.

Richard's sensors picked up the lead pipe smashing down towards his head. He shifted his weight, and caught the pipe. Continuing the momentum, he pulled the man with the broken nose down to the ground, and in front of him. He brandished the boning knife on his throat and yelled out,

"One cut, and I'll gut this son-of-a-bitch."

The two men glanced over and saw Richard on the ground with the knife. The Mountain was standing off to the side still nursing his shattered hand.

"Let 'em go," the Mountain said, staring straight at the bandaged-up eye behind the left goggle. "We're out of our 'eagues."

They let Zecona go, and Richard shoved the man into the ground.

"Let's go," Richard said standing up.

They continued down the main line past the guards who had been watching and left the camp.

***

Following the roads again, they passed streets with multiple craters left in the middle of the road. Most of the holes were shallow, others punctured straight down into the sewer lines, subway tunnels, and water pipes that were thankfully empty or turned off. Richard continued to scan the buildings and cell towers they passed. He had noted a soldier had been following them from the camp, but they had lost him after taking a few too many turns around the streets and buildings. Eventually, they reached an overpass.

A Rasvelg classed VTOL's floated overhead under the deep orange sky. Zecona watched the black mass of the ship sail along on the skyline with its four thrusters over the city streets. A host of missiles and weapons clung to its thick underbelly. The sun sank into the horizon with each step they took.

Night crept up on them, with the moon starting to creep in between buildings casting shadow's on the street. Zecona was walking down the road staring over the building tops. "What now?" he said. Zecona hadn't bothered with a flashlight.

Richard was walking beside him "You head back to D." he said stopping. "I need to meet up with my contact."

"Need me to help?"

"No." Richard turned and walked away. Zecona shrugged, and continued down the road. While he had gotten enough familiarity for where he was, the digital map in his pocket was going to help as well.

CHAPTER NINE
DEMON

D watched Zecona as he walked around the building at the end of the street, before hopping off her hole in the wall and rushing towards the bathroom. Throwing open the door she caught a glimpse of her shattered figure in the mirror. The rucksack was still on the floor, with their clothes still intact. Grabbing it by the strap, she raced down the stairs, out the front of the building, and down an alleyway to the back of the building towards a metal barrel drum. She dumped the clothes into it and stared down as they settled with the ash that came before. Her hands gripped along the edge. How many times had she done this?

She jerked herself back up away from those thoughts, snatched a ripped-up shirt from the bottom, and tore off a ribbon of fabric. Chucking the shirt back into the drum, she pulled out her lighter, lit the rag, and tossed it into the clothes. The bottom of the drum glowed orange, as she sank against the wall of the alley and lit a cigarette watching the smoke rise. D took a deep long drag, letting it provide a needed warmth in her chest, before letting it go.

D started her routine check of the building. The War Devil may have filled her in if anything was suspicious, but that was no reason to get lazy. The rooms were still empty, nothing had changed in the time she'd been there. Each of the rooms still showed signs of scavengers that had passed through before her, and methodically ransacked each of the rooms. Heading down through the lobby, she grabbed hold of the wooden planks nailed up across the windows and gave them a solid jerk, and studied the wall. Some parts were starting to crack from the stress from the collapsed floor above it. It seemed like the building would hold out, but she couldn't say for how long. She knelt down beside the Prowler and double-checked the energy levels. Finally, she made her way down to the basement, and checked the plank of wood propped against the back door by jerking the handle. The door didn't budge.

She walked into the supply room and grabbed her metal case from her back pocket. Counting the used vials, she tossed them and the used syringes into a bucket and started thinking through the actions for the next couple of days. D pulled out the MC from her coat pocket and put it into the terminal input sticking out of the wall. The screen beside it lit up with a percentage of elements available for the building, with an aluminum compartment beneath it to grab generated items.

Turning the MC on, she froze. The eye of Overman wasn't staring back at her. A cracked emblem of the Federation popped up instead. Her hand jerked back into her pockets and she grabbed another MC. She flipped it on and was met with the eye of Overman.

She glanced back at the cracked Federation. Marcus's MC. Pocketing her molecluizer, her hand continued to hover over his. She navigated to the main menu. Vehicle repair components were present as usual, but something else caught her attention. Explosives were present among the data. Class 7 Elite battle armor, micro grenade launchers, specialized demolition explosives with associated detonators.

She ripped Marcus's out and replaced it with her own, forming a new set of syringes, and vials of her cocktails. She pulled out a fresh set of vials with blank labels. D put the new vials and syringes back in her metal case and stuck it back in her back pocket again.

Overman forces took intellectual security seriously. Any molecular data obtained from the rebel forces was deemed illegal to possess. Any registered Agent caught possessing or using any data they were unauthorized to have access to would be fined excessively. Far more than what she'd get for completing this contract. It was the reason why she'd been so meticulous in erasing any data she'd been in contact with that she was not authorized to use. Her retainers would use any excuse to fuck her over if they found out.

"It wasn't personal," Alice originally told her, "it was just business. If an Agent utilized unauthorized tech, then they were practically providing free work to the Federation. If the Federation wanted to take advantage of the best available tech, then they could pay for the best available tech."

D pulled Marcus's MC back out and took a deep breath. Her legs felt numb as she stared at the screen again. She'd been following the rules up to this point, and this is where it'd gotten her. Pushing the thought out of her mind, she put the MC back in her pocket while keeping the data intact.

D still had Michael's rifle. If she was going to keep it, it would be best to practice with it. Climbing the stairs, she grabbed it, along with a case of beer she'd smuggled out of a bar last week, before walking back down the alleyway beside her building. Dropping the case of beer down by her feet, she lined her shoulders up against a row of empty cans lined up against a ledge and held up the rifle. Am I authorized to use this rifle? Hugging the stock of the assault rifle against her side, she pulled the trigger. There was a loud series of cracks cutting through the air, a beer can exploded. D pulled out the clip and reloaded. Aiming it back at the cans, felt the recoil kick her arms up as she unloaded another burst. Two more cans exploded off the shelf.

Scooping down into the case, she snatched a couple of beer cans into her arms, and cracked open one. Throwing her head back and drank the whole can in a matter of seconds. Am I authorized to drink this beer? She put the empty can, along with the unopened ones on the shelf.

Cracking more shots at the wall, warm amber shot out in all directions, spilling to the ground. Dust of concrete bled into the air. The smoke from the barrel waned. She unloaded clips, shooting and drinking through the 24-pack as the sun reached it's peak. Grabbing her last clip out, she pulled some extra bullets from the rucksack to top it off, before strapping the rifle to her back and walking back inside the building.

What difference does it make? She thought as she pulled out Marcus's MC, and stared at it. If she continued playing by their rules, she'd be dead within a month at most. If she used the data on the MC to get the explosives she needed, she might be able to pull off what she needed, but she'd be dead if they found out what she did. If they found out.

Walking back upstairs again, she took a look at her notebook, flipping through the pages, until her eyes shot up to a road around a warehouse and processing plant. Tapping her pencil on the page, she made a quick mental note of the roads in the area, before slapping the notebook closed, and grabbing the rucksack.

She jumped back down the stairs. The sun was well on its path down across the sky. D dumped out the rest of the supplies from the rucksack. Strapping the now empty bag to her back, along with the rifle, she patted the compressed Marlow against her inner thigh. She patted the metal case in her back pocket, then grabbed Marcus's MC out of her coat pocket and stuck it into her front jean pocket. Taking one last glance around, she hopped onto the Prowler.

***

The mechanical maul of the rusted, deteriorating crane towered over her. Walking forward, she had her hands shoved into her pockets with her back straight. Piles of twisted shipping containers lined her right side. To her left was a massive warehouse that had crumbled apart. Its roof had collapsed into the building, and a massive hole laid through its side. The asphalt under her feet was cracked and broken from bullet holes and mortar craters.

Walking between the crane's tracks, she stepped over a piece twisted by a crater to its side. She kept her eyes on the orange light from a street light ahead of her, before spotting a group of six soldiers standing beneath it. Brushing the top of Marcus's MC with the tip of her finger, she kept her head pointed forward. A dog lying in the dark beside the soldiers popped its head up from her footsteps. The empty bag bounced off her back as she picked up the pace.

"Hey!" one of the soldiers yelled out, "There ain't nothin' for you over there."

D turned around. "Sorry, I usually take a walk through here."

"Well, walk somewhere else. This is a restricted area."

She walked towards the group. "But that's such a long way out of the way," she said, slipping on a smile. "Wouldn't it be quicker to just search me?" Stepping into the light, she could feel the weight of the Marlow strapped to her inner thigh grow. "Or if you wouldn't mind, would one of you boys like to escort me so that I don't get into any trouble?"

"I'm sure trouble can find you just fine."

A soldier with a round face piped in, "Are you afraid of a girl?" He turned back to D. "Where you heading?"

D smiled. "Straight through. From here and out the other gate."

"I'll walk you through," he said.

"Karolek, stay here until we get further orders."

The soldier just shot him a look as he walked towards D. The two walked away from the group following the rows of shipping containers along their right.

"Sorry about Cargan," Karolek said. "He's a prick trying to act like a Captain."

"Oh?" D said. "He's not the one calling the shots?"

"Nah, Jackson's walking around somewhere. This area's pretty quiet." He shifted the weight of the rifle on his shoulder. "Although you might want to clear out of walking in this area after tonight. Things will probably be heating up soon."

"Thanks for the heads up." She glanced back at the street light. "I'm Michelle by the way." She held out her hand.

He smiled and shook it. "Nice to meet you."

"You seem like the kind of guy that knows how to have fun."

Karolek laughed. "So what were you before the war?" he said, glancing over at her.

D shot a quick glance and smiled. "I was a doctor."

"Ah, you know we could always use more of those around."

D just smiled and nodded. "What were you?"

"I was a policeman."

"Protect and serve," D said, smiling.

"I do what I can." They turned down a row of containers. "So do you think when this is all over, you'll go back to being a doctor?"

"I don't think we'll ever be able to go back to what we were," she said.

"Yeah, I suppose not." He turned his attention to the rifle on her back. "Can you shoot that?"

"Of course." D nodded.

"Really?" He raised an eyebrow. "Where did a doctor learn to shoot an assault rifle?"

"Small gun club outside of the city," she said. "I think it was called Brookersons?"

"Oh yeah." His eyes lit up. "I've been there."

"You have?"

"Yeah, I used to practice there with a few guys from the precinct a couple of times a week." His eyebrows furrowed. "Funny. I don't seem to remember seeing you there."

"Well," D said, letting the word roll off her tongue, "I tended to practice at night after my shift."

"Weird." He shook his head. "We tended to stop by at night too. I would've thought I would have run into you at least once."

"Well, you know, there was that one section with heavier weapons? My fiancée was in the military, so we got to practice in those lanes. Away from the normal ranges."

"Yeah. I know about those lanes. The precinct provided access to those. We practiced a lot in them."

Every step that hit the ground shook through her in between the silence. Taking in a quick breath, she brushed a strand of hair behind her ear.

"Where's your fiancée now?" They turned the side of a building.

"Oh." She said with a quick breath. "He's... gone." The wind brushed between them, and it ignited a faint ember in her chest.

"I'm sorry to hear that."

"Not your fault."

"Are you making by on your own?" he said, turning to her.

"Yeah, I tend to." She thought for a moment. "Scavenge for things in the outskirts of the city."

Karolek was shaking his head. "That's no way to live. It must be pretty rough."

D laughed. "You could say that." She was biting her lower lip. From the corner of her eye, she spotted a portion of the main control building, and turned to Karolek and said, "So what do you think this place was used for?"

"Well, this whole area used to be a high-volume materializer. Raw materials would be shipped in and reformed into products and sold in the city. This building was central control for the surrounding buildings. Hook up an MC, have the right stuff, and you could create anything."

"I take it the thing's ran out of juice?" she asked.

"Not exactly, it has a small reserve of materials left, and its micro fusion reactor is still operating, but it doesn't have nearly enough of either for the major operations we need. We keep it in our patrols, though, so that if we run into trouble we can maybe stock up."

D studied his face before saying, "How long until they start to worry that you're gone?"

He laughed. "Not long, why?"

She smiled. "Just curious if you were up for a little fun."

"I don't know," he said. "My group might get a little worried."

"Oh." The smile fell from her as she was staring at the outline of the control building. She slipped her hands into her pocket. "I mean. I just wanted to show some gratitude. Since you volunteered to escort me and all." Her fingers traced along the corners of the compressed Marlow. "I know you boys have better things to do than dealing with this kind of trivial bullshit."

"What did you have in mind?"

Her smile widened, staring at him. "It'd be quicker to show you."

He let out another laugh as they walked. D's finger brushed the trigger of the Marlow.

"Nah." He shook his head. "I really can't right now. Maybe some other time? Do you know where the Orcanna Camp is? We could meet up then."

She walked closer to him and wrapped her arm around his. "Shame."

"Why's that?"

D pulled out the Marlow and pressed the barrel beneath his jaw, and said, "We'll have to do this the hard way."

Before he had even processed what had happened, she'd snaked her finger behind the trigger of his rifle.

She nodded towards the central control building. "Let's take a walk."

They made it to a clearing on the other side of the shipping containers. Red light creeped out of an opening in the ground in front of them. The ground opened into an incline large enough for two trucks to drive through. They had entered a wide empty loading bay. D shifted her attention to an open hallway to their left and jerked Karolek towards it. Damp concrete struck her nose, as they moved deeper into the control building. Entering the hallway, they were surrounded by the exposed metal piping a part of the massive subterranean cooling system. Along with their footsteps echoing through the long empty hallways, they could hear the sound of water dripping from condensation building up on the pipes.

"Let go of the rifle, and hands in the air," D said pressing the Marlow harder under his jaw.

"What exactly is your plan?" Karolek said, "If you shoot your gun in here, the rest of my unit is going to hear it and check things out."

"I'm waiting on a friend," D said as she took out the rifle's clip from the rifle. "Lift the strap over your head. And drop it onto my arm."

He shook his head. "It's going to be awfully hard for them to get through the unit outside."

"They're pretty resourceful," D said firmly grabbing his rifle. "Keep your hands up, and stand against the wall."

"Are they?" Karolek asked, "They're going to need to get here soon. My unit will start to worry if I'm not back soon."

D leaned against the wall and set down his rifle, and proceeded to grab the metal cigarette case with her free hand.

"Thinking about it, I'm pretty sure Cargan was planning on topping up on some supplies down here soon."

"Then I guess we'll have to deal with when that situation comes up," she said popping open the case with one hand.

D still had the Marlow pointed at him, but she turned her attention towards the opening they'd just walked down while feeling around the vials with her other hand.

He glanced back at her. She instinctively pointed the gun at him from the movement, and yelled, "Keep facing the wall!"

"Nervous?" he asked turning back towards the wall.

She didn't say anything as she looked back at the opening and manipulated the syringe over the lid.

"You should be." He started to shift his weight to his left leg. "If you keep yelling like that, you'll give away where we are."

"I think we'll be fi--"

Karolek jumped to his left, and D pulled the trigger. A loud bang shot through the hallways as a bullet struck a pipe where he'd been standing. Steam shot out of the broken pipe and filled the hallway. She dropped the syringe and vial to the ground to shield her face. As she swung the gun towards where he'd jumped to, Karolek tackled her through the steam. D's head slammed into the ground. His hand was gripped around her neck.

"Drop the gun!" he shouted, as he hugged her arm gripping the gun tight against his side.

She coughed for air as he crushed her esophagus. Through her blurred vision, she could still see him staring at her.

"I said drop it!"

D's other hand flailed along the ground searching for the syringe.

He lowered his head, and she felt a drop of water hit her cheek. In a lower voice, he said, "I don't want to kill you."

Her hand landed on the syringe and wrapped around it. On pure instinct, she jabbed it towards where she thought his neck was, and pushed in the plunger. He jerked back, releasing his grip on her throat. She coughed as she sucked in the stinging air. Karolek's body toppled over, motionless, as D scrambled to her feet.

D aimed the Marlow watching the opening they'd come from again, but couldn't hear anything above from the hiss of steam still shooting out from the broken pipe. The sound of the gunshot was still present in her mind. How far did the sound travel? Who heard it? What was the situation outside? She kicked Karolek's body, but he didn't flinch.

Sweat mixed with tears ran down her face, as the span of time she was just staring at nothing dawned on her. She came for the explosives, and she had no intention of leaving without them. Scooping down she grabbed the syringe and metallic case, before sprinting down the hall.

CHAPTER TEN

DELUSION

As D ran deeper into the facility, the tangle of pipes of the cooling system vanished into the walls, and gave way to offices and abandoned security checkpoints. Turning a corner, at the end of the corridor, she spotted the heart of the facility. The main central processor, an octagon shaped room at the fork between two other corridors, with three glass walls facing towards her.

She slammed into the glass door, and grabbed at the door handle to open it. Locked. Beside the door was a keypad. She grabbed Marcus's MC from her pocket and pressed it against the keypad. It recognized Marcus Greeve as an authorized user on the network. With a sharp click from the mechanized lock, the door opened.

Rushing into the room, it was filled by a bolt of blue light from the screens turning on. Three screens were embedded into the wall in front of her. A console extruded from the wall below them, with a touch screen display surface, and an input for the MC front and center. Embedded into the walls on either side of her were compartments with signal lights installed over top of them.

Touching the console, she powered on the main processor. The hum of the machines filled the room. She glanced over her shoulder for any movement. As screens began flipping on, D noted one showing a periodic table with percentages, one showing the electrical build-up throughout the facility, and one filled with numbers she couldn't understand. Taking Marcus's MC, she plugged it into the terminal and navigated through the various explosives stored in it before selecting the ones she needed.

The console's interface changed, and she saw the whole map of the area. Large sections on the surface were dark red. D looked towards the top corner of the map and located the room she was sitting in. Touching the surface, she zoomed into the room, and saw the compartments around her were still active and selected one. A large green button appeared, with the single word ENGAGE. Her finger hovered over the interface as her eyes widened. Since walking through the front gate, she noticed the facility didn't appear to have any noticeable upgrades since it was initially established. All of the tech seemed to be a ham-strung recreation of tech from Ancient Earth. This process was not going to be quiet.

Gritting her teeth, she jammed her finger into the interface then turned her attention back to the hallway. There was a deep hum somewhere deep within the facility as she sank to the ground gripping Michael's rifle. D glanced back at the screens to keep an eye on the status. An internal fusion reactor started by charging up eight rows of parallel super capacitors. The system measured out the required matter for the synthesis process and delivered it to a prepping area within a matter of seconds. A row of super capacitors released their energy payload to kickstart the MROX reaction, sending a surge of energy to rip apart the molecular bonds. Loose atoms were then filtered into a large heated chamber deep underground labeled, Micro Alpha Chamber.

362 Parallel Quantam computers jumped up to maximum usage as they calculated the required MRAC reaction. D recalled a brief moment in college when her physics teacher was discussing the process. His back was turned to the class as he was writing some type of formula on the chalkboard.

"Imagine a tornado ripping its way through a forest, and then through sheer happenstance, creating a hundred-story structurally sound skyscraper made from the wood. Complete with stairs and floors. Now, statistically speaking, this scenario is unlikely to happen naturally. However, If you knew the exact position of every tree in the forest, and found a way to perfectly manipulate how the pressure acted within the cyclone's core, while still keeping it's rotation stable. Well, then it becomes much more theoretically possible."

She watched the computer mainframe work through the process of organizing the very molecular makeup for the explosives she needed for sixteens seconds before seven more rows of super capacitors dumped their energy simultaneously. Within a fraction of a second, the chamber heated up to beyond 2 billion kelvin. In the next instant, the chamber rapidly condensed the super heated plasma, while simultaneously using NFIA chilled liquid nitrogen to extract the heat from the chamber. Excess heat bled into the water system. Screams echoed through the hallways. D snapped her attention back towards the hallway and pointed rifle with the finger on the trigger.

It was just steam. She thought, lowering the rifle again. Looking back at the monitor again, the steam bled out of the system, but she wasn't entirely sure from where. The system had entered its final stage and delivered the explosives to the internal navigation system. D sat sweating with her back pressed against the console watching the halls. The screams of the steam traveling through the pipes had been silenced and were replaced by the hum of the monitors.

As she focused on the silence around her, she began to hear other noises. The sound of creeping mechanations from somewhere below her. Tracks and gears began to shift in the walls around her. A bead of sweat rolled down her cheek. There was no movement in those blacked halls outside those glass walls. A loud buzzer sounded off her left. She fumbled for the gun before holding her chest to calm herself. A green light flipped on over one of the compartments.

Jumping up from the floor, she opened the side compartment and pulled out a metal crate. D slid the top off, and a cocktail of gases blasted out, leaving behind a crate filled with small white pellets. Digging around, she pulled out a bulging circular metal disk covered in white dust. She brushed it off and looked for any abnormalities in the metal casings.

D placed the device into her rucksack and continued digging through the crate to grab the rest of them. When she was done, she zipped up the bag and slung it over her back. Rushing back to the console, she cleared the production history, before making her way back out.

D retraced her steps through the facility while going slow to keep the noise down. Peering around every corner as she went, she checked for any movement. The halls were quiet now. Eventually, she made it back to the loading bay, and walked out of the concrete maw of the underground structure. She froze to check her surroundings as she breached the surface. Nothing around her moved. Every shadow between the shipping containers was motionless. Even the wind was still. Hugging her coat tight, she followed the road with the row of containers to her left. After being underground, the outside air felt much cooler. Turning a corner, she could see the western gate up ahead of her was unguarded.

The bullet ripped through her right shoulder blade and exited through her lung.

Her eyes flashed wide, as she threw the bag of explosives onto the ground, and threw herself between a row of shipping containers.

Scrambling to a crawl, she threw her back against the metal box as she struggled to breathe from one lung. A few more shots rang out. They pinged off the box and whizzed through the air. She kept her eye on the bag. Resting her head against the barrel of the rifle as she flipped the safety off, she pulled out the Marlow. It expanded into its lethal state.

She tucked the Marlow into her pants and grabbed her metal case. Scooting her way to the edge of the container, she listened to the silence. D angled the reflective metal against the edge, and saw disfigured forms hugging close to the row of containers making their way towards her.

Her eyes shot back towards the bag lying on the ground, then back to the reflective metal case. A soldier ducked into the containers a couple of rows behind her, while the rest continued forward. D's eyes shot for the bag one more time then back to the metal. The figures had stopped a row short of where she was. She pocketed the metal case, and pushed herself up the container. Grabbing the rifle with her right hand, she walked towards the cluster of shipping containers away from the explosives, with the assault rifle pointed forward.

A figure popped out in front of her rifle. Sprinting towards him, she fired a burst. He let off a volley of bullets, ripping through her abdomen and thigh as he fell to the ground. A gunshot from behind her ripped through her left arm. Ducking behind the end of the metal container, she hobbled down to the next row, and deeper into the maze of containers. The sound of footsteps behind her were broken by more gunshots. She ducked down another row of containers.

Spotting an open container, she ducked into it. Her right arm was numb, and she couldn't move any of her fingers. Hugging herself against the container, she pulled out the Marlow with her left hand and pointed it at the open door, and stood listening. The footsteps ran up the side, then silence. They had stopped somewhere. D was holding her breath as she watched the door, trying to keep the Marlow from shaking against the container. Her heartbeat pounded against handle of the gun.

Her eyes locked onto the shiny trail of blood at the mouth of the shipping container. Blood was still dripping down her sides onto the floor. She could hear mumbled voices from outside. The barrel of the gun popped in through the opening and shot at the right wall of the container. D didn't return fire, but watched the rifle and waited.

The soldier poked his head in, and she fired three quick shots with the Marlow. The soldier was down. Stray shots tore through the container. She threw herself down onto the ground, as the last soldier was belting the sides with bullets. All that she could hear was a constant ringing. Crawling her way towards the door, she slung the rifle to her back and gripped the Marlow firmly in her hand.

The flashes of the bullets stopped as she reached the door, but the ringing consumed everything. She pushed herself up; no one was to either side of the door. Her rifle was ready. D could feel her right hand again. Walking around the side of the container, she peered around the edge and saw no one.

A burst of gunfire ripped through her abdomen from behind. She held onto the Marlow as she fell to the ground. The soldier was on top of her and kicked the assault rifle out of her hand. Her fingers twisted around the handle of the Marlow, and the trigger. D was coughing and sputtering up blood as she lay on the ground. He pressed the barrel of the gun against the back of her head.

"Don't move!" the soldier yelled over her, as he assessed her bullet-riddled body.

D didn't hear past the ringing; she was focused on holding her breath, but kept gasping from her one good lung.

"Did you hear me? Don't move!"

D continued to cough on the ground. She kept a death grip on the Marlow.

He pushed the rifle off of her head and stood up. "Target is contained and disarmed. What's the next move? Over."

She pulled the Marlow up to her chest as she forced herself up with her right forearm. The soldier pushed his boot between her shoulder blades. He was still holding the radio, listening. D pressed the Marlow against her right chest. Static was sounding off over the radio. She was still coughing for air.

She fired a shot through her lung. The soldier shot back, shouting, "Holy shit!"

D rolled over with the Marlow pointed at him. He let off a spray of bullets from his rifle, ripping across her chest, and popped the other lung. She fired the Marlow until the trigger uselessly functioned.

He was down.

D laid there, arching her back as her body desperately tried to suck in air from two collapsed lungs. She rolled over and pulled herself against the container. Trying to watch her left and right sides between the spasms, she was only caught off guard when her left lung popped back.

D sucked the air in and coughed. The ringing hadn't stopped in her ears. Between gasps of air, she pushed herself up and walked down the empty rows of containers. Going back to the road, she looked around and spotted her bag still lying on the ground. She was watching for any kind of movement as she moved forward towards the bag. Nothing was around. Picking it up, she made her way out of the compound.

***

Richard followed the steam of data over the airwaves to a short office building. Pushing his way past the foyer, he jogged up the fire escape and marched through the burnt-out floor. Popping open the door to the bathroom, he saw a woman with red hair staring into a mirror poking at her iris. He could see them changing from green to a dark brown.

She stopped to stare at him in the mirror. "What's with the outfit?" She smiled.

"I needed a way to move around."

She laughed. "Are you trying to scare away the crows? Didn't you hire a Federation Agent for that?" She straightened up, turning towards him.

"I did, but we needed to cover more ground."

"Cute. Who's the agent?"

"Zecona Giovanni."

She tilted her head towards something outside her mind. "Could be worse. Is he around?"

"No. I didn't want to disclose any of your identities."

"Right," Silver Gecko said, turning her attention back to the mirror, "what's your report?"

"Not good," Richard said, leaning against the door beside an assault rifle. "She's taken out the engineers heading the Maintenance for convoys, and erased their molecularizers."

"Sounds like a good start. What's the problem?" She was stroking her hair now; it was changing to a sandy brown.

"She says she was expecting a demolition team to take out the convoys." Richard looked at the duffel bag at her feet.

She shook her head. "She wouldn't have that kind of clearance to ask." She pushed her hair up from the bottom. It was getting shorter.

"I know."

She wiped the makeup off her face with a paper towel. "What's your next move?" She dropped it into the sink and started pulling at her cheekbones and chin.

"Any chance you can authorize demolition clearance for me?"

"No," she said. Her hair was now a buzzcut. She started to take off her clothes. Richard shifted his weight between his legs and focused on another part of the room. There was no logical reason for this reaction in Richard's mind, but somewhere deep within what was left of his soul, was an appreciation of the female body. Even though there was nothing he could do to act on those emotions.

"Even if I did have clearance," Silver Gecko continued, "I wouldn't authorize it." Looking back at him, she pushed her breast into her chest. "You'll be putting multiple Agents in the area at risk." She grabbed hold of a bar across a toilet stall, and pulled herself taller.

"What can you give me?" His mind's eye wandered as he watched her hands traveling down to her waist.

She was focused on her clit now. Spreading her lips. "How about troop details? Movement, patrols, whatever you need."

"That's a start." He said, watching her push her index and middle finger deep inside her. With a pop, a dick and a pair of balls flopped out of her. Richard physically recoiled and refocused on the far corner of the wall.

Silver Gecko hadn't noticed and was looking in the mirror flexing their muscles. They bulged out as it flexed them. The thin frail sound of the woman's voice said, "That's all I've got?" The android grabbed the front of own his throat, focusing on the ceiling for a moment, and rubbing it with his thumb and index finger. A deeper voice came out. "I can maybe get you more details in a week or two. This is all abrupt."

"Give me what you can."

He was rubbing his arms now. As his hands passed over the skin, hair seemed to spring up. He slid his hand over his face, and a five o'clock shadow appeared. He squatted down to the duffel bag on the floor and ripped open the zipper. He grabbed a thin rectangular device and handed it to Richard. "This has been the troop movement for the past month. On the surface. Also, there's the communication frequencies generally used, and more importantly, who uses them, for what." He was pulling out boots and military fatigues.

Richard popped the device into his wrist. "How'd you get a hold of this data?"

"I'm stationed within the central sector. I have access to most of the communication that passes through the system."

Richard looked up at him. "Only surface movement? What about the Subway?"

"Not a part of my sector," he said, pulling up his pants. "Would need a couple of days tops to get in contact with another operative." He threw on a jacket and started pushing and pulling his forehead and eyebrows, making them broad and thick. Richard was staring at the name **Lt. Kurt Seawood** embroidered above the jacket pocket. He pulled on his ears, making them slightly longer

"Anything you can tell me about about this Black Dog?"

"You have her dossier?" He said buttoning up his shirt.

"I know." Richard said. "Just curious if you knew anything else that wasn't included with that report."

"Well," Seawood thought for a moment turning to face him. "I do know that she was working directly with Ada for at least a year before being reassigned into the field."

"Ada? The acting Consul?"

"Yea," he said, putting on his Kevlar vest.

"Seems like a long time. Aren't new Agents typically assigned to the field within a week?"

"They are. I only know about it because a few of the others that'd been on assignment in the area had passed it along to me when they'd heard she was reassigned to this area. I'd assume it had something to do with what happened to her and Adam, and she wanted to do an extended Diagnostic. But I'd never heard of that kind of examination going past a month."

"I thought that incident was caused by a rouge terrorists cell?"

"It was more complicated than that." He said strapping on his tactical helmet. "Weren't you updated about that situation?"

"I think all that occurred before I woke up." Richard shrugged. "Besides it was well outside my normal operations onboard the federation stations."

"Right," Seawood nodded, "I can see about getting you the details if you want to get caught up?"

"Maybe," Richard said picking up the assault. "I've got enough on my plate to deal with right now, and we're stretched thin as it is." Silver Gecko turned towards him, and he held out the rifle to him. "Any chance I can get some backup?"

The android took a deep breath, looking at the stock of the gun. "No." He gripped the handle, but Richard was still holding firm.

"Then this contract doesn't have a chance in hell," Richard said; his sensors were locked onto him.

Seawood sighed. "What do you want?"

"Either someone who can assist me, and make this work. Or you help me get out of this contract."

He pulled the rifle out of Richard's hand. "Everything's a bit too hectic right now." He turned back to the mirror.

Richard had his arms crossed, staring at the floor.

"No promises."

"Wasn't asking for one."

Seawood scooped down and grabbed the bag off the floor, slung it on his back, and looped the rifles strap over his shoulder. "Careful out there," he said, punching Richard in the shoulder.

"Thanks."

Seawood was gone. Richard waited until he was out of range. He stared at the reflections from his armor in the mirror. After fifteen minutes, he scanned over the general communications of troops in the area on the radio waves, and picked up a transmission.

"I repeat, be on the lookout for a tall woman, with dark hair and brown eyes, carrying a military Rucksack. Last seen North West Kalgu. She is armed and dangerous. Use extreme caution. Don't hesitate to use extreme or lethal force."

Richard stood staring at the mirror before leaving the building.

***

Zecona was sitting on the cot listening to music when Richard walked in.

"D isn't back yet?" Richard said glancing around.

"Apparently not," Zecona said, putting away his headphones.

175

He scanned over the area. "I see her now." He walked over to the hole. "I had heard the Prowler."

"Wonder where she's been."

Richard remained silent as he scanned her, and the bag of explosives. Sensing her walk up the stairs, and taking a detour into a bathroom. Zecona jolted at the door slam down the hall.

"What was that?"

"D." Richard walked down the hall. Pipes in the wall started singing with running water as Richard opened the door. He saw the explosives lying on the ground, and a pile of bloody torn-up cloths on the ground. D was already in the shower.

Richard stared at her. "Can we chat?"

D didn't say anything back and continued to wash the blood off.

Not waiting for a response, he spoke, "You realize you were spotted, right?"

D glanced at him with her head held under the water. "Then I guess it's a good thing my job is done."

"How's that going to help us?" Richard said. "If they review what you took from that compound, they'll be expecting bomb hits. Not to mention the fact we really could have used an extra hand with this."

D was shaking her head. "It'll be fine. Just trust me."

"You don't think you're going to be making our jobs just a little bit harder?"

"I got the explosives," she said.

Richard shook his head. "That's not the point."

She kept her head under the stream of water. "Can we please talk about this later?"

He slammed the door as soft as he could get without breaking it and walked back down the hallway.

Richard walked back into the room, and turned his attention to the road. Watching the raven across the road, he monitored the increased traffic across the communications network.

CHAPTER ELEVEN
DIVIDE

"Up." Richard stood over Zecona. Zecona opened his eyes to a dim gray room. He could hear feet scuffling around him, along with a soft rain smacking against D's tarp.

"What time is it?" he said, not moving his head off the pillow.

"Up," Richard said again. A high-powered flashlight kicked on from the helmet.

Zecona squeezed his eyes closed. "Fucking asshole." He shielded his eyes with his forearm as he sat up. D turned on an electric lantern in the middle of the room, then took a seat on the crack in the wall. A stiff wind whistled through the room. Richard was already wrapping his head up again and already had his overalls on.

D dropped the rucksack in front of Richard and said, "There's your first batch of explosives."

Richard scanned the bag and counted them up. A low growl of thunder rolled through the street.

Zecona looked over at D and said, "So what'll we be doing today?"

"We're going to need to split up our locations," D said, glancing at Richard.

"Why's that?" Richard said as he sat down across from her.

"There's going to be too much movement in this area. You two need to be closer to the action. Jump in and strike quickly from a central point, and that'll leave me open to gather more materials for the explosives. Any location you're using as a launch point for attacks is bound to draw attention. On top of that, I'm on their watch list. If I'm bringing in explosive materials while the area's being watched, then we're all compromised."

Richard threw on his coat. "How are you going to get the explosives to the secondary locations? The patrols will be looking for you."

She tapped her pencil on the notebook. "We'll make a drop-off location."

Richard crossed his arms. "Isn't that complicating things?"

"How's that?" D said.

"What if someone finds the drop-off location?" Richard said he stood and walked across the room.

"I'm willing to take that kind of gamble," she said.

Richard turned staring straight at her. "I'm not."

"Look, I know it's just not that simple, but a dropoff location is reasonable. It'll be halfway between our two locations. I'll drop off and keep watch until we exchange supplies. You'll just need to keep vigilant over who's around you, with only you entering and leaving your location, and me only entering and leaving my place. There's less of a chance we'd all be compromised. Besides which it doesn't matter if you two are compromised. I can't risk it." She pulled a breath from her cigarette. "I'll hit their communications. You'll cut them off at the legs." She flicked off the ash. "There's six major points and about twenty minor points."

Richard shook his head. "This is becoming a bigger project."

"I'm asking for three days," she said staring at him. "I can reasonably get a hold of some more explosives, which'll help us tremendously." She flipped a page of her notebook.

"Won't those be protected?" Richard said.

"I can get past them."

"Why not take out their central power?" Zecona said, glancing over. "That'll knock out their communications."

D shook her head. "Nothing's really centralized. Each location probably has their own generator and engine. Which means each location will need to be knocked out individually."

"Wouldn't knocking out the communications increase patrols?" Richard said.

"Probably." D took a longer drag off the cigarette. The rain continued to beat against the tarp above her.

"How are you going to deal with that? They're already looking for you," Richard asked.

"Easy." She flicked the butt of the cigarette to the corner of the room. "You're going to start with the minor locations first. I'll knock out the communications arrays while they're positioning the forces to man what's leftover. Then you'll hit their major locations. The army's cut off at the knees. They'll have no way of repairing their systems, and the rebels patrolling the outskirts lose their supplies. The troops patrolling fall, and the Federation sweeps in to clean up the mess."

"What if they strengthen their major sites when communications go black?" Richard asked.

She was staring at him. "You can handle it."

He didn't say anything. Another low growl of thunder rolled through the building.

She twirled her pen in her hand. "It'll be a combined focus on the minor locations, the communications array, and the major. Plus, they'll likely keep forces watching weak points within the wall. Attacking multiple points of contact will keep them on edge, cause them to overreact and spread their forces thin trying to protect their assets."

"Why would they do that?"

She was still spinning the pen. "'Cause they don't know the enemy."

Richard was staring down at the map. "We should hit the overpasses." Grabbing the pen from her hand. "Here." He put an **X** over Fourth Avenue. "Here." An **X** over Dmitrievich Street. "Here." An **X** over Moshern Street. "And here" A final **X** over Kasigan Avenue. "Those roads are major routes towards the outside of the city. We can take them out today, and maybe take out a few convoys in the process." He marked another **X** over a street and said, "We'll hole up for the night on this block here, and I'll engage the night patrols in skirmishes in these three Zones." He **X**'d over three streets towards a major base. "Meanwhile." He stopped, looking at the cell towers that were marked. "How much range would you estimate these towers would have?"

"I'd guess... half a mile radius?" D said.

Richard calculated in his mind and drew the radius on the map for each tower. Twelve in total. "You'll need to take out at least eight of these towers within the first two days."

He marked off the eight he was referring to. "This'll throw the rest into over-capacity unless they have mobile temporary setups." He clicked the pen back. "But Zecona and I can take those out when they come out. They'll be a part of the military convoys."

"First day, be discreet. Knock out three if you can. Shoot the computer components, I don't know. Be creative. Start in the early

181

morning, with this one." He marked one near Fourth Avenue. "That's where we'll be striking first. Second day, blow them up. Hit five of them. The morning of the second day, our skirmishes will be escalating to the smaller bases. South of the Highway here, east of the 220 Bypass, west of the Intersection at Monroe and Gumbit, and a little bit north of 420, here." He was circling the points. "These are more important because they're touching past the normal bridges and can allow a quick pass through Highway 98. Taking them out will slow them down, but not by much." He circled another block. "Zecona and I will move our operations to this block here. And resume skirmishes through the night to keep the military on their toes. Communication will likely be kept to a minimum. We'll make a direct strike on this base, here." He circled a large block over the community center. "And deliver a payload, blowing their transports." He drew a line down the road. "We'll make our way west and grab another payload, head to the bank here, and deliver a second payload to their vehicles situated here." He circled within the area of where the base walls had been drawn.

"One problem," D said, holding up a finger.

"What's that?"

"How can I be taking on the cell towers if I'm gathering the explosives?"

Richard thought for a moment, then said, "Zecona and I will be taking on the cell towers and bombing the bridges today."

"Seems like a lot to deal with," D said, staring at him.

"It's the only way it'll work. Besides which, you already have been spotted once, if you get caught during this, it's not going to help us."

She pulled out another map. "Here's the current subway system. They can circumvent the bridges getting taken out here and here" She pointed to Fourth and Dmitrievich. "And blow past these bases on the west side and get a clean jump southbound along these four tunnels."

"We won't have time for it," Richard said. "After attacking the Dorbich Building and the Community Center, they'll be far more vigilant."

"Then it's worthless, because the train yard, Borch Tower, and the Kimal Building can ship supplies through the subway more efficiently than by truck or convoy. The subway is just as important as the road."

"It's too much to attack at once within three days."

"Then I'll hit the damn subway on the third day with the leftover explosives. I'm not going to let this fucking work go by the wayside."

He was looking at the subway map. "There are too many key locations to hit, and we don't know when they're even running."

D was staring at him, and leaned in and whispered, "Do you really need Zecona with you on the third day?"

His sensors stared back at her, his voice was quiet when it answered. "He's a greenhorn. He'll be dead as soon as he steps foot out on the tracks."

"This is war. There are casualties."

"Not needless ones," he said as another groan of thunder passed through.

She sighed. "I can use whatever explosives I have left to take out the tracks."

"You have more to worry about. If the tracks were designed to work around broken parts, you'll need to cut across a whole row. Not only that, if they have sensors to note irregularities with the lines, they could stop the trains altogether and fix the lines before

183

our job is done." He leaned forward. "Optimally, you'll need to destroy and derail a train on the tracks. Hell, maybe even explode its payload to damage the tunnel. This'll slow them down. But we don't know when they move, or even what they'll be transporting."

"I'll handle it," D said. "What's the run down?" She rested her chin on her leg. "I'm grabbing the materials today and tomorrow?"

"Correct," Richard said. "While you're doing that, Zecona and I will hit the bridges and knock out the communications on the first day. On the second day, we'll be attacking patrols and convoys along alternate routes. We'll meet back up that night, then start delivering explosives to the bases, and anything left over will be thrown at the subway system."

D shrugged. "Sounds like a plan to me."

Zecona shook his head and grabbed a cup of coffee from the food dispenser. Richard was checking the rifle clips, loading them in, and chambered a round.

"I want to start hitting sites as soon as Delta is set up," Richard said, looking at Zecona.

"Great," Zecona said, taking a sip.

"Shouldn't take more than an hour to have everything set up." He strapped the rifle to his back.

Zecona gave a thumbs up from behind another sip of coffee. "Is she coming with us?" he said nodding to D.

D piped up, "No. Haven't you been paying attention?"

"It's your show." Zecona shook his head. "I've just been waking up." He bent down and zipped up his bags.

She shook her head. "Just don't fuck it up."

"Right," Zecona said behind another sip.

"Drink on the way," Richard said.

"Fine." Zecona threw the bag over his back, still holding the coffee in his hand.

They didn't say goodbye to D. She sat motionless watching them behind her cigarette as they walked out the door.

***

The rain had let up as they traveled, but it stayed mostly cloudy. Eventually, they approached a squat gray building.

"This is it?" Zecona glanced around the front of the office building Richard was walking towards.

"What's wrong?" Richard glanced back at him.

"Nothing," Zecona said, catching up to him.

Under the noon sun, its three floors looked like a stack of cracked porcelain plates. The surrounding parking lot was getting overtaken by the roots of what used to be decorative trees. At one time they would have needed a keycard to get into the building, but they walked through the busted double doors into the lobby.

"Get things set up now," Richard said as they made their way through the foyer into the main hall. "We won't be back until late, and you won't have time to set up then."

They jogged up a staircase and made their way past the remains of a cubical farm. They stopped in a hallway outside a row of office rooms, with a long row of tall tinted windows beside them.

Zecona plopped down the bags. "What's the plan?" he said, bending down and unzipping one of them.

"You're bombing the bridges. I'm shooting the cell towers."

"I thought I was shooting the towers?" Zecona glanced up.

"Too risky. I'll take the heat from those targets. You focus on taking out the bridges. I'll provide the distraction, while weakening their communications."

"Anywhere in particular I should put these bombs?" He pulled out a roll of athletic tape, and started to wrap up his left hand.

"The bridges will have a couple of fail-safe components on them. You'll have to take out multiple beams beneath the underside of the bridge to cripple them. After the explosives are attached, you'll want to activate their receivers so we can detonate."

"How many will it take to bring down a bridge?"

"Probably three or five at least. The structures will probably need some level of weight on top to take them down all the way."

Zecona stopped wrapping his hands and stared up at him. "Are you saying I'm going to have to carry all of the bombs with me to each bridge?"

Richard stared at him. "What's wrong with that?"

"Fuck all, apparently," Zecona said tightening the wrapping. "Carry around a big ol' bag of explosives? I don't see a damn thing wrong with that."

"Don't get shot, and you won't blow up."

"Great. I was just worried about getting shot for its own sake." Zecona was starting to wrap his right hand. "Are we really going to take on a fully armed military base?"

Richard was setting up a computer on the ground. He shook his head. "No. That would be suicide."

Zecona kept wrapping his hands. "That's not what you told D."

Richard was typing something into his computer. "I know."

"What's the plan, then?" Zecona finished wrapping his hand.

"We'll take out the cell towers. Hit a couple of bridges. Cause some trouble with the patrols tonight, and tomorrow. Then we'll wash our hands of it. I've already asked for reassignment from my contact."

Zecona was nodding his head. "What'll we tell D?"

Richard glanced over at him and shrugged. "We tried."

Zecona was punching his taped-up hands into his palms. "If we're just going to take the money and run, why are we even trying?"

"I'm still under contract. I feel like this part of the contract is at least doable." He paused standing up straight. "But honestly, I'm just bored." He was staring at Zecona now. "I've been locked onto the wrists of some fat politician for the past two years." He looked away and stared out the window over the city. "The opportunity to assault a military force with unchecked supervision? This is what I was born to do. It's a shame we don't have more manpower."

"Doesn't sound like much fun to me." Zecona was standing straight up. "How am I getting up under the bridges?"

Richard looked around the office before saying, "Follow me."

They walked up to the locked door in the corner of the building. Richard grabbed hold of the keypad, and his onboard computer hacked through the interface, opening it to a messy closet. Cleaning chemicals lined the shelves. Sponges and mops were thrown about, but Zecona's eyes were drawn to a picture of a kid taped on the wall. Richard was already interfacing with the materializer embedded in the back wall.

"Got just the thing." Richard input the correct code, the machine hummed alive, and the drawer clanged. Opening the hatch, he grabbed the device. "Maintenance Rope," he said, turning, and handed it to Zecona. "Scan a distance. Wait a minute, and it'll create the cable from the surrounding carbon to whatever length you need. They'll latch onto any surface, and they're designed to allow you to get into any angle you need to work from." He reached over and grabbed a vest. "You'll also need a harness so you won't fall and die."

"Fantastic." Zecona held the lime green safety harness in his hand. "It definitely won't stick out while I'm hanging under the bridge with a big bag of explosives."

"Would you quit worrying?"

***

Zecona walked alone along the lower roadway. The first overpass for Fourth Avenue loomed in front of him, and in the distance, he could see each successive bridge he needed to climb under in order to prep the explosives. Each one connected the two portions of the city together, and all of them provided the fastest route from the central encampments to the Rebel forces surrounding them.

The lower highway was peppered with abandoned vehicles that looked to have been partially salvaged, potholes, and shallow pools of stagnant water on the edges of the road with pale white tubes of Croca-weeds sprouting from the asphalt. Above him on either side of the road, he could see what looked like rows of townhouses. Just from the plain concrete form each building shared, he assumed that they must have been built when the city was first established. Most of the windows had long since either been boarded up with plywood or had tarps covering them as though they were bracing for a storm.

Fourth Avenue appeared to be six lanes in total, broken into two bridges side by side. He'd have to place explosives along each one to bring the whole road down. Zecona gripped the maintenance cable tight as he walked up the concrete slope under the first bridge. Glancing across, he lined himself parallel to the supporting beams. The bag of explosives hit the ground with a thud. Holding the maintenance cable, he scanned the distance and pressed the button on the side. A light flashed red, and air sucked in through the surrounding vents, vibrating in his hands. When it finished, the light flipped to green.

Zecona held the device above his head and fired. A hook and a cable shot out of both ends. One embedded itself into the ground behind him; the other shot across the length of the bridge. More air sucked in at an alarming rate. Zecona was shocked that it didn't slow down as it sailed through the air. The hook of the cable dug itself into the other side. Throwing his coat to the ground, he did a quick check of the athletic tape over his hands before strapping on the lime green safety harness.

He clipped the bag of explosives to his back and did another check on the cable by pulling down on it with his full weight. It didn't budge. Gripping the cord with both hands, he pulled himself up. Every part of his body ached from the gravity, but he pushed past it. Wrapping his legs over the top, he hung there studying the hook embedded on the other side for any sign of movement. The bag on his back was swinging with him. He clipped the safety harness to the cable and started pulling himself across the bridge.

***

Richard had his sensors on monitoring the block around the cell tower. His face wraps limited the distance he could see, but it was far enough. Taking the time to calculate the shot from the window across the street, he took a quick potshot with the pull of the trigger. His hand gripped the door frame, and he threw himself down the hall as the bullets hit the tower. Monitoring the area, he watched the guards running down the streets around him, before hitting the last landing and running out the back door.

"Another one down." He heard the chatter on the network say. "What the hell is going on down there?"

"Don't know, that's the fourth one."

Richard rounded a corner down a block.

"Where's our Arct? We'll need some repairs ASAP," Central called out.

"Arct here. Is it those fucking kids shooting the damn things again?" Another voice hopped on the network. "Shoot 'em back, see how they like it."

"We're supposed to be the good guys, Ted," Central said.

"This is a fucking war. They're helping the Federation, damnit. Pop the suckers if you catch 'em," Ted said over the channel.

"Archo here. I think I saw the fucker in the window this time." A voice called out. "Quick little shit, already left the building."

"How many shots were fired?" A deep voice called out.

"Five or six, I think," Archo called back

"That's all it took?" Ted said. "Lucky bastard."

"Maybe we should be recruiting them?" Central popped in.

"Defector?" Archo said.

The deep voice boomed back in. "Set up checkpoints around the remaining comm towers. Secure surrounding buildings. Central Comm, meet in my tent in five."

"Yes sir," Central called back.

"Anyone not on the roads, shoot on sight," the deep voice said.

"Seems a little extreme."

***

Zecona was finishing up the third bridge under Moshern Street bathed in the deep orange of the setting sun. Just like with Dmitrievich Street, this crossing was a single four-lane roadway, making the work easier. Opening the bag, he grabbed the braces, another explosive, the bolts, and the wrench. He stuck the pump screws into the bottom brace and pushed it into the cross beam of the bridge. A quiet, metallic pop rang as he pushed the buttons along their sides and they drilled themselves through the metal. He put the explosive and the brace in their position, then began the arduous task of screwing in each of the bolts.

As he worked, a small herd of Aeoki made their way up the lower roadway. He'd read about them a long time ago while studying aboard Viridi Araceae Station. The strange coloration on their face made it look like they had three more sets of eyes than they really had along their long and narrow heads. Wind traveling down the artificial valley would ripple across their golden barbs, in a way that mimicked golden crackle-back grass. Some Aeoki were eating the croca-weeds, as they weaved their way through the abandoned cars with their four thin legs. Others took the time to pop their long necks through broken car windows, and rip up the seat coverings. Despite their four curved horns jutting from the back of their heads, they were able to eat the seat foam with ease.

Zecona took a second to wipe the sweat from his face with a shaky head. His back was aching from constantly hanging for so long. The added stress of gravity sickness wasn't helping. Taking another break to lay out under the bridge and take in the now clear sky was ideal, but he was behind schedule. He twisted the wrench one last time on the final bolt, and gripped the brace to see if it was secure enough, then grabbed hold of the mic and asked, "How's it looking out there, Richard?"

"Troops haven't bothered with those roads," Richard said in his ear.

Zecona crawled his way back towards the concrete slope. The herd of Aeoki were long gone. Explosives had to be placed across three main beams, along with an extra one along the failsafe beam to ensure the bridge would collapse on itself given the right weight. Climbing down from the cable, he deactivated the cord. Air blasted out of the vents. When the device was back to its original size, he put it with the bag of explosives. Squatting down, he grabbed the mic again. "Still clear?"

"Hold on a sec. I think I heard there's a patrol sweeping through."

Richard had been swinging back around the bridges after every cell tower he hit. On top of that, he was monitoring the radio traffic to note where troop movement was going to be next. They were rather infrequent, and they didn't seem to be looking under the bridges as they went through.

Zecona could hear the footsteps walking above his head from multiple people. They stopped, and he suspected they were taking in the view. Glancing westward, his eyes were drawn towards the dancing swarms of gravits that had started to come out. From this distance, they looked like specs of orange light against the setting sun. Flying between the croca-weeds, he could see a few Sicklebees hovering above the water, then flying up to land on the tubular lavender flowers. In between the calls of a nearby Krobi, he could make out a muffled conversation from above him, before hearing them continue down the road.

"You'll tell me if they send a rail gun across one of these things, right?" he whispered into the microphone.

"Quiet."

He focused on the far side of the bridge. The older concrete townhouses from before had slowly morphed into smaller houses that were far more damaged. Their wooden frames where scorched and exposed to the environment. From listening to the patrols, they were generally short. It took them maybe fifteen minutes to get across most of the bridges. One every half hour it seemed.

"You're clear," Richard said.

Zecona grabbed his coat and the bag before running down the incline and making his way towards the last bridge. As far as he knew, Richard was somewhere in the general vicinity. Zecona picked up to a jog. He kept an ear out listening for Richard under each bridge for any hint of footsteps, or movement when he got a second to look up at the road. How he was keeping so quiet baffled him. Richard moved onto the next batch of cell towers.

***

As Richard ran through the alleyway, he could sense the patrol walking on the road through the building. The next comm tower was coming up. He pulled the KRISER off his back, and calculated another shot. Spinning in mid-air, he let his body fall a foot, aimed through the gap of the building, and fired off another quick burst. His boot slammed into the ground, and he shot down the alleyway behind him.

"Another one down."

"Where the fuck is he?"

"Delta, Bravo, station between the western towers now," the deep voice commanded.

"Spotted someone running." Hearing that, Richards sensors kicked, and he spotted a soldier to his left. Richard gripped the KRISER. Instincts kicked in, and he fired a quick burst behind him. The bullets tore through the soldier.

"Enemy Fire." Another soldier popped onto the Comm.

Richard launched himself down an alleyway.

"Man Down!"

"Mobile Unit's assemble." The deep voice boomed, "Dead Air."

Richard was left listening to his footsteps hitting the pavement. Jumping into the back door of a building, he shot out as many sensors he could in every direction. Despite the bandages dampening his sensors, the rebels had veered off the chase. A Jeep monitoring the alleyways and the road picked up the downed soldier and circled back towards the broken comm tower. The rifle pulsed and clicked away the minutes as more bullets formed in the clip.

"Mobile Unit's in route to Western Comm Towers." Central popped back on. "ETA, thirty minutes"

"Should we engage target?"

"With extreme caution," The deep voice called back.

***

Zecona crawled over the six-lane highway under Kasigan Avenue, as another herd of Aeoki passed below him. The clear sky steeped in a deep orange sunset had been reduced to a sky fading to gray under a cloudy sky. Similar to Fourth Avenue, Kasigan Avenue was eight roads split between two bridges. He'd already finished the first bridge, and was finishing the second one. Richard had been radio silent for far too long. After this one, they would meet up at a safe distance, and detonate the explosives. After eight solid hours of climbing around under bridges, his hands had a hard time lining up the bolt and the socket. Pushing it in, he grabbed the wrench again. Four more bolts on this crossbeam, then another four on the safety beam he hadn't touched yet: that's all he needed to get through, but he needed to pick up the pace while he still had sunlight.

The growing shadows from the surrounding buildings did not help either. Kasigan Ave was seated at the heart of the business and commercial buildings. He'd only caught a glimpse of the sheer extravagance that was molded into each building towering over him when he had rushed his way towards the bridge. Despite the personality they'd been built with, they were only hollow shades of their former selves. No lights showed through their windows. No movement could be seen from the roads. They stood silent watching the city around them. This area seemed to stand defiant to the city decaying around it.

He tightened the bolt down and grabbed another from a pouch on his stomach. Twisting another bolt tighter into the hole, then another bolt along the top. Footsteps echoed on the asphalt above him. One last bolt. The radio was still dead quiet. He expected at least a little bit of a heads-up about the patrol. This was the last bolt, and he wasn't making enough noise to begin with, so he pressed on with his work. As he tightened the wrench, he felt his arm start shaking from the tension, before it slipped off the bolt. He punched the support beam. The loud clang as the wrench hit the side of the bridge split the air. Zecona curled up, clutching his hand.

Dead air rang out over the radio. The echoing footsteps stopped. Zecona hung on with one hand, watching the flashlights cut across the ground below the bridge.

"Did any of you guys hear that?" one of the soldiers muttered.

Zecona heard the radio static above him, but couldn't hear what was said.

"Yeah, it sounded like it was down there. Ichiro, why don't you go down and check it out?"

Richard popped back in. "What happened?"

Zecona didn't move. He swayed, suspended above the ground. A column of light was floating down along the side of the bridge. He held his breath and clutched his closed fist tighter. Gravel crunched next to the bridge.

The soldier was going to see him in his lime-green reflective vest. There was no way they wouldn't. Zecona looked forward and backwards along the cord. Forward, or back?

Ichiro stopped midway down the incline, and called back: "Looks clear."

No time, Zecona realized. He was exactly in the middle. There was nowhere to hide except on the top of a trailer a few feet behind him.

"Mack," Ichiro called out, "cover my six. I want to take a closer look."

Tightening the explosives to his back, he unhooked the safety latch from the cord, and hung upside down by his legs. Zecona kept an eye on two pillars of lights floating their way down the bridge. With a snap, the safety harness detached. He twisted the bag around his abdomen. His legs ached with each passing second.

"Fucking hell, Mack. Get your ass over here already."

Zecona jerked his head to the base of the bridge. Nobody was there yet.

"On it!" another soldier called out.

The rope stabbed into the back of his thighs like knives, and the strength in his legs was starting to give. Shoving the safety harness into the bag, he bear-hugged the cord and watched them walk down onto the road below him. The lights flashed everywhere below him. Shifting the weight back to his upper body didn't pull out the knives in his thighs.

Zecona wouldn't be able to hold on for much longer. As he glanced back at the truck, he thought of a time when he was a young chilikie aboard the Alnus Telum. He and his calarose would race through the maintenance ways where the pull of the station's artificial gravity would be weaker or stronger. They would race through those tunnels jumping between ladders and odd-angled hallways. The gravity seemed comparable, and falling here didn't seem as complicated as grabbing hold of a ladder under double the force of that gravity. All he had to do was fall, twist his body around, and land gently on top of the trailer.

He began inching his way towards the trailer. The two soldiers were primarily searching the ground, but while they were still farther out in the road, he would at least be partially concealed by the bridge's beams. However, if they glanced up in his direction, it would all be over in seconds. Each time he pushed himself towards the truck reignited the pain in his legs. Both soldiers were in plain view under the bridge as he positioned himself over the middle of the trailer. Their flashlights scanned the ground below him.

It was now or never.

He let go of the rope and fell with the grace of a log into a river. His back hit the top of the truck with a loud metallic thud.

"The fuck was that?" Ichiro shouted.

Zecona's entire body writhed in agony, while he contained any noise he wanted to make. Gravity was a bitch. Flashlights were whipping around the top of the truck as Zecona rolled over. This was it. If he gave up, maybe they'd treat him fairly. The frantic lights turned their attention back down, and Zecona followed them, watching a sole Aeoki bound over abandoned cars.

"It was just a damn Aeoki," Mack exclaimed.

"I don't know," Ichiro said, "I always thought they were more graceful than that."

A voice called out from over the bridge. "If there ain't anything down there, let's keep moving. We need to get back to basic in the next hour."

"On it sir," Ichiro said.

They were walking back up the incline back to the main bridge. Zecona let out a deep breath, listening to their footsteps fade away. He laid there letting his muscles rest. All that was left was to apply an explosive to the safety beam; after that, he would be done.

***

They were perched on top of the office they'd set up in. Zecona was watching Fourth Avenue through a pair of binoculars. He clung to the detonator in his other hand. Richard removed a portion of the face wrap to see the distance. From the line of concrete townhouses, rows of headlights began crossing the bridge.

"Wait for it," Richard said.

"Just tell me when." Zecona rested the binoculars on the ground.

Richard raised his hand, then sliced it down. "Now!"

Zecona pressed the switch.

Nothing happened.

"I said now!"

"I pressed it," Zecona said, looking at it. He pressed the button harder.

They saw the multiple blasts from the corner of their eyes. Zecona looked up, as the sound of the blasts reach them. The headlights were pointing up from the lower roads. More explosions as the munitions aboard the trucks detonated from the impact.

"So far so good," Richard said staring at the silent carnage. His sensors scanned over the horizon, at the other bridges that were hit.

Zecona sank against a part of the air-conditioning unit. Richard listened to the radio chatter in his mind. The moon passed behind some clouds.

"You good?" Richard said, glancing down at Zecona.

"Yeah," he said. "Just exhausted."

Richard nodded his head. "Can't blame you." The suit crossed its arms and stared up at the stars through a clear bit of sky.

"What do you suppose this looked like?"

"When? Before the war? Or before it was urbanized?"

"Both." Zecona shrugged.

"I haven't a clue." The suit was staring off. "I didn't get a chance to see any of it." Richard paused, "Shit."

Zecona looked up. "What?"

"It didn't trigger the other ones."

Zecona grabbed the binoculars and stared out in the direction Richard was looking. He could see Dmitrievich Street, Moshern Street, and Kasigan Avenue were still standing. Glancing down at the detonator, he smacked it, and pressed it harder. "Could it be the distance?"

Richard was shaking his head. "If it triggered one, it should have triggered all of them. Did you activate the receiver on all of them?"

"Yeah, I..." He trailed off. "Shit." Zecona sunk down, shaking his head and staring at the faint pulses of red on the horizon behind them. "I'm such a fucking idiot."

"It happens," Richard said. "We'll just have to head out and activate them."

"I can't." Zecona shook his head. "I can't deal with this. Over the past couple of days, I've had my ass kicked, I've been shot at, and almost had my throat slit. This is just too much to handle. I thought I could work through this, but fuck. I thought today was going to be 'easy', and I still managed to fuck it up."

"Nobody said today was easy," Richard said, staring at him.

"We put bombs on a bridge and blew them up. How is that difficult?"

Richard shook his head.

"It's not like we were attacking a convoy or a patrol. We had all day to set up." Zecona was looking at him.

"Everyone makes mistakes." Richard was still shaking his head. "You're still getting used to working planet side."

"That's not what I meant." He ran his hand over the top of his head.

Richard remained quiet, glancing back at the distance to the bridges.

Zecona was shaking his head. "I didn't want this." He stood up. "I wanted to join the Federation and protect the stations. I didn't want to be..." He trailed off staring back at the bridges. "What I've become."

Richard looked at him. "And that would be?"

"I wanted to protect." He turned his attention to Richard. "I wanted to show that the Federation was a force of reason." He waved off into the distance. "What is this?"

Richard remained quiet, glancing back at the horizon.

"Then the war broke out. I guess that's what changed things. I wanted to get into the pilot's division, but Abots aren't allowed to enlist. I guess I was expecting to be just assigned to a sector, and keep the peace. Maintain order. I was supposed to make sure things ran smoothly. Then this." Zecona waved back at the roads. "I didn't expect this."

"Then why did you volunteer to come here?" Richard said.

Zecona shrugged. "I don't know. I thought... I thought I could help."

Richard stared ahead at the flickering horizon. "You should get some rest."

Zecona took a deep sigh, staring at the burning bridge ahead of them. The moon appeared back from behind the clouds. "What are we going to do about the other bridges?"

"I'll take care of them."

Zecona took a deep breath. "Fine." He got up and walked towards the access door.

CHAPTER TWELVE
DOWNPOUR

A pillar of red smoke rose up against the black sky. Richard saw another patrol show up at the mouth of the road. He kept his body in the shadow of a pillar gripping the KRISER as he monitored the group's movement. Zecona was asleep on the cot. No vehicles were within range of his sensors. All units appeared on foot.

The patrol tossed down a smoke bomb in front of his building. Richard picked up chatter over the radio.

"Dango 2. Targets? Over."

"None. Over."

"Copy That."

Zecona rolled over. Richard watched the group continue down the street, before walking down the hallway and out the front door. He had the KRISER in hand, and the pistols ready in his coat pocket.

Sending out a pulse through his hand, the gun transformed into a much higher-powered assault rifle. Richard grabbed the clips from his pocket and sent out a different pulse, reprogramming the majority of ammo into carbon bullets. At 200 meters he saw another group appear at the mouth of the street.

He sprinted down a side alley, and ran in between buildings into another road a block away, before continuing his way to the bridges. More movement became clear as he got closer to the roads. Shoving his gloves into his pocket, he extended the claws in his hands as he came up to Dmitrievich Street.

He sent out a quick, short signal to ensure the explosive wasn't already armed. Everything remained silent. After a quick scan to see where the bombs were planted, he launched himself into the underbelly of the bridge and dug his claws into the metal, arming one, two, three, and four. Jumping and digging his hands into the metal for each one on both sides, the steel screamed out.

"I'm hearing something on the bridge southwest of my position. Checking it out now." a voice on the radio called out.

Richard threw himself off onto the road below.

"Dispatch, could you get some more units into the area."

He resent the signal to the bombs. A blast shot through the area as the bridge went down.

"Shit! The bridge was just hit."

Richard sprinted down the road towards Moshern Street.

"Dispatch get mobile units in the area on the double."

Richard spotted the soldier to his left too late.

"Dispatch I see movement on the road below my position!"

Richard fired the rifle, and the voice became garbled.

"Who was that!?"

"South of the bridge here. Must be heading eastbound?"

Richard could see the next bridge in front of him. The motors wound beneath him, as his pants tangled and ripped apart with each step he took.

"We're seeing a line of bridges on our map. Units need to get on those bridges and watch for the target."

Richard launched himself up under the bridge. The first one he checked was already armed. He threw himself across the bridge, tearing across the steel underbelly to activate the second. Hearing the jeep speed up above him, he threw himself to the third.

"Mobile Unit here. Watching southbound from the bridge."

Richard ripped across the steel glanced at the third. It was already active.

"The hell was that?" A soldier cried out over the radio. Richard threw himself towards the last bomb. Above him, he heard one of the soldiers cry out.

"Off the bridge. Now!"

Arming the last bomb, he threw himself back towards the east. The wheels of the Humvee squealed as it jolted forward.

He activated the bombs before even bothered hit the ground. He hit the ground running at 45 MPH.

"Movement spotted eastbound!" He heard a motor over the radio. The Humvee barely came into view on his sensors.

"Go faster!" one man said over the background on the radio. The Humvee was already to his left. They sped up on his right; he had the rifle aimed as his mind calculated and pulled the trigger. Four shots for each soldier of the unit.

A garbled mess tore over the radio as the Humvee jumped the rails, spiraling straight towards him. The grill was staring down at him as he jumped up, and kicked himself away. It crashed into the ground, as he sped along to the final target.

"Units in position." He heard the call come in over the radio. Kasigan Avenue crept into view, with a row of soldiers lined against the side. He sent a pulse over the radio waves. Half the bombs exploded, causing the bridge to buckle.

KRISER in hand, he shot at the scrambling units, hitting three and missing two. Propelling himself up, he scrambled along the swinging bridge. It groaned under its own weight.

One more active. He swung along to the last one. He heard a Humvee above him start to back up. Pulling up beside the explosive, he hesitated when he saw it was already active. As he launched himself east, he could hear the Humvee's wheels squealing. Shooting out one last signal, the bomb blasted through the air, and half the bridge went with it.

Richard continued east, watching the sunrise with each step.

***

Zecona woke up to the automated tinted office windows dulling the morning light. It must have been at least 8:00 AM given the position of the sun. Richard was nowhere to be seen. Getting up, he walked past the offices to what were once rows of cubicles. At the far corner of the floor he was on, he found a breakroom with a working food dispenser. Even though the system had been reduced to emergency services, it was still offering basic functionality. He selected a basic breakfast, and watched as a bagel plopped out along with a cup of coffee. Standing in the door way, watched over the halfwalls as he ate.

Walking back towards his cot, he grabbed a roll of athletic tape from his bag, and started to rebind his hands and wrists. As the sun rose along the window, the glass reacted, and worked to reduce the glare. Tightening the final wrap, he flexed his fist after finishing to make sure his hands where binded tight enough.

Picking up his MoCae from his pack, he flipped it on, and angled the camera lens.

"Hi everyone!" He flashed a smile. "I know it's been a while since I last uploaded a video. Like I said in my last video, I'm on Verra now." He bit his upper lip as he mulled over the words.

"Honestly not sure what I can really say. The drop to planetside went fine. The people I've been working with have been treating me well. Things have been going pretty well!" He said, then rolled his eyes. "Well, about as well as a war zone can go." His eye's locked to the lens again and said. "It seems like the work I'm doing here will wrap up soon, so I should be able to relocate to a safer posting. So I can start reuploading again. I hope you all are doing fantastic though! Can't wait to hear from you all again!"

Moving his other hand he pretended to turn off the MoCae as he had always done, but left it recording for a few more seconds, then continued talking.

"Hopefully I'll remember to edit this out later. But..." He looked away from the camera for a moment. "If this should end up lying on the side of the road somewhere, and this message somehow finds its way back to you. I just wanted to let you know that, I'm sorry." Forcing a smile, he stopped the recording.

Zecona tossed the MoCae back into his pack and collapsed onto the cot. He was half asleep again when heard the footsteps coming from the cubicles. Dropping his hand to the floor, he rested his hand on the pistol beside his cot. Richard walked through the door frame.

"Where have you been?" Zecona said sitting up.

"Cleaning up, then scouting the area." Richard leaned against the doorway. "Scouts had been out tracking the area all night."

Zecona nodded picking his coffee back up. "What's the plan for today?"

"I'm going to need you to be my extra set of eyes today." Richard kicked off of the door frame, sat down beside him, and projected a map of the area onto the floor. "The layers of clothing are affecting my sensor's, I can't see as far as I usually can. You need to patrol the rooftops in this area." He pointed to a city block that appeared to be close to where they had been. "Give me details of troop movement and any convoys along this street. We'll cause trouble for them there, then we'll move locations and set up here." He moved his finger to another city block a great deal away. "You set up first, and let me know when you are ready for me to engage.

"Seems kinda dangerous." Zecona shrugged taking a sip of coffee.

"How's that?" Richard looked up at him.

"I'm standing out in the open for one," Zecona said. "We're not exactly using a secure channel. We're using a radio signal right? Since we've knocked out the cell towers in the area. They'll pick up on it most likely, right?"

"I doubt it," Richard said. "The radio is set to encrypt the signal, I'll decrypt it. When I pick up on it."

"I'm still running around the rooftops. I'm sure to get spotted."

"I'll be keeping their attention." Richard waved his hand. "We'll be far from each other."

"This is a shit plan." Zecona shook his head. "We should just cut our losses now, go back to D, and say we did what we could."

Richard was standing beside the pane glass window. Looking out at the parking lot of the building, he shook his head. "I at least want a little bit more action."

"Is that all this is to you?"

Richard shrugged. "Things will go smoothly. We've just got to keep moving and hit these areas and we'll be good. After that, we're done. We can't do anything else, and D can't ask for us to do anymore. This is the best we can do."

Richard scooped down into Zecona's bag and grabbed his head radio, and tossed it at him. "Gear up. The sooner we head out the faster we can be done."

***

Zecona ran towards a wide four-story building as the sun reached its peak in the sky. Despite the broken windows and doors, it appeared that the buildings in the area were still intact, lacking any major structural damage. The last two building's he checked didn't have the proper roof access. It looked like an old office building as he entered the lobby through the broken door. Damp plaster rushed past him as he ran past the reception desk out front, and into the remnants of a cube farm, he found the emergency stairs towards the back of the building, and sprinted up the flight of stairs. He rushed towards the roof access on the final landing, and was met with a chained locked door. Fumbling with the padlock, Richard piped in on the radio.

"Are you in position yet?"

"Working on it," Zecona said.

The lock popped open a second later, and he threw open the door. He was met with a wide rooftop with tangles of air ducts stretched over the plastic gravel. Zecona sprinted forward, stopping short of the edge of the building. Dropping to his stomach, he crawled up to the edge, and squinted in the afternoon sun while scanning the streets, before he saw a group of three men toting assault rifles walking southbound along the road far to his right.

Checking his location on his digital map, he grabbed the mic and reported, "Richard, you've got a few guys on South Broxton. Over."

Turning to his left, he ran towards the other side of the building. The hard plastic chunks crunched under each step. He clambered over a tube of aluminum ventilation, and ran up to another ledge, checking his position as he went. Looking down, he was met with an empty street.

"I see 'em," Richard responded.

"See where they're walking? Over," Zecona said.

"West."

Zecona took another quick glance along the streets but didn't see any troop movement. Gunshots rang out from the streets behind him.

***

After taking out a patrol of five soldiers, Richard flung the KRISER back onto his back and ran back down an alleyway. He monitored the transitions.

Central command called out, "Delta? Respond. Delta."

"Anything from Bravo yet?" another voice over the air called out.

"Nothing. Dead air," Central responded.

"What the hell is going on? Any eyes out in that area?"

"Nothing yet. Did I hear them right? It was just one guy?"

His radio receivers suddenly picked up. "Cells are nearly down!"

A deep voice boomed over, "Switch to radio transmissions. Frequency 233."

"Understood," Central called out.

"Roger that," another voice called out.

"Get that goddamn convoy out of there! It'll be a sitting duck."

"We picked up some gunfire over chatter."

"Duck Pack, stop where you are and bunker down," the deep voice called out. "We've got trouble in the area."

"Roger that, central. Duck Pack is unloading the payload."

Richard called out to Zecona, "Any eyes on a Convoy?"

Zecona whispered, "Not yet."

"Let me know when you see it," Richard said. "Careful, they're expecting movement."

"Support incoming, Duck Pack," the deep voice called out.

***

Zecona burst through another roof access and could already hear the chatter over the edge of the building. As he ran closer, he could hear engines idle from the trucks. Ducking down, he crawled to the ledge and glanced over the edge. Below him, he saw the military trucks stopped, and the troops clumped beside them. He crawled back in and ran the opposite direction.

"Found it," Zecona called out over the radio. "It's in the middle of..." He glanced down at his location. "Madison Street."

"How many?" Richard asked.

"Like I'm sticking around," Zecona said, running down the rest of the stairs. "I think five trucks of soldiers?"

"Fine," Richard said, "Let me know when you're a safe distance away."

"Don't need to tell me twice," Zecona said as he landed on the bottom floor, running for the door.

"Get to our secondary location. I'll clean up here."

Zecona stopped in the middle of the road, and caught his breath, before answering back, "Is that really a good idea? Let's not be greedy here."

"They'll increase activity here, which will free up the secondary. We'll be fine."

Zecona shook his head as he sprinted down the alleyway, stopping on occasion to check the map to see where he was going. A gust of wind ripped through the street around him.

***

"I'm good to go," Zecona called out over the radio.

"Got it," Richard said.

The War Devil had been watching the convoy with a host of other sensors inside of a building. Arming the KRISER, the gun breathed to life expanding into an assault rifle. His programmable clips thumped against his chest as they created new bullets. He scanned the area again and picked a handful of targets to fire at on the vehicles, along with one very important point within the flanks of rebels.

He jumped off a loading port and walked into the alleyway. His sensors took into account the wind speed and the direction, along with the strength of his own motors and other variables. Using that data, he calculated the distance, time for the rise and fall of mass of an object, along with the speed, and the time that he needed to get into position. He grabbed hold of a grenade, reprogrammed its onboard computer, primed it, set the timer, and then chucked it well over the top of the building.

Richard made one last check of his rifle as he walked out into the street. The rebels were spread out into two groups on either side of an armored truck. They spotted him instantly.

"Hold it!" one of them cried out. "Put your gun down, and stay where you are!"

Richard opened fire on the group positioned to the left of the convoy. Three were shot down. The grenade detonated midair amongst the group of soldiers on the right of the truck. Two were killed by the blast, three more were thrown to the ground injured.

The War Devil had the rifle firing full auto carbon-based bullets. The rebels at the back of the convoy ran forwards. He could see the back of a truck was left open.

The suit pulled out another grenade as he fired at the new batch of rebels, and ducked back into an alleyway. He calculated the next throw while continuing to scan the immediate area. His rifle was breathing in the air; new rounds beat quickly into the programmable clips. The rebels continued to lay suppression fire as they moved up and took cover at the end of the forward truck. A stray bullet cut through his rubber rain-coat, but it was deflected by his armor.

Richard threw the grenade over the building. By normal standards, it would have been a million to one throw. It bounced off the side of a building, and landed inside the back of the truck containing the ammo cache that was being delivered, and wedged between two explosives.

When it detonated, it took a squad of rebels with it.

Richard felt a sudden gush of wind rush past him. The breeze came from the block east of his position, but his sensors didn't detect anything unusual. Walking back into the street, he opened fire down the street again at the rebels as they were falling back to another armored truck.

He was caught in the middle of the street as the Rasvelg popped over the rooftops. It fired a quick burst of bullets, ripping into his rubber raincoat, and masking tape mask. A bullet had wedged its way into his crescent moon eye. His sonar sensors popped up for auxiliary sight as his auto-repair systems began to mend the damage; his armor deflected the rest of the rounds. The Rasvelg floated motionless in the air.

His sensors could now pick up the Rasvelg, but not the pilot. Guessing at the location and variables, Richard popped another burst up towards it, missing the pilot and only clipping the sides. That's when he heard the hiss of the missile firing off. He had just enough time to jump out of the way as it howled into the road, engulfing the area int an inferno. He clutched the KRISER tight to his side as the shock-wave of the blast rippled through him. His raincoat melted off like wax in the flames, the denim and masking tape caught fire and shredded off him.

The cameras onboard the Rasvelg caught a flash of silver from the dust.

Richard adjusted the power supply on the clips. They sucked in more air around him, and pounded more rounds into the rifle. His vision sensors flashed back on and he fired a full clip back at the Rasvelg. It had already taken evasive maneuvers and had flown further back. The radio chatter had risen from excited to yelling over multiple frequencies.

"Shit." He rescanned the area and sprinted towards a door to his west. A full spray of bullets from the Rasvelg rained down on him. The remaining squad of soldiers opened fire from down the road. Shouldering the door with full force, he sent it skidding across the floor the wall.

He was running down a hallway when he heard a voice shout over the radio traffic loud and clear. "War Devil spotted on the ground!"

The howling of two more missiles pierced the air above him. He shouldered through a wooden door and splintered it to pieces. He sprinted the short distance through the old janitors closet and punched through the back wall, a foot of concrete. Missiles tore through the front of the building. He flung himself against the back wall of another building, embedding himself into the bricks.

Explosions from the missiles ripped through the air. The shockwave caused the two floors of the building he came from to collapse, and a cloud of dust burst out of the hole his body had made to meet him. Kicking off the wall, he sprinted full speed down the alleyway. Opening his radio channel to Zecona, he shouted:

"Fall back!"

***

Zecona was climbing up a short ladder to a higher portion of the roof he was on when he heard Richard's order. Freezing at the top, he looked back at the horizon. A solitary siren sang out. He watched as the Rasvelg floating in the distance shot another volley of missiles from the rooftops. More sirens joined in around him, and gray smoke rose from the building. The solitary VTOL volleyed more missiles towards the roofs.

Colored smoke began to rise from the surrounding streets. They began rising in near synchronization, gradually mixing with each other, and the body of dark gray enveloped the center. The sirens sung louder around him, encasing him in a horrific noise of panic.

Trucks tore through the road below him. A sudden burst of air ripped past as more Rasvelgs flew over head. Over the sirens, he could hear with sudden clarity the popping of gunfire breaking out in the city. Fire climbed up to the roofs in the wake of the Aircrafts paths, and a synchronous volley of missiles rained down from them, blanketing the horizon with an orange blast.

Zecona pushed the mic closer to his mouth. "Where are we falling back to?"

He stood alone in the radio silence.

***

The screaming death of another missile cut through the air above Richard's head. Zecona's voice was drowned out as it tore through the roof of the building, blasting apart the floors above him.

Richard ran towards another back alley, and pushed through the dust to cut across the street. The sirens from the nearby base were ear-piercing. Radio traffic hadn't let up either, as panicked voices shouted over the channels.

Another Rasvelg raced low over the tops of the buildings.

He raced back out of the back alley and was in the middle of the street when he noticed the massive, green, coiled barrel sitting at the mouth of the road. The air around the barrel deformed and blasted out the sides as the rail gun shot. With no time to react, his arm was almost torn off by the bolt as it ripped past him. Glass from the windows rained onto the street. The bolt sailed on and tore through the front side of a building, and it folded into itself.

Richard scrambled down yet another alleyway as more howling death screamed above him. Running down the narrowing corridor, he gripped his arm together with his hand.Another shockwave from the rail gun rocked the walls around him, with bits of plaster raining down on him. The walls began collapsing on him, and the buildings behind him toppled and flattened in his wake.

He heard the manic screams over the radio, "Red and green! Red and green. Funnel? Funnel!"

Richard called out over the radio, "Where's the smoke?"

***

Zecona heard Richard call back but didn't make out what he said. He stood against the edge of the building now, leaning over to catch his breath, watching the smoke and fires rise. The alarms were screaming louder. The truck tires squealing over the asphalt with the engines roaring behind them. The Rasvelgs ripped through the air. Blasts tore through the wind, and he watched the air boil, followed by dust jumping into the air, and entire city blocks leveled in seconds. Every muscle in his legs begged him to run, but he still had a job to do.

"Did you hear me?" Richard called back out, "Where's the smoke?"

"Everywhere," Zecona said, lowering his voice to a whisper, and pushing the button on the mic.

A loud screech screamed over the channel. Zecona instinctively ripped the headset off from the sound before sinking to his knees. Garbled noises came back over through the radio, followed by silence. Zecona didn't bother checking back and hugged his knees to his chest.

"Where's the smoke?" Richard cried out.

Zecona gripped the headset until his knuckles turned white and yelled straight into the mic, "Everywhere!"

"Colored smoke!"

Zecona had his head back in his hands. Another screeching sound pierced through the radio.

"Red and green?" Richard called back.

Zecona had his eyes closed, shaking his head.

"Do you see red and green smoke?" Another explosion sounded off over the radio.

Zecona snapped his head up looking around. The roar of another Rasvelg overhead, followed by the wind ripping around him.

He held the mic up to the mouth, "Just gray."

Silence. He looked around some more. "Black and gray."

Zecona was clutching the mic. A blast rocked the building below him. He fell over, dropping the mic, then scrambled for the fire escape.

"Fall back. We'll regroup before we meet with D," Richard called back. Zecona was already gone.

***

Richard was caught off guard by the sudden burst of light as he exited the alleyway. As his foot left the sidewalk, another barrage of missiles struck the road in front of him. The ground buckled, and he was weightless in a cloud of smoke and dust. Wrapping himself in a quick flash of blue, he transformed into a spider and crawled amongst the rubble as more missiles struck around him. A slab of falling asphalt buried his leg. Twisting it out, he strained his motors even more as he dug deep into the debris, and found an exposed pipe. As he pulled himself into it, fire engulfed the crater.

He crawled his way forward. Dust, smoke, fire, and steam followed him. Muffled blasts continued to thunder behind him until he was only aware of the vibrations of the metal, and gusts of wind rushing past. Richard accessed the map of the area in his mind, reorienting himself in the underground terrain. His legs clicked through the darkness toward his next location.

***

It was well into the night when Zecona walked into D's room. He was still shaking as he supported himself against the door frame. The room was dark except for a few embers glowing in the middle of the room. Walking in, his foot kicked his cot, smashing it into the wall. From the darkness, he saw a silhouette sit up from D's couch. Zecona froze.

"Hello?" D said. He could see her figure rigid in the dark. "Nadia, is that you?"

Zecona stood frozen, staring at her.

"Hello?" D said she fumbled around in the dark. "It's alright if you had to step out for some air." She picked up something from the ground. "I see you standing there." She flipped on the electric lantern, and was staring straight at Zecona with a weird grin. The smile fell, as she was staring around the room.

Zecona relaxed his stance. His legs went numb as she walked across the room. She was looking dead at him. The smile was crawling back.

"D, we--"

"Holy shit," she said, the smile grew. It was the first time Zecona had seen her really smile.

"Holy fucking shit," she said staring straight at him. "You did it?"

"D, we--"

She was laughing, dropping the lantern, and hugged him. "God damn, you actually did it?" She hugged him harder. "Holy shit! Just..."

The strong smell of whiskey filled his nostrils.

She was waving air at her face. Quickly turning her face to the street. "Do you have any idea?" She was laughing again. "Where's the suit?" she said, grabbing his shoulder. "Where's your suit? I've got to thank it."

"He's..." Zecona was staring at her beaming face. "He's cleaning up. He'll be back in the morning."

D was shaking her head. "I can't believe it."

"I can't either," Zecona said.

She hugged him tighter and hopped up and down. "You have no idea," she said. She was crying now. "You have no idea what this means to me." She sank down to the cot and took a deep breath then let out another deep laugh.

Zecona sank down beside her.

"Yes!" she cried out jumping up from the cot.

She stood over where her fire had died throwing more wood on top of it. She lit a quick match, and Zecona saw the fire come back to life.

She clapped her hand. "Oh God, this is great." Her eyes darted around the room. "Do you have any idea how hard all of this was?" D grabbed a bottle of whiskey from her collection, letting out an obnoxious laugh.

"Come, come!" She motioned for him. Zecona stood up. "Holy shit." D was shaking her head. He sat down beside her as she opened the bottle.

She shook her head suddenly harder. "No, no, no! We need cups! Only the unworthy and worthless shits of the world drink straight from the bottle." She handed the opened bottle to Zecona as she went over to the food dispenser and grabbed two coffee mugs.

She sat down and handed him a mug, grabbing the bottle back from him.

Zecona felt his chest tighten up as he gripped the mug. He avoided eye contact by staring into the empty cup, before shaking his head and handing it back to her.

She frowned. "What the hell is the matter with you? You've earned this! Just--" She was smiling again. "Come on, just drink with me. Just for tonight. This one time." She poured him a small amount, then did hers the same. She cleared her throat, staring around the room. "Toast, a toast." She stared at the floor, then held her mug up over the fire. "For what we lost along the way and the sacrifices made. For the cost of freedom and for a brighter future." Hesitating, she stared into the fire and added, "For what was necessary for love." She downed her mug.

Zecona hesitated for a second and did the same. She set the mug on the ground below her. Staring back at the fire. "I didn't think you bastards would be able to pull it off."

Zecona watched the light dance across her face. She was smiling again. He remained silent.

"I know," she said. "I know. When you told me." Her eyes wandered around the room. She let out another laugh. "Unbelievable."

She stared back at him, then grabbed hold of his hands. "Thank you." She was looking at him straight in the eyes. "Thank you so much. For all you've done."

Zecona nodded. "It's been a long day."

D leaned back, still staring at him. Then she let out a laugh. "Right, I'm sorry. I just lost my mind. There's still work to do."

Zecona smirked.

D was waving her hand at him. "We'll talk more in the morning. When I've sobered up."

Zecona stood up. "Good night, D," Zecona said, staring down at her.

She looked up at him, and said, "Right." She nodded, smiling again. "Good night. And thank you again."

Zecona paused staring at her, before turning back to his cot and laying down with his back to her. He could feel every inch of his body weighing him down, as his mind raced through what he needed to do next.

CHAPTER THIRTEEN
DURABLE

D rolled out of bed with her eyes half closed. She shuffled her way over to her food dispenser and slapped the general area for where the buttons ought to be.

Zecona woke up facing the wall listening to D moving around behind him. Hesitating, he turned over and watched D sitting on the wall, before standing up and making his way to the food dispenser.

"Morning, slim," she said to him, taking another sip. "Where's the War Devil?"

Zecona froze. "Beats me." He felt his stomach sink, staring at the flashing green light. "I think he's meeting with our contact."

D shrugged. "Shoulda figured." She was smiling behind her coffee. "I can't wait to hear his report." Taking a sip, she glanced over to the two bags sitting in the middle of the room. "I've got explosives ready to go for today. When he gets back, we'll head out."

Zecona tried to push a few buttons on the interface, but kept missing. He was too focused on what D was saying. Then he smiled, and said, "So, who's Nadia?"

She froze staring at the road mid-sip. Turning her head to him, and stared. "What did you just say?"

"Nadia? Who is she?" he said, picking up his bowl of oatmeal; he pivoted around. His smile faded when he saw her face.

D's eyes were dead on top of him. She gripped the coffee cup in one hand so hard the tips of her fingers were white. "You think you're some kind of goddamn comedian?" She pinched her lips, tilting her head. "You little piece of shit!" She threw the coffee cup at Zecona's head.

He dodged and the wind rushed by his head. She stormed across the room and punched the bowl out of his hand. "Who the fuck told you?" She pinned him against the wall by his throat. "Who?" Zecona gasped for breath. "Who? Goddamnnit, Who?"

D backhanded his cheek with her fist. He fell onto his cot. His chest caught the bar.

Richard jumped in behind her and grabbed her.

"Let me go. Let me go!" she yelled out. The War Devil gripped her arms and pulled her away from Zecona.

Zecona was on all fours. He coughed, trying to catch his breath.

"Goddammit! Let. Me. Go!"

Zecona glanced over his shoulder at her. Richard let her go. She took a couple of steps forward, taking in quick, shallow breaths before kicking the food dispenser. It clattered to the floor. Dissatisfied with the result, she ripped off the back hose and metal plating, and tore off the face plating, before smashing the touch interface shattering the glass.

Zecona was staring up at her.

She hunched over, panting, before muttering, "Get out."

Zecona moved towards the door.

"No." Richard stared at her. The suit crossed its arms.

She glared at it and stormed straight into its face "Get out!" Her eyes burned straight into its cold black sensors.

"No."

Her fist clenched, and her whole body shook. She spat on its crescent moon eye and stormed past him. Zecona tried to get out of the way but got shoved against the wall. She was gone down the hall. He sunk to the floor, shaking, and stared out the door.

The suit wiped off the spit, then glanced down at him. "I told you we needed to regroup <u>before</u> we talked to her."

The Prowler tore out of the building, and down the road.

***

The roar of the fusion engine tore down the empty unfamiliar highway. D swerved around ruined buildings. Two wheels of the Prowler lifted off the ground. The speedometer was edging against 50. Taking an off-ramp, she kicked up the speed. Spotting an intersection, she slowed the Prowler to a crawl, and parked it in the middle of the street.

She stood outside a storefront with the broken sign **Vic's Fashion**. Walking through the busted double doors, she stood staring at the rows of empty clothes racks with blood beating against her ears.

Walking over to the first row of clothes racks she kicked it to the ground, then turned grabbed another one, she hurled it across the floor. The clattering of metal hitting the fake tile and concrete sounded off the surrounding buildings until only the sound of the Prowler's engine idling remained. Lighting up a cigarette, she sank to the floor and watched the smoke linger to the ceiling.

D noticed a mess of webs in the corner of the store. She could see the outline of the spider, but something seemed off about it. The spider just hung there. It had one leg caught on a single thread over the room. Its other legs were limp and weightless beside its body.

She stared at it through the drifting smoke from her cigarette. The more she focused on it, the more she could make out the green and blue fuzz breaking down the body between its abdomen. Dead and rotting away, suspended above an empty store, surrounded by the only thing it was capable of creating.

D flicked the cigarette to the floor and walked over to the Prowler. Putting her sunglasses back on, she did a quick scan of the road up ahead before getting back on the Prowler and speeding off. Cranking up the throttle, she weaved in and out of ruined buildings along the road, with the shapes slowly blurring together. D started to laugh, and leaned off to the side on one turn, pushing the speed again. An explosion launched her off the Prowler. She skidded briefly across the ground a few feet, before the Prowler crashed down onto her lower back, pinning her to the road. The breath got knocked out of her, and she blacked out.

***

D heard the faint sound of footsteps. The Prowler was resting on top of her lower back. Her hands could still feel the ground, but she couldn't feel her legs. Forcing her eyes half-open, she stared out of her shattered sunglasses. Through the web of cracks on her lens, two dark figures walked towards her from around the edge of a ruined building. She closed her eyes.

The two men approached her with guns drawn. "Heh. Typical woman driver," one man said.

The other elbowed him in his ribs. "Check for signs of life."

"On it." He took his boot and started to nudge the side of her right hand. D didn't flinch.

"James, that's not how you... just move over." He bent down holding two fingers against D's neck, checking her pulse. "She's not dead, and I think she's still breathing."

"So what are we going to do?" James said.

He looked around the area before pointing to another building off the highway. "We'll hold up over there, and radio into operations for a civilian evac. If we're lucky, we'll get her back alive."

"Davis, come on now," James said looking over D. "With this much damage to her legs, she might be better off with a bullet to the head now. Is she really worth the effort?"

"James. We've got to maintain some of our humanity, we need to at least try."

James shrugged.

"Here," Davis said gripping the Prowler. "Help me get this off of her."

They flipped it off of her, shifted it into neutral, and rolled it off to the side of the road.

Davis knelt down beside D, examining her legs, and said to James, "Check the Prowler for anything we can use."

"Right."

"She's in pretty rough shape," Davis said, looking her over. He took off her coat and wrapped it around her legs. "Anything in the Prowler?"

"Not that I see."

"We're going to have to pick up the pace. She doesn't have a whole lot of time. Grab her shoulders."

***

They set her down on a ratty old mattress.

"Right," Davis said, looking around. "Keep her secure."

"Where are you going?" James said.

"I can't get a good signal here. I'm going to back-track to see if I can get something better. Stick around here. I'll be back once I've gotten orders on what to do next."

D lay still while controlling her breathing.

"Keep the area secure," Davis said walking out of the room.

"Right."

D cracked her eye open to see James leaning up against the doorframe. His head was facing down over the landing, down to the front door to the motel building. Her unbroken hand crept to her side. James shrugged his shoulders and re-positioned himself at his post, and peered down the hallway. She arched her back and slid her fingers slid along the smooth metallic case in her back pocket, and pulled it onto the bed.

Arching her back again, she flipped the lid open. James's eyes shot over towards her. Furrowing her brows, she turned her head to the wall. Her fingers moved along the happy slender needle. She let out a low, excruciating moan. James turned and walked over to her as she felt the bumps along the vial labels for the word <u>Paco</u>.

"Keep it down," James said, "Help is on the way."

She positioned the needle over the vial. She shook her head and cried out in fake pain.

"Relax, everything's going to be alright." The needle punctured down into the vial as she gripped the sides with her pinky and ring finger. She pulled the plunger with her thumb and index finger. Her eyes fluttered around the room, and she screamed. "My Legs!"

"Quiet! You'll give away our position!" he said flipping the safety off of the rifle.

D pushed down the plunger to let out any excess air and screamed louder. Adrenalin pulsed through her as she held the syringe. James rushed to the side of the bed, propping the gun at the edge of the bed. He grabbed hold of her and put his hand over her mouth. "Listen! You--" Before he could finish, her arm had snaked around, and the needle punctured straight into his neck. Instincts kicked in, and he jolted back before she could push the plunger down all the way. He clawed at his neck for the needle.

Her eyes darted to the rifle, and she pushed herself off the bed towards it. She slammed into the ground and tripped the rifle out of her reach. Blood gushed out of his neck in bursts before the needle finally fell out. The tips of her fingers grazed the strap of the gun. James stood staring at the needle. Gripping hold of the rifle's strap, she dragged it towards her. James glanced up pale hearing the death rattle of the rifle against the floor.

He grabbed his pistol and chambered a bullet. D rolled over, facing him. The pistol's bullet tore through her abdomen. She let out a quick burst of shots that ripped across his chest. Foam started pooling out of his mouth, and he collapsed to the ground. Chambering another round, she shot James again just to be sure.

D turned her attention to the door and coughed up some blood. It felt like she'd been lying there for hours. Her body shuddered sporadically, and on occasions, she would pass out no matter how much she fought it. She'd have to rough it. There was another one out there. Coming in with a convoy of other soldiers. She couldn't be caught. At the very least, she couldn't be caught alive. After getting enough strength, she unwrapped the jacket around her legs. They weren't fully healed yet, but they'd take the pressure. Stooping down, she grabbed her needle and packed it back in the metallic holder. She grabbed his pistol and strapped on the rifle.

No signs of Davis around as she walked through the building and out the front door. Looking at the Prowler, she listened to the silence around her. She rolled it into a nearby building and left the area on foot.

＊＊

Davis heard the screaming and doubled back before he could open a signal. That's when he heard the gunshots. He waited in the building across the street watching the door. James was dead, he was sure of it. Opening a local signal to inform command of the situation seemed risky. Radio command had started to warn against it as it seemed the channels had been compromised.

Standing in the building across the street, he had been watching where he had left James ever since then. Nobody had left, but the Prowler was still sitting where he and James had left it. It was just a matter of time before they left the building. Spotting movement, he moved closer into the shadows and grabbed a pair of binoculars. A woman with the rifle emerged from the doorway, looking cautiously around. She was still limping badly. Instead of riding off, she rolled her Prowler into a nearby building and walked back towards the highway. Davis and James had their vehicles tucked away a few meters away, but it would be too obvious if he created that much noise. He left through the back door of the building and followed her on foot. Grabbing a piece of green chalk out of his pocket, he marked an X at the mouth of the road.

＊＊

Richard was waiting for D on the first floor. He'd been waiting well past sunset, but it didn't faze him. D walked in, catching sight of his crescent moon eyes across the black room.

Richard spoke first, "What gives you the right, to hit my consultant?"

D shook her head and said, "When you're done with your portion of the contract I want you both gone."

"Did you hear what I just said?" Richard said crossing his arms.

"I don't care," D said straightening up. "I'm done. I'm tired of dealing with this fucking nonsense with you mindless soul-sucking monsters! I've had it with all of this goddamn bullshit. I hired you for help, and this is the kind of shit I get?"

"That's what we're here for!" Richard's audio clipped as he spoke. "That's why you hired us. We are here to help you, and given the circumstances, we did the best we could."

"Right," D said shooting her hands into the air. "Good enough. Adequate. It's all the fucking same to you assholes. I'm not bound to that though. I have to make do with what I've got, and dammit, that's not a lot. And I've got to make decisions I have to live with!"

"Right! And, given the circumstances, I think we did as well as we could. What the fuck are you expecting from us?"

"You know, honestly... I..." She shook her head. "I expected a little bit more professionalism. I would have expected you to keep my personal details private, and I certainly wouldn't expect you to tell that fucking asshole up there." She pointed at the ceiling.

Richard was just staring at him. "What the fuck are you talking about?"

She froze with her hand still stuck in the air staring into the duel crescent moons. "What do you think we're talking about?"

"Hitting the convoys went south. They now know I'm here, and probably have fortified the bases in case of an attack."

Her arm fell slapping her knee. "What?"

"Where do you think I was this morning?"

"Bullshit. That fucker told me you were meeting your contact."

"All night? Why the hell would I meet with my contact after hitting the convoys? I was losing a group of Rasvelg hunting me down," Richard said.

They both stared at each other.

"The fuck were you talking about before."

She physically batted the question out of the way. "Nevermind that." She brought her hand up to her forehead. "So." Shaking her head. "How did he..."

"What the hell did he say this morning?"

D jerked her attention back towards Richard. "Why don't we have a chat with him."

She pushed past him, running up the stairs, and down the hallway. "Why the fuck didn't you tell me?" D screamed.

Zecona bolted up from the cot, and looked around, the suit had followed D into the room and leaned against the wall and watched D walk across the room.

"Fucking honestly? Why the fuck didn't you tell me? You failed? You worthless--"

"You should have known better," Richard said.

"Fuck you! The plan was solid. You just weren't good enough!"

"The hell it was!" Richard shouted back. "You realize how much shit we're in now?"

"D." Zecona said looking up at her.

D glared at him "Shut up." She was shaking leaning over him. "Shut the fuck up." She spun back to Richard "And you, you're a fucking War Devil! For fucks sake, you can't even take out a Rasvelg by yourself. That's one of the things you were designed to do!"

"I'd like to see you take out a VTOL without any flight capabilities. Like I said before. We're under-equipped, under-manned, and we lack the intel we needed."

"Quit with your fucking excuses." She slapped the metal helmet with her bare hand. Richard didn't flinch. D ignored the pain.

"You think taking on the full rebel army's a fucking cakewalk? You don't think anyone else has tried what you're doing now? Did you honestly think it would be <u>that</u> fucking easy?"

Zecona was sitting up now.

"Unfucking believable." D was shaking her head. She turned her attention back to Zecona. "And you, who the fuck told you about that?"

Zecona met her glare with a blank expression. "What?"

"You know damn well." D's eyes had cooled staring at him.

Zecona thought it over, before saying, "About Nadia?"

"Yeah," D said.

"Nadia?" Richard said, he pulled up D's dossier and scanned through the details.

Zecona cocked his head staring at her and said, "You did?"

D stared at him frozen in place. "Don't fucking lie to me."

"It was the other night, you just... I don't know."

"Who's Nadia?" Richard asked staring at her.

D took a deep breath, "Forget it." She was tapping her index finger against her forearm.

Zecona clenched his fist and said, "No, you know what, fuck you. It feels like I've been walking on eggshells around you so that you won't fucking slit my throat! First by slamming me into a wall when I ask you if you wanted children someday, then punch me in the face for asking about a name you called out in the middle of the night."

Richard stood with his arms crossed analyzing the dossier on D again.

"Just," D said shaking her head. "Fucking drop it." She turned to Richard. "What's the status of the plan?"

"Un-fucking-believable." Zecona sighed and slouched back down.

Richard snapped his attention to D. "They're aware I'm here."

"What do you mean by that?"

"I mean, Rasvelgs have pictures of me. I've been noted as existing in the network. Every soldier in a fifty-mile radius is looking for a Silver Class Three War Devil wandering the streets."

D was holding her head. She kicked at the burnt embers, and cried out "Shit!" She turned back to him. "There goes the whole fucking element of surprise. You fucking asshole."

"This isn't our fault," Richard said snapping his attention to the hallway, watching the wall.

"How isn't this your fault?" She glared at him. "If you couldn't do the fucking job, you should have just walked away from it." She shook her fist at him as she sank down into the hole in the wall.

***

Davis could hear talking as he moved up the stairs. Making his way past the second floor, he could hear the voice's above him. He walked up the last flight, and saw an open door at the end of the hall. Hugging the wall, he followed the crimson trail along the floor. As he edged closer, the voices got louder. His gun was already drawn.

"I don't know what the fuck we're going to do now," he heard the woman say.

He saw the end of a cot through the door. He could make out someone sitting there from the moonlight.

"I mean I've got little ideas, but nothing to real--"

Davis jumped in the room and pointed the gun at Zecona's head. He didn't have time to react as a silver flash punched his forearm into the wall. Richard pulled out a silver gun out of its thigh.

"No!" D shouted.

Richard and Zecona looked at her

"Take him downstairs."

***

Richard and D tied Davis to an office chair down in the basement of the building. Zecona stayed up in the room. D was holding the Marlow in her right hand, looking down the barrel. Richard stood in the corner with his arms crossed. The only sound was the hum of the fluorescent light above them.

"Who did you report to before engaging in a possible hostile location?" D said.

"No one," Davis said eyeing the gun. "I'm acting alone."

D glanced over to Richard and asked, "Is that true?"

Richard nodded. "I didn't pick up any radio signals."

D smiled staring at Davis. "See? We're already off to a good start." She stood, up walking over to him. "It's not that it matters though." D sat down in his lap. Davis gritted his teeth glaring at her. "I mean we can kill you, pack up what little we have and clear out of the area before anyone even bothers looking for you. But I distinctly remember you saying you were going to get in contact with a convoy." She reached down into her back pocket and grabbed a scalpel. "Now why would someone go into an area knowing full well it'll probably be hostile without informing anyone about it?" She held the scalpel just above his wrist. He wasn't saying anything.

"You know, I used to be a butcher," she said, eyeing his arm. "A gun is just so unnecessarily blunt in this situation. I could carve you up like a sculpture without even hitting a major artery." She nodded her head back to Richard. "My friend here can cauterize the wound to make sure you don't bleed out too badly."

"What are you trying to pull?" Davis said with a smirk. "Cut the bullshit. What kind of android are you?"

D laughed. "I'm not an android, I'm one hundred percent human."

Davis shook his head. "Nah, I'm not buying that. You wouldn't be commanding around a War Devil if you were human. I've been honest with you this far. Why are you trying to treat me like I'm an idiot?" He tilted his head staring at her. "I bet you're one of those Silver Gecko's I've heard whispers about?"

"You're wrong." D stood up. "I'm completely human."

Davis glanced at her, then at the War Devil before saying, "Prove it."

She let out another laugh, "And how am I suppose to do that?"

"I don't know," Davis said, staring at the suit. "But I'm not going to give any information to an android."

"If you really think I'm an android, then I guess that's the end of our conversation." She pulled out the Marlow and pointed the barrel at his head.

"Give me something, and I'll give you something." Davis said. "But I'm not saying a word with that thing in the room." He nodded to the War Devil.

D mulled it over before turning to Richard and said, "Leave us."

Richard nodded and walked out the door, and his footsteps faded up the stairs. When it was quiet D turned her attention back to Davis and said, "Alright." She dragged an extra chair across the floor and sat in front of him. "Let's chat."

"Prove that you're human first."

"And how can I do that?" D shook her head. "Don't I look human? Don't I sound like a person? If you gave me time, I could certainly show you that I feel like a person."

"I saw you torn to ribbons by a land mine, and crushed by a Prowler. And in less than an hour, I saw you walk away from that building like nothing even happened. There ain't nothin' 'natural' 'bout that." Davis shook his head as well. He tested the strength of the rope on his hands.

D smiled. "I was sick. Overman saved my life, and modified me so that I would work for them. Plain and simple, now I owe them a debt. I'm just working to get my life back."

Davis laughed as he tightened the rope on his wrists. "Just that simple?"

She nodded.

"And they just handed you a War Devil without a second thought?"

D took a deep breath. "It's more complicated than that."

"Oh, I bet," Davis said nodding, his index finger traveled towards the knot. "I'd imagine it'd be pretty hard for a Silver

Gecko to put together a convincing story after getting caught repairing itself."

She shook her head, lighting up a cigarette. "Silver Gecko's play the part." D took a deep drag, and blew out the smoke. "That's why they're so good. Shoot 'em dead, they'll play dead. Otherwise, I bet you could just knick them and expect them to heal up. That wouldn't exactly fit in with a group of soldiers, would it?"

"Sure." His fingers fumbled with the loose cord of the knot. "But then, that doesn't exactly prove you're human."

D took another long drag off the cigarette and blew the smoke at him. "And I'm just supposed to accept the fact **you're** human?"

He raised an eye brow. "What?"

"The Rebellion has already been compromised by Overman. Since day one. You could also just as easily be a Silver Gecko."

He laughed. "If I was, wouldn't this be easier to just say who I am, and we can be on our merry little way?"

D smiled. "It's not that simple. Like I said, Silver Gecko's play the part. Not only that, but we're in direct competition with each other." She held the Marlow against her hip, and pointed it at him. "A Silver Gecko would see the value in selling me out to get more info from a military group." She smiled watching his eyes. "Maybe you should be the one to convince me that you're human?"

Davis froze in place, staring at the gun. "If you're not a Silver Gecko, then what are you?"

"I told you." D sighed. "I'm just a girl, paying off her debt."

"I don't buy that," Davis said, shaking his head. His index finger and middle finger gripped the loose piece of rope.

D took a deep sigh. "Then how can I convince you?"

"Why?" He said cocking his head.

"We've got plenty of time to get to know each other." She said, "And I know who I am."

He was staring straight into her eyes. "Tell me about your childhood."

"Well, I grew up west, my parents were second generation. I did well enough in Primary and Secondary School. I got a full Scholarship, and moved East and to study medicine and surgery. Went through normal internships at hospitals, and began practicing four years ago." She held up her hands. "And here I am."

Davis smiled as he tried to tug on the loose piece of rope. "Seems a little short."

"We've got all night," she said, smiling.

"I guess we do." He felt the tension of the knot around his hand give a little. "Why a doctor?"

D shrugged. "I don't know. I guess I wanted to help people."

"Weird way of helping people."

She smiled. "You can't always choose the path you walk." D took another drag off her cigarette.

"Which hospital?" He winced as he felt the knot grow tighter.

"Mmm, no." D shook her head. "I've been nice enough to answer your questions. Now it's your turn."

"Fine." He readjusted the knot again. "Ask away."

She smiled staring at him. "What group do you report too?"

Davis laughed. "I thought you were worried if I was a Silver Gecko?"

"I'm not worried." D shook her head. "It just doesn't make a difference to me."

He was still wearing the smile as he re-loosened the knot. "I'm a part of central division."

D's eyes sparked at the words. "Shame."

He cocked an eyebrow. "Why's that?"

She flicked some ash off the cigarette, and stared down at the floor at his feet. "I already have plenty of information on that group." D shot her eyes up, and locked into his. "Who runs that group again?"

Davis laughed. "Don't you know?"

"Of course." She smiled. "I just want to see if you've been telling the truth so far."

He mulled it open, looking into her black eyes, and said. "Jeremy Samson."

She took a deep breath smiling. "That's right."

Davis worked hard to contain his smile, as he began to feel his hand wiggle in the loosening knot. He froze, and sat straight up staring at her. "You really think you're human, don't you?"

D laughed. "I am human."

He rolled his wrist around, and grabbed the knot with his other hand while he stared at her. "Then why are you helping Overman. Don't you know what they are going to eventually going to do? We should be working together? Not fighting. You said so yourself, you wanted to help people."

She smiled and shook her head. "I am helping people. You bastards released the Blue Lotus into the general public. You firebombed the streets. I was in the hospital helping all those people you were 'helping'. Because of you, I'm here. I'm helping the Federation bring you fuckers down."

Davis was shaking his head. "We didn't release the Blue Lotus." He gripped the loose cord from hitting the floor.

D was shaking her head. "You terrorized the public to your side, and still expecting to come out as the hero."

"You're wrong. We didn't bomb the streets. We didn't release the virus. We're fighting against our own annihilation!"

"Funny how you have to kill your own people to fight against annihilation."

Davis laughed. "Are you going to believe everything you've been told?"

"I wasn't told. I saw it. First hand. In the hospitals."

"Listen to me!" Davis said raising his voice. He gripped the cord in his fists. "If there's any ounce of humanity left in you. Help us. You've got to."

D shot up out of her seat. "You're the ones that gave Overman the position they needed! Don't you get that?" She stood over him shaking her head, gripping the Marlow in her hand. "It's funny to hear you say I'm the one that lacks humanity."

He stared straight at her, keeping the Marlow in the back of his mind. "You're not human."

She thrust the gun towards him. He whipped the cord around around, and knocked the gun out of her hands as she fired into the wall. Davis could hear the distant thunder of the metal boots through the floor above him.

He locked eyes with the Marlow on the ground, and kicked D out of the way. She was back on her feet as the metal boots struck the stairs. Davis dove for the ground. D towered with her fist aimed at the back of his head. In one swift motion, he was off the ground, and had spun her around, with the Marlow pressed against her temple. Richard was in the doorway, pistol drawn, and he could see it finishing its transformation into a high-powered revolver.

Davis had his full attention on the War Devil as he said "Now--"

D smashed the back of her head into his face. The Marlow fired ripping off her lower jaw. Richard blasted six rounds through her and Davis.

CHAPTER FOURTEEN
DAMAGED

Zecona had heard the string of gunshots from downstairs. He didn't know how long he had been sitting on the edge of the cot watching the doorway. Staring down the hollow barrel was burned into the back of his mind. Everything drifted by as he focused on the on the solitary bullet hole embedded in the wall.

He saw the smoke rising from the street below out of the hole. Wandering over to take a look, where he saw the body engulfed in flames in the middle of the street. Running down the hall, he jumped down the stairs, to the landing, and bounded down another flight of stairs into the lobby.

Zecona shot out the front door, past D sitting on the stoop, and past Richard. The body was burning brighter.

"What the hell do you think you're doing?" Zecona said gawking at it.

D glanced up at him holding her jaws together. Zecona had already ran inside and back up the stairs. He burst into the bathroom, and ripped the blood stained shower curtain off its rings, before jolting back down the stairs. Back out into streets, he beat out the flames with the thin plastic.

He spun around and glared at them. "Don't you understand!?"

D and Richard just stared at him.

Zecona tried to lift the shower curtain, but it had melted to Davis' flesh. His body clung and peeled to the plastic surface. The smell of cooked flesh smacked him in the face. He threw it back down, and worked his hardest to wrap the body avoiding the soup spilling out onto the road.

Walking over to Richard, he held out a hand and said, "I need a shovel."

It reached down to the ground, sent out a small shock wave, grabbed a hold of a box containing a shovel, and handed it to Zecona. He dragged the body off.

Zecona walked back down to the intersection dragging the plastic transparent sack behind him, with the shovel propped up on his shoulder. With each step he took, the thin plastic threatened to split open, and leave the body behind. He pulled it down the road, spotting a hardware store along the way. Walking further, he hit a bare field behind a row of burnt out buildings, and started digging. The moon had hit its peak, and was starting to set as he worked. When it was three feet deep, the realization that he'd have to put the dirt back sunk in. Climbing out, he pushed the body in. Pondering as he scooped up the dirt in the shovel whether to say anything in memory, but shook his head against it, and refilled the grave.

***

D and Richard were still sitting out front. They hadn't moved since Zecona had stormed past them. D watched the moon fall behind the row of buildings, as her bone and muscle fused back together. When she was able to feel her tongue again, she reached into her coat pocket and pulled out a cigarette.

"How was he able to get out of that knot?" she said.

Richard was scanning the areas around them for any movement. "I wasn't programmed to tie knots."

243

D shook her head, sparking the lighter. "I'm noticing you weren't programmed for a lot of things."

Richard continued to scan the area, while she watched the smoke drift by her. "I'm getting tired of this bullshit," D said taking a drag, she noticed Zecona walking back down the road.

Zecona moved to walk past them, before stopping and shooting a look. D stared right back at him.

"That smoke could have been seen for miles," he said finally. "We're already dealing with enough without scouting parties giving us trouble."

"We needed to get rid of the body. He nearly blew your fucking head off," she said flicking the ash off the end of her cigarette. "And mine."

"I'd expect him to do the same for me then."

She muttered, "He wouldn't have wasted the time."

"I don't care," Zecona said, clenching his fist. "I can only control my actions."

D nodded, then glanced back into the road taking another shot of whiskey. Zecona was still standing there. She smiled shaking her head. "Is that why you lied to my fucking face the other night?"

His eyes widened staring at her. "I didn't lie to you."

"You didn't bother correcting me." She flicked ash at his feet. "Did you?"

Zecona took this as the cue to head inside.

***

Zecona woke up staring at the wall. He rolled over to see D sitting on her usual slab of the wall, smoking a cigarette, looking over the road. She glanced over and saw him staring at her, but jerked her head away keeping her eye on the road. Zecona just stared at her, before getting and up glanced down at his wrist. It was considerably lighter.

"Where's Richard?"

"Who?"

"The War Devil?"

"He's meeting with a contact." She let out a column of smoke. "Reassignment."

He Got a bowl of oatmeal, and glanced at her; she was still paying attention to the road.

"Hey, listen," he said.

"Hmm?" She turned to him.

"I'm sorry for what I said happened the other day. I didn't realize how touchy of a subject that was for you, and," he was staring down at the ground, "I guess I still don't exactly understand, I was just trying to change the subject for at least a little while."

She cocked an eyebrow at him and stared for a moment. "Go fuck yourself." She hopped down and headed for her couch.

Zecona nodded. "I give up."

"Good." She grabbed a scrap of paper from her notebook.

"I try to be nice, and you explode at me. I shut up, and you suddenly become nice."

"See? You're getting it." She flicked her attention to the paper and was doodling something down.

"Fine, I'll just shut up then."

"Fine."

Zecona crossed his arm, walked to the hole in the wall, and watched the road. "Fuck you," he said.

"That's the spirit." She was taking a drag off her cigarette.

He turned around and looked at her. She was writing something else down. "What do you have against me?"

"Gee, I don't know, maybe the fact the two of you completely fucked everything for me? Beyond that, how about your chirpy can-do attitude? Or how you are desperately trying to get accepted." She was glancing up at him now. "How you try to act like a total badass and completely fuck it up. All the stupid questions you ask me." She had set down the pencil and was counting the reasons on her fingers. "How you just trail behind like a lost puppy everywhere I go, like a needy child afraid to be left home alone for too long. The way you smile in the morning. But honestly, I could look past all of that. Maybe. And work with you, if it wasn't for the fact, that you lied to my fucking face, and cost us a day of action to fix the mess that you two made."

He stared at her a moment, "What were you expecting?"

She took one last drag off the cigarette before flicking it out the window. "Honestly, I don't know what I was expecting. But I certainly wasn't expecting getting a dysfunctional death machine, dragging along some fucking tourist."

Zecona narrowed his eyes at her and crossed his arms. "Really? I'm the tourist."

Flicking her attention back at him, she narrowed her eyes at him, and said, "Are you really going to pull that?"

"What am I going to pull?" Zecona shook his head. "You act like so much time has passed, we're barely into the second century since ya'll just showed up and took the planet, and already I'm the tourist."

"I was born here, you were born on a Space Station I assume?" She was pointing her pen at him.

"So? That just completely erases Generations of Abots that were born and died here before you Apes showed up? I didn't get to choose where I was born."

"For fuck's sake. It's not like I chose where I was born. Do we have to do this now? I have a mountain of other shit I need to deal with."

"Oh, right," Zecona said laughing towards the ceiling. "You're dealing with the problems you dragged with you. I guess the Abots should just sit in a corner and wait for those things to get resolved before we ask for our planet back."

She slammed the notebook closed and pointed to the door. "There's the door. I'm not stopping you from going out and claiming the planet back."

He just stood there shaking his head at her. She kept her hand pointing at the door.

"That's what I thought." D opened the notebook back up turned her attention back to the paper, and started to jot down more notes. He turned and stormed out of the room.

***

"That's it then," Richard said to Seawood as he loaded the intel into his wrist.

"That's it." Seawood buttoned up his shirt. "You did the best you could given the situation. You and Zecona are to report West to the HQ located in Marlona. You'll station there until reassignment. You can head out in a day or two until we get D reassigned."

Richard paused for a minute. "Do you have any details about any sort of relationship between someone called Nadia and Black Dog?"

"What?" Seawood threw on a beret and stared at him.

"Nadia." Richard was staring out the window. "I didn't see anything listed in Black Dog's dossier, but I wanted to double-check my intel."

Seawood was shaking his head. "No. You're right. There's no record of that individual with any sort of relation to Black Dog."

Richard turned back. "Interesting. I haven't noticed any sort of monitoring in the area. Could she have met this person in secret in some way, and we missed it?"

"No." Seawood was studying him. "That doesn't seem right. All Agents are required some form of monitoring per their contract. Why do you ask?"

"Just looking into a situation that came up recently. Is there a chance monitoring was removed for this particular Agent?"

Seawood was shaking his head. "No. That would be glaringly obvious to the Federation. What was the issue?"

"I don't have all of the details on it at the moment. All I know is that Black Dog freaked out when the name Nadia was mentioned. Are you familiar with any sort of issue with the other stray dogs?"

"I mean, there was that situation I mentioned before with Adam? A Black Dog Agent got a hold of a restricted weapon and killed Adam, and nearly killed Ada. But that was a couple of years ago and I haven't heard of any issues since then."

"You said before Ada had left this Black Dog in review for a year?"

"Right." Seawood nodded, "but again, I'd just assume it was out of an abundance of caution after almost getting half her head blown off."

"I see."

"Unless," Seawood stared at the wall, "I suppose it's possible that any information regarding Nadia was just withheld."

Richard cocked his helmet. "What do you mean?"

Seawood shrugged. "I'm just saying. Intel is passed down by the higher-ups. It could be possible someone is aware of Nadia, and just didn't put it into the dossier."

"I see." Richard was silent for a moment looking at a smooth patch of blue tile on the floor. "Is there anyone planetside that would have access to those details?"

Seawood let out a deep sigh staring around the room. "I mean Ada springs to mind locally. But I doubt if they'll just hand out the info liberally. What are you looking for specifically?"

"I want any monitoring intel for the Black Dog Agent I'm currently assigned to."

"I don't know if she'll give you 'all' of those details. Are we only talking about information about Nadia?"

"Just get what you can," Richard said.

Seawood laughed. "That might be getting a little out of our league. I don't have that much pull. But I'll see what I can get." He paused glancing out the window.

"Thanks," Richard said.

"Yea, We'll meet back up the day after tomorrow morning?" He grabbed his MC out of his pocket and entered in coordinates. "Patching you an address we can meet up at. I'll fill you in on what I can get a hold of."

Richard got the coordinates saved in his mind. "Thanks, this might answer a few questions I've been having."

"You owe me," Seawood said scooping down and grabbing a Rucksack.

"I know." Richard was standing straight. "I need to head back and start gathering up what supplies we have."

Seawood nodded. "See you around Barbatos."

"Yea. See ya." Richard was out the door.

***

Zecona could still smell the burning flesh. Trying to ignore the stain the body had left in the middle of the road, he walked a couple of blocks, but he could still feel the heat that came from it behind him. Coming to an intersection with a crumpled spotlight lying in the middle of the street, he looked across at the crosswalk that would have told him when it would have been safe to walk across on the deserted street. Leaning against the pole, he stared at a circled green <u>X</u> marked at the mouth of the road in chalk wondering what significance it had, before glancing up the road.

He didn't want to deal with this anymore. Originally when he had volunteered, he had hopes of seeing what was left of his world, and here he was on the downward spiral of a nation. Spotting the hardware store again, an idea crept into the back of his mind and he wandered over to it. Wandering around the isles, a lot of the rows laid bare from scavengers grabbing what the could, but he found what he wanted. A small broken plank of wood, and a hammer.

Zecona walked back to the grave and hammered the piece of wood. He took out a switchblade from his pocket, resting on top of the mound of dirt above the grave. Staring at the wood, trying to think what to write, he attempted to carve out the letters in Abotian. In the back of his mind, he knew nobody would be able to read it, but it didn't matter. Standing back up, he brushed off the dirt looking at the message. There was no direct translation, but it roughly meant "another shadow". Pocketing the switchblade, he dropped the hammer and headed back to D.

***

Richard walked into the room and spotted D still sitting on the ledge, he glanced around and said, "Where's Zecona?"

"He's off visiting the body."

"Why?"

"I pissed him off."

"How's that?"

She glanced over at him. "Don't worry about it." She hopped off the wall. "When he gets back, I want to head over to the hospital."

"What for?"

"I have one last lead, and I want to keep my options open." She grabbed a bowl of oatmeal from the machine. "How'd your meeting go?"

Richard stood staring at her shaking his head. "Zecona and I are due to move out two days from now."

"I see." She took a bite of oatmeal and walked back to her ledge in the wall. "I wanted to talk to you about what we're going to be doing tomorrow."

"We?"

"From what I've heard, Central Division controls the anti-air portion of the Rebellion over the city. I think we should strike there as hard as we can throw everything we can, so that a few of the Federation ships can scape on through and hit parts of the city."

She sat up straight. "You and Zecona will go out in the open and attack flat out just outside of the Skyscraper there. While I sneak in with explosives and take out their armory, comms, and any stragglers."

"That's suicide," Richard said.

She glanced up at him for a moment "That's not the point. They're completely vulnerable at this point."

"Based on what? Your plan is to take on the entire Rebellion head-on?"

"No. Only part of it, and only the important parts of it."

Richard was shaking his head. "I'm sorry, but I'm going to have to decline at this point."

"What? But you're still under my contract."

"You're asking me to put my life and Zecona's life on the line, and for what? We've been given new orders. We've been reassigned. We don't have to worry about it."

"Fine. I'll do it all myself."

"What the hell is the matter with you? This isn't your damn war. Just sit back and wait."

"That's easy for you to say," D said shaking her head.

"It's a shit plan, and you know it. Just go back to your Overman contact and see if they would be willing to forgive a portion of your debt, and continue doing what you did before?"

D kept shaking her head. "That's not an option. I'm kinda committed at this point."

"You don't even know if that soldier was from central."

"That doesn't matter." She set down her bowl and walked over to him. "If I can knock out what's left of their communications, and if there's any kind of air strike, they're sitting ducks."

"Lots of 'ifs' in that plan. How do you know striking there will knock out the rest of their communications? Do you even know how the anti-air works?"

Her eyes glanced up at the wall for a moment. "I know enough."

"Bullshit. So obviously central division is the best to hit?"

"Hitting one will weaken the whole network. Central divisions is the closest one we're near. They're stretched thin as it is, knocking one out will just cripple the state further. Their communications are weak. Most of their supply lines have been hit. Their patrols have been left in shambles, so they're being forced to reorganize. Combined with the falling of the outer perimeter, it'll be enough to knock the revolution on its ass."

"I'm not helping you this time."

"Just trust me, alright? Can I at least get that?"

He scanned over her vitals, before saying, "You must think I'm a complete fool."

"No. Why?"

"I see that second MFC you have."

D's eyes widened staring back at the cold black eyes of the devil.

Richard continued, "What do you think they will do once they realize what you're doing with that?"

"Don't know," she said, shrugging. "I'll cross that bridge when I get there."

"No. You know exactly what they are going to do."

"I'm doing what I need to do to survive."

"So am I," Richard said. "They will figure out what you did. When they do, they'll kill you, and If I continue to help you with that knowledge, they'll kill me as well."

She rolled her eyes. "Just forget about it."

The sun was getting lower in the horizon, and the suit just shrugged. Zecona walked through the door.

D smiled and said, "Just in time."

Zecona glanced at her. "What?"

"We need to head back to the hospital. I need some quick Intel."

"I'm staying here," Richard said crossing his arms.

D glared at him, pursing her lips. "Fine." She glanced back at Zecona. "Are you still coming?"

Zecona shrugged. "Sure. I guess."

***

The sky was a brilliant orange as D and Zecona approached the hospital. D hadn't spoken a word since they left Richard behind, and Zecona had given up trying a few blocks back.

"I'm sorry for the way I acted earlier," D said, keeping her eyes on the outline of the hospital. "I've just been under a bit of stress with everything going on, and it's been a while since I had a choice to act sensibly."

Zecona sighed. "It's fine, I guess." He put his hands behind his head. "What did I walk in on between you and Richard?"

"We had a disagreement regarding his contract."

"Uhh huh," Zecona said.

"What's the deal between you two?" she said glancing at him.

"What do you mean?"

"Like, is he contracted to protect you on behalf of the Federation or something?"

"No," Zecona said shaking his head. "He's made it pretty clear to me that I'm only here to move him around discreetly. If I purposely get into any sort of trouble, he's not going to help me out at all."

D nodded. "Gotcha."

They didn't say anything else as they made their way through the hospital. D handed off Michael's rifle to Zecona, and disappeared into one of the offices, leaving him alone to peruse the hallways. Zecona started off patrolling the hallways, but as the evening began to set in, he settled in the nurses' station reading some old documents and memo's left behind under a table lamp.

After hours of searching the hospital records, D rested her head in the palm of her hand. Staring back at the computer monitor, she let out a long sigh. "How many ways are there to spell Jeremy Samson?" she asked, looking over the list of names. D shut down the computer, and leaned back into her chair.

Zecona glanced through the scattered papers on the desk and picked up another report. A receipt for medical equipment for room 205 was stapled to the top. The patient came in reporting trouble breathing. He glanced up when he saw D walking out of the door.

She stopped just short of the door with her head bowed. Grabbing hold of a medical cart sitting beside the door, she threw it to the ground, beakers shattered on the floor, cabinets spilled out.

"Fuck!"

Trays slid down the hall. Zecona raised Michael's rifle and pointed it at the door at the end of the hall. D kicked a drawer. It skidded across the hall, smacking against the wall.

"There's at least twenty of the fuckers... <u>Twenty</u>!" She grabbed hold of a jar that didn't smash and threw it to the ground.

Zecona turned his head around and called out, "Would you keep it down before the locals come"

"To hell with them!" She threw another jar at a wall. "You think I honestly give a shit about those animals? Do you?"

D kicked the cabinet a few inches along the floor. "Let them fucking come! What the fuck do I care?" She stopped kicking it and rested her forehead into the palm of her hand. Turning, she sat down on the cabinet and took a deep breath. "I don't know what to do." Bringing her hand down, she wiped off her lips. "I don't know the guy's age for starters. Any sort of identifiable features, like hair or eye colors. Fuck, I'd love to have a blood type. I don't even have a full name." Taking another deep breath, she glanced at the ceiling. "God damn, I don't even know if that's his real name, or even if he's a <u>he</u>. I don't... fucking know..."

Zecona couldn't hear any footsteps from the stairwell. He turned his attention back to D. "Did you just try the surname, Samson?" he said lowering the rifle.

"How would that help? The list just jumps to seventy." She shook her head at him.

"I tried Jerry, Jeremy, Jeremiah, but without an age or anything like that, I can't narrow it down. I'm looking at close to twenty to thirty different people all named Jeremy Samson."

"What's the big deal?" Zecona said shrugging. "Why are you trying to locate this guy?"

D was just staring at the floor.

Zecona waited for some kind of reply, before walking out of the nurse station and said, "We probably ought to head back before it gets too late." He walked up to her and held out his hand.

D glared at it momentarily, before gripping it, and rose to her feet.

*****

It was late at night when Zecona and D returned to D's base. They hadn't spoken a word since the hospital. Zecona was exhausted from the hike and collapsed onto his cot. Richard hadn't moved from the side of the doorway since they'd left. D huddled up on her couch, with an electric lantern. He drifted off to sleep watching her scramble through her notebooks.

"Wake up!" D hissed as she tapped Zecona's cheek.

"Uh?" Zecona said opening his eyes in the pitch-black room.

"Shhh!" D held a finger to her mouth.

Richard was looking out the hole over the road, clutching one of the bags of explosives. It was still dead of night, but he could make out the heavy mechanical whine of multiple heavy motors from the streets.

"What's goi—"

D slapped him. "Shh!"

D had her Marlow out. Standing, she glanced over at Richard. He saw her and nodded. She pocketed her Marlow, and ran over to her bed.

Zecona walked over to the hole and looked down the street. Something big was moving at the mouth of the road. Amongst the shadows, he could make out what looked like several large legs moving in strange synchronization. The low bass of multiple massive mechanical motor's pulsed through the floor as the mass of shadow moved through the street. It was a spider tank. He backed away wide eyed. D grabbed his arm and motioned for the door. Richard watched them, then looked back towards the road.

D strapped the other bag of explosives to her back. She and Zecona ran down the stairs, through the lobby, and down another flight of stairs into the maze of rooms in the basement. Pulling Zecona behind her as they ran down the corridors. They came to a dead stop in the last hallway, at the makeshift barricade blocking the back door.

She kicked at the wooden barrier, but it didn't budge. Smashing her heel into it again didn't help. D handed Zecona the bag of explosives, put Michael's rifle on her back, grabbed hold of a long wooden piece sticking out of the pile, and pushed it forward. After several loud pops from the wood, the whole pile collapsed in front of them. The walls around them shuttered. Kicking away the broken bits, they burst through the back door and sprinted up a short flight of stairs, before running down an alleyway behind the building. Stale beer smacked Zecona's nose. That's when they heard a whirling noise from above them.

"Fucking hell!" She shoved Zecona off to one side and dove to the other.

He looked back at what was making the noise, and saw the spider tank crouching on top of the building. Two guns were whirling right beneath the large spherical cockpit. The roof collapsed, taking the tank with it. Lasers fire cut through the night sky.

D laughed. "Take that ya lit--"

A leg of the machine ripped through the back of the building. It tore through the back wall like a dull knife through bread.

"Shit!" D got up, grabbed Zecona and they sprinted down the alley again.

The building crumbled from its weight, and the tank jumped up onto the roof of another building, before galloping along the rooftops. Dust raced down the alley behind the two. They could see the end of the alley ahead as the dust engulfed them.

The tank crashed at the mouth of the opening. D Shoved Zecona off to the side. It turned and faced down at them flipping on a floodlight. Zecona could see behind the light, resting on top of eight tan and gray sharpened legs, the obsidian sphere where the pilot was sitting. D Shot the light out with her rifle.

The alley went black again. She was walking towards it, shooting another burst. Stopping at the mouth of the alleyway, she spread out her arms.

"Com' on! You want a piece of me?" She dropped her rifle. The tank shot at her arm ripping the flesh to ribbons, before taking one of its legs, and stabbed her thru the stomach, pinning her to the ground.

"Identify yourself." A voice spoke from the machine

Zecona saw the gun on the ground.

"Who are you working for?"

Zecona crouched up against the rubble, looking at the tank.

"If you do not cooperate, we will extract the information through other means."

Zecona turned his attention back to D. She was struggling to get the leg off of her. Feeling each breath leaving him as he crouched there. He clutched the bag of explosives on his back, and bolted down the alley. A gun from the tank whizzed up.

"No!" D shouted. Zecona grabbed the rifle, and ran straight through the massive legs under the tank. The tank pulled its leg out of D and turned towards Zecona. He sprinted down the road, before spinning around and took aim. It was almost turned towards him.

"Run you fucking idiot!" D screamed at him. Both mini guns started to whirl. Zecona stared at her. "Run!"

Zecona paled as he saw the guns pointed at him spinning. He tossed himself down an alleyway. Lasers ripped through the building. D pulled out her Marlow and started firing at the undercarriage of the tank.

The obsidian sphere shattered as Richard flew out of the front of the spider tank, while clutching the upper body of the pilot. He slammed into the ground, and dropped the body behind him. Richard stood up, walking towards Zecona and sent out a radio pulse. The spider tank exploded behind him from the inside, with a column of fire chasing after him from the cockpit. It's burnt husk sagged to the ground. Zecona crawled back into the street looking at the flaming wreckage.

Richard reached down helping Zecona up, and turned back to D.

"Everyone alright?"

"Fuck no! What the hell took you so long?" D said, getting to her feet as she gripped her stomach.

"You can't rush perfection."

Zecona grabbed D's rifle. He tried to hand it to her, she shook her head.

"What the hell am I going to carry it with?" she said.

Zecona stood gawking at the open wound in her stomach, and the ribbons of flesh and muscle that dangled where her arm was. They gathered in the middle of the road in front of the building inferno of the spider tank.

Richard said, "Where to now?"

"I have no fucking idea." She coughed up blood onto the street.

"Don't worry about it," Richard said, looking around. "We can hold back up where me and Zecona set up a base camp."

"Is it far?" she said, glancing over at him.

"Not exactly."

"Then lets get moving."

She started hobbling down the road. Zecona reached out for her, but Richard stopped him, shaking his head. Richard led the way.

CHAPTER FIFTEEN
DOLL

Richard held the door open, and D followed Zecona up the stairs to the hallway. She sat against a piece of rubble. Richard struck a match and started a fire in the barrel in the middle of the room.

"We'll attack Central Division tomorrow."

"You can't be serious?" Richard said.

She nodded over to her mangled arm. "This'll be fine by morning." She was still clutching her stomach. "This too." She adjusted her shirt across her abdomen. "How much of the explosives did you use?"

Richard cocked his head at her. "All of it."

Her mouth hung open. "Are you fucking kidding me? An entire bag full?"

The suit stood still with its arms crossed.

"Fine. Whatever." She sat up, shaking her head.

"Doesn't it hurt?" Zecona asked.

"No shit," she said.

"You don't act like it."

"You get used to things when they happen enough." She leaned her head back. "You should get some rest."

When he didn't move, she shook her head and leaned back, watching the fire.

D reached into her pocket and grabbed a cigarette, and put it in her mouth. Grabbing her lighter, she smiled looking at the D engraved on it, before letting the cigarette fall out of her mouth.

"I bet you're wondering who Nadia is."

Zecona glanced over to her.

"A long time ago. Before this all this mess started. Would you believe I was a doctor?" She grinned looking over at him, but he was just staring at her.

"Well, I can't believe it." She looked back at the fire. "I wanted to help save people. You know? Gave shots to little kids. Cast broken arms. General surgery if I needed to. Save people from their pain. There were mistakes of course, but dammit I made a difference when it came down to it." She watched the flames. "Jacob was my fiancée. He was in the military with the Federation. Along with a few others I knew. But I've known them practically my whole life. I loved him."

She opened her mouth and focused on the words. "I didn't want kids starting out. I mean, if it just happened during the marriage I wouldn't..." She trailed off, looking around the room for the words she needed. "I had a career. I needed to focus on that." A laugh forced its way out. "I didn't need a kid messing things up."

She put the lighter away. "I didn't get a chance to marry Jacob. When the revolution started, it was just small terrorist attacks. Buildings getting bombed. Car bombs. Rebels taking the airwaves dictating their message. Freedom through fear. They eventually got hold of Blue Lotus. One accident in the hallways, and I was infected."

She glanced over to the side of the room. "I thought that was the worst day of my life. Later when things began to escalate between the Rebellion and the Federation, we made our way to the evacuation points outside the city limits. The streets were clogged with cars, we had to leave by foot. Things changed so fast."

She started to cry. Zecona could only tell from the fire; her face didn't change. She let out another laugh. "I'm getting so far off track." She was shaking her head. "What he did..." She trailed off watching the fire. "What he did was another story." She was shaking her head.

Her tears gave way, and she tried to laugh. "You know!" She couldn't laugh anymore. "You can't forget pain like that. A friend that close. That deep. Just tearing you down and ripping into you like that. Like he doesn't even know you. It never goes away. When he was done, I told him I was going to tell them everything. What he did to me. They'd leave his sorry ass. That fucking bastard. The love of my life. And my best friend. Chocking me and bashing my head onto a rock. The look in his eyes. He wasn't the same man I knew. Who I grew up with. Who I fell in love with. I got a hold of the gun and with one shot... Gone."

She tried to smile. "I passed out from my injuries after that. I don't know what happened next. I just remember waking up to Ada." She closed her eyes. "I wish she hadn't found me."

"Ada said I belonged to Overman. The treatment they needed to use to save my life had put me into debt within their system, and she told me I needed to work for them to pay back that debt. Otherwise, Overman would 'repossess' everything they had put into place that saved my life." She took a deep breath. "So they sent me back here, to gather information, that they would, in turn, buy from me.

"Starting out, the information I got sold well. Just walking into a bar, and chatting up a soldier. It seemed like I could get back to my life in as little as a year. What they don't tell you about, is the diminishing returns for each piece of information you give them. On top of that, you're competing with other Agents in the area for the same information. So if someone you'd been able to sweet talk into access to say the communication arrays got killed by a fellow Agent, that made getting information even harder. What looked like a quick year of work turned into two. Then three. Then maybe after ten, if you're careful. Then it dawns on you that you'll be lucky to work over twenty years. All the while you're fucking and drugging any information out of anyone you can get your hands on. Watching the dollars of your life slip away."

She took a deep sigh. "About a year ago, I started keeping some of the information I gathered. I had to work twice as hard to keep my debt manageable, but I needed something to work with. Something I could use. To plan with."

They both stared at her.

She laughed. "When I got sick, I didn't even consider the fact that couldn't 'get' sick. I just thought I had a stomach bug. I started to throwing up on those rare occasions. It dragged into weeks, but it didn't slow me down. I needed to get out. And then I felt the kick."

Zecona watched the fire dance in her amber eyes.

"Six months ago, I had an abortion," she said. "I believe it was somewhere within its second trimester. Maybe twenty weeks into it?" She said looking back around the room again. "I don't know the exact timing because..." She trailed off again. "Well, I don't know who the father was. Ada had told me that they had 'sterilized' me, so I didn't use any protection while I was... gathering information. Because I thought that couldn't happen. But I guess something fixed itself down there and..." She shook her head. "There was no way I could keep it.

"I was shooting up at least five times a day just to keep my head straight through everything going on. Drinking in between the times I used the needle. And the sheer number of fights I had gotten myself caught up in. How that fucker made it along that long without a miscarriage is beyond me." She readjusted herself sitting straight up. "Actually, for all I knew..." She trailed off staring into the fire. She could feel her right hand pulse at the thought. Forcing out a laugh, she brushed her hair back with her right hand. "I had to get rid of it. I couldn't take the chance." She focused on the words again. "It would've left me too vulnerable in the field. That's if it survived to birth. And what then? I was fighting as hard as I could to keep myself alive." She shook her head. "But maybe worst of all, what if Overman got a hold of it? Then it'd be trapped like me. Fighting a losing battle. Living only half of its life before they killed it, after they used up everything it could offer them."

Her head was sinking lower to her chest. "So I stole a scalpel from a hospital and ripped it out of me." She threw her head back taking a deep breath. The tears were back. "And... I remember looking down at it and thinking, 'This is what I've become.'"

"That destroyed me," she said staring at the wall. "I..." She was lost in her words. "I decided then that I wasn't going to be forced to make that kind of decision. I know that it was the right decision. And if I had to make it again, right now, I would do it. But one way or another, I was going to ensure that I wasn't going to be forced to make that decision again. And when my other options failed, I found only one remaining."

Her eyes fell on Zecona, and said, "But you were asking about Nadia." A strange smile spread across her face against the fire. "I found her being beaten by a group of men down an alleyway. I killed those fuckers, and got her out of there. When she came to, I..." She swallowed her words for a moment. "She had nowhere to go. So. I took it upon myself to adopt her. I thought I could help her. Save her. But..." She locked eyes with Zecona, and in a whisper said, "I shot her in the face, and burned her body in the middle of the street. Because I thought she sold me out." She shook her head. "And I see that even if she did, it wouldn't have mattered."

Zecona didn't say a word, he didn't know what could be said. Her fist was clenched and shaking. He laid down on the floor and continued to watch her for a couple of minutes. She closed her eyes, and laid her head back on the slab of concrete behind her.

***

Richard stood in the corner. As the fire raged on in the middle of the room, he watched D's body heal up as she slept. His twisted shadows froze as the fire cooled to embers. Within hours, the morning light began to seep in, peeking through the cracks of the building. D popped her head up and saw him staring straight at her from the shadows.

She lit up a cigarette. "What?"

His arms were still crossed as he watched the glow of D's cigarette. He glanced over checking the vitals on Zecona, and looked back at her.

"I'm just trying to figure out what your goal is," he said, looking at her.

"I'm sorry?" she said looking straight at him.

"You can sway the kid with that kind of story, but you should know better in thinking that you can change my mind."

She was shaking her head. "You fuckers are all the same."

"You're expecting me to just throw away my life for you?"

"That's not my intention." D snapped

"Really, because it seems like regardless of today's outcome, as you say it, you won't need to worry about having to be forced into making a possible future decision."

"I'm cleaning up the mess you made."

"No, you're being forced to follow through with your shit plan."

"It wasn't a shit plan." She shook her head. "You just weren't prepared to work hard enough to help me."

"I'm not being paid enough to lay down my life for you. What makes you think your life is worth more than mine?" Richard said.

"So, what, I'm not good enough to live?"

"Don't you know what you are?" Richard asked.

"I know exactly what I am," D said, clenching her fist. "I'm a human being."

Richard stared at her, glanced over at Zecona lying down on his cot, and walked out of the room.

"Aren't I?" D said, standing up to watch him walk away. She stormed towards him. "Aren't I?" She raised her voice.

Zecona turned over in his cot.

She followed Richard down the stairs to the first floor. "Don't walk away when I'm talking to you!"

Richard stopped in the lobby of the office and held up his hands. "Better here than getting the kid involved."

"Are you going to answer my question?"

"Close the door"

"Fuck you!" she said, slamming the double doors behind her. "Are you going to answer my fucking question?"

Richard shrugged, "What do you want me to say?" It folded its arms and leaned against the front desk.

"The truth," D said.

"Really? 'Cause I thought you would have been able to figure that out on your own."

D crossed her arms and cocked her head to her side. "And that would be?"

"Cut the fucking act. You're an Agent of Overman. You were designed for a sole purpose."

D forced out a laugh. "Designed? So what, all those..." She waved her hand in the air. "Events from my life are, what, made up?"

"No. They happened. I have no doubt about that. Just not to you."

She stared at him, trying to get some sort of read from the still silver helmet and crescent moons staring back at her. "I don't know where this is coming from. I would have expected more professionalism from a War Devil under my command."

"I'm speaking as an Agent of Overman, to a fellow Agent."

She continued to stare at him before breaking a smile and laughing. "You're completely serious, aren't you? I mean, one hundred percent. You legitimately believe I'm, what, an android, or something?"

"No, I read your dossier. You're a Delta Clone with nanobots and a modified set of DNA."

"Even better," D laughed again. "What the fuck is a Delta Clone?"

"Well, it's important to explain what an Alpha and a Beta clone are first."

"Oh, believe me. I'm all ears," D said with crossed arms.

"Your Alpha is where your baseline DNA and memories come from. I don't know the particulars of your case, but I would assume it would be that she either approached or was approached by Overman Agents concerning a life-threatening condition. She was offered free treatment to save her life at the cost of donating her DNA, and a mental dump for 'further research purposes'. Your Beta Clone started out as a direct clone of your Alpha, but they were mentally and physically 'stress tested' to pinpoint weaknesses. The clone would have been pushed well beyond their limits, to optimize you in the field. Mentally your memories would have been augmented to better suit an Agent, and tested for stability in case you went insane or your mind outright rejected the inception of new thoughts. Since your body would be reequipped with the ability to rapidly heal itself, your body would need to be subjected to an ungodly level of pain to recalibrate your nerve and brain activity. I'm sure by now you've repressed those particular memories, but I'm also pretty sure that the first week when you woke from your 'coma,' you had vivid night terrors, right?"

D's eyes widened at the memories of those nights, but she remained otherwise motionless with her arms crossed listening to him.

"Being shot, being skinned alive, being set on fire, dissolving in a base substance, exposed to high degrees of radiation? That's where you come in as a Delta. You're the product for the Federation. Scrapped together from a collection of identities and memories to perform short-term contract work. You're even designed to terminate yourself at the end of the contract. Failing that, an Agent will pick you off. Then your body is recollected and broken back down for other purposes. Hell, as a Delta, you're probably not the only one of your kind. There are probably ten or twenty others just like you, sharing your same memories, all running around different cities around Verra doing the same exact thing you were doing."

D shook her head. "I'm not going to entertain this idea anymore. I know what am."

"Really?" Richard said. "And how do you know that? Gut instinct?"

"I just do."

"What separates your idea of free will from mine?"

"I wouldn't know," D said, pushing her tongue against her lower lip. "I'm not a machine."

"Oh really? Where did you learn to shoot and handle an assault rifle?"

"I went with--" She paused for a moment. "Jacob. To the firing range on weekends."

"And you shot assault and battle rifles? Fully Automatic? Why not settle with a small caliber pistol?"

"I liked something with a little kick to it."

"Shotguns, too, I imagine? Ever throw a grenade there, or use a grenade launcher?"

"As a matter of fact, yes. There was one time mid-summer they had a demonstration, and I was one of the lucky few to attend."

"Seems kinda odd," Richard said, cocking his helmet, "that a public firing range would have access to explosives and fully automatic assault rifles."

"It required special fees and waivers signed, along with a monthly payment for members. There was a public portion for regular firearms and a private portion for more exotic weapons."

"What kind of doctor goes to the firing range on the weekend? Wouldn't you be on call 24/7 by the hospital?"

"I went when I was off call. Only had a few instances off hand where I was pulled away from the range for an emergency."

"You didn't consider guns to be a conflict with your profession?"

"No, I needed something to release my stress, and I wanted to spend time with..." Her eyes widened for a brief second and she let out a deep breath.

Richard stared at her for a moment. Her expression had become like a stone. "What kind of doctor were you?"

"I started out as a General Practioner after college, then when terrorists attacks started to ramp up in the city I switched into Trauma Care to help out in emergency situations."

"I've seen the blank labels in your metal case with the bumps. Where did you learn Braille?"

"I had to work with blind patients, and had to work with them to develop their reading ability."

"Really? Wouldn't that be the job of a language specialist? Why would a practicing surgeon be teaching the blind how to read Braille? Especially in this day and age when the visual responses in the human eyes can be so easily repaired."

"Look, I don't expect you to understand all of the human aspects of our decisions. Some people who are blind just opt out of surgery because they believe their loss of sight makes them unique. Either they're just born that way, or some accident occurs, or they're paranoid about the surgery. Loads of reasons. The same thing happens with deaf people. They form a community around it. I picked up Braille and sign language as their doctor to better help them through the transition process."

"So you're a brain surgeon?" Richard said, pointing a finger at her.

"No." She thought for a moment. "I didn't say that. I practiced on multiple parts of the body."

"Strange. I'd expect you to focus on one particular aspect of the human body, rather than attempt to be a jack-all-trades. Wouldn't that make sense?"

"I trained for what the hospital needed." D glared at him. "I hadn't really picked an area of interest within my practice, but I most certainly had to develop a knowledge of multiple areas of the body."

"Right, and you trained in Braille and sign language for a select minority."

"Right."

"And you had time to train in assault artillery on the weekends amongst all of this."

D nodded her head.

"Amazing. How well do you handle a syringe?"

She raised an eyebrow. "What do you mean?"

"I mean, how long does it take you to find the right vein on another person? Few minutes? A few seconds? Does it take you a few tries to get it right?"

"I might be a little above average." D shrugged. "That's always been the case. I've just been lucky."

"Really?" Richard said nodding his helmet at her. "I would say hitting the vein the first time after taking a second to look is luck. The second time is extremely lucky. The third time is unnatural. And that's in a hospital setting. Not drugged up, with a gun pointed to your head while fucking a guy."

D glared at him. "After a while it just becomes--"

"Muscle memory, right, I know. A skill like that pops out of no-where, and it's like riding a bike. Always the same with ease. All the while, your colleagues may take a minute to pinch the arm a few times, flex the skin, poke once, and realize that they missed the damn thing once, and try again, might miss it again. Not you though, you have the muscle memory to find the vein in any person you've never even seen before. Right?"

D was shook her head. "Let's say you're right. You're not, but let's say you are. Why give me such vivid memories of..." She stared at a wall. "Why make me remember that level of pain, why not just glance over that like the rest of it?"

"Isn't that obvious?" Richard said, staring at her. "What was Jacob? A policeman? A soldier? I bet you see him when you wrap around a soldier. You feel that intense sense of rage build up at times, and it makes it that much easier to do what you 'feel' like you need to do."

D was visibly shaking. "Jacob was real."

"I'm sure."

"He was. I went back to my old place. I found the photos. Of us. I looked up his medical information. Don't stand there and tell me that didn't fucking happen!"

"It probably did," Richard said, staring at her. "Just not to you."

D sank to the ground.

"You're a clockwork actor, D," Richard said, walking towards her. "Built for a solitary short-term purpose of gathering intel and killing specific targets."

"Why the fuck did you take my contract if you knew all of this?" D said, staring at the floor.

"Who am I to argue about easy money?" Richard folded his arms looking down at her. "If a stray dog wants to have one last hurrah before they get refabricated, who am I to object? Come planetside, have a little fun of my own. And then take the money and run."

"And Overman is so infallible, so far removed from making mistakes that he wouldn't accidentally modify an 'Alpha' and send it in the field?"

"That's quite impossible," Richard said, "I've already checked. And Overman would never ruin the original. Besides, there are no Agents keeping watch of your situation. And I've been searching for them too, which tells me that what you're doing has no consequence to the greater mission."

D took in a deep shallow breath. Richard stood up straight and walked towards the door.

"Then answer me this." D still stared at the floor.

Richard had his hand on the handle as he turned around.

D had turned around and looked up at him. "If Overman designed me with every aspect of my consciousness and 'free will', and I'm destined to kill myself, why is it every fiber of my being committed to fighting this and living rather than just lying down and dying?"

Richard took a moment to scan over her. Her facial expression, respiratory system, heart-beat, pulse, eye dilation, sweat, and tears. He wanted to find something that would change his mind. He said nothing as he turned and opened the door and left her sitting on the floor.

***

D flexed her arm new arm as Zecona started to wake.

"Wake up," she said, swinging her arm around.

"I'm gettin there." He stretched his neck and rolled his shoulders.

"Looks like this is where we're parting ways."

Zecona's stomach rumbled. "What do you mean?"

"It would just be better if we separated. You have your next orders, and I have my own mess to deal with. I don't need you anymore," she said, glancing over at him.

He yawned. D reached down in one of her bags. Richard was standing back at the entrance. Zecona got up and stretched.

"Here." D chucked him a bag.

It caught him in the stomach. He sputtered and the bag clattered to the floor.

"What's this?"

"Parting gift," she said, "I don't have anywhere to go back to. Better to give it to someone so it's not wasted."

"I feel so privileged," he said, looking at her. Glancing down, he noticed her lighter, the notebook, and the metallic case. "What is this?"

She looked back. "Junk."

He was studying her expression as he strapped the bag to his back. "Oh, thanks. Just what I need."

D strapped the bag of explosives to her back "If you don't want it, throw it away. You can probably sell some of it for some extra cash if you need to."

Zecona glanced at Richard. "Where are we going?"

"I'll tell you when we get there," Richard said.

Strapping the rifle to her back, she turned to Richard. "Can I ask one favor?"

"Depends," Richard said staring at her.

"I need a combat knife."

"What kind?"

"I don't care."

"Fine." He pressed his palm against the wall and collected the iron and carbon from the surrounding elements. He grabbed the formed handle and handed D the jagged steel combat knife.

"Thanks."

Zecona finished strapping the bags to his back and followed her as they walked out into the road. The sun was still low in the sky.

"Looks like this is the end of the road," D said glancing around the street. "You going to jump out in front of any more tanks?"

"Of course not," Zecona said smiling.

"Mmhm." She glanced at him. "Well, if I don't see you again..." She gave a half salute. "It was fun."

She turned and started to walk away.

Zecona watched her. "I'm sorry," he said.

She stopped and looked back. "For what?"

"For the way I've acted."

She cocked an eyebrow. "Quit being such a fucking tool." She strained a smile and kept walking down the road.

Richard said, "Let's get packing." He turned back towards the building.

Zecona stared after D, before turning and following him.

***

"We need to get moving."

"Why's that?" Zecona said, sitting on the cot.

Richard held D's lighter in his hand. "Odds are that when D gets caught, she's going to try to pull us in by giving them our location," he said as he walked across the room.

"Shouldn't we get moving then?"

Silence.

"You're not planning on going in after her are you?" Zecona continued. "Let's just get out of the city the best we can and let the cards land where they fall."

Richard didn't say anything as he hit his back against the wall and folded his arms. "No." He sighed. "There's just a few things not adding up."

"Well, I don't see how that's our problem anymore." Zecona stood up and started packing the bags. Richard hadn't moved. "I'm figuring," Zecona said with his back to him as he zipped up a tote bag, "if we move fast, we can probably reach the southern checkpoint." He turned back to him. "Mind dissolving the cots?"

Richard was watching as a raven flew down and perched down on top of a lamppost in the parking lot.

"It's interesting." Richard stared at the black bird cleaning its feathers. "How Verra could have evolved something that looks so close to a Raven."

"What?" Zecona turned and scanned over the empty roads and rooftops along with the bare lampposts and traffic lights, before saying, "What's a Raven?"

All of Richards sensors were firing on the bird before he said. "I need to go."

Zecona was staring at him. "What?"

Richard was still leaning against the wall. His head snapped, up meeting Zecona's stare. He pushed off the wall, and said, "I'll be back later this evening." He opened his thigh and dropped D's lighter into an empty slot, and grabbed a pistol.

Zecona's eyes widened. "What the do you mean?"

"I need to meet up with my contact. I need some answers."

"Are you insane? You just said we had to get out of the city!"

"Stay here," Richard said pointing to him.

"Stay here? The Rebels will probably be swarming the fucking streets soon!"

"Then leave the damn city for all I care," Richard said, running down the hallway.

CHAPTER SIXTEEN
DEVIL

After taking a quick detour, D tossed the bloody combat knife down an alleyway and stopped by where she had ditched her Prowler the day before. She drove down the road towards the toppled Borch & Kasigan skyscraper marking the Central Division. Weaving her way around the concrete barricades, the main gate loomed over her, with sniper towers set up on either side. The wall was built from large broken slabs of concrete and metal beams from what was once the surrounding buildings. Stopping at the gate, she waited as a soldier approached her with a rifle drawn.

"What's your business here?"

"Just need a place to crash for the day. Need food, gas and sleep," D said, glancing over the horizon.

"Now's probably not the best time," The guard said lowering his rifle. "I'll need to clear it with the inner squad."

"Can we skip the bullshit?" D snapped her attention back to him. "I haven't had a break in two days."

He stared at her, before pulling out a PDA and holding it up. As he was messing with the display, she saw his eyes narrow, before he nodded towards a man at the controls and said, "You can head on through." The gate started to inch open. "Follow the road to the tower, and the secondary guard will give you further instructions. I'd advise you maintain a low speed."

"Thanks." D revved the engine

The guard didn't say anything, but watched her head through.

***

Clumps of tents lay scattered about inside the wall. Soldiers were out in mass, packing combat rifles and armored head to toe in thick ballistic armor. She came to a smaller secondary gate, and another guard came up to her.

"You boys getting ready for a fight?" D said, looking around at the soldiers.

"Just routine, ma'am," the guard said.

"Doesn't look routine to me."

He stayed stone-faced staring at her.

She patted her Prowler. "Where can I park this?"

"Someone will be by to escort you."

She raised her eyebrow. "Why can't you just tell me where?"

"Standard procedures ma'am."

D shrugged. "Alright." She hopped off. "Get much action this far in?"

"All the time." The guard signaled to two guards as they approached her. "Follow, them ma'am."

"Yeah, yeah." She switched it to neutral and walked with the guards.

"Do you always escort visitors?" She glanced at one of them. "Or is it only with the ladies?" she said with a smile.

He didn't respond, and she turned her attention back to the camps. When they reached the upper level of the parking garage, they were met by another squad of soldiers signaling them to stop.

"We'll need to take that rifle off of you," one of the soldiers said.

D smiled, clutching the bag. "Sure."

He took her rifle. She kept her eye on the three other soldiers rifles. They went down into a parking garage underground.

As she rolled her Prowler into the twenty-first space on B level, she clutched the bag of explosives closer to her shoulder. The guard motioned her to follow, and they went towards a central elevator.

With an audible ding, the doors opened and inside where squad of soldiers stood. Rifles drawn, cocked and loaded. One of the guards she was with grabbed hold of the bag. The other swept her feet, and slammed her head into the ground.

***

Richard had been running towards where he had agreed to meet Seawood. It was the crumbling remains of a cathedral. A raven cried out as he ran up the stone steps. He threw open the double doors, and saw a figure sitting in the middle of the pews.

The white and black eyes of Ada met him as he walked down the asile. "Hello, Barbatos." She floated up and started walking towards him. "SG96 isn't here, they got pulled into an assignment last minute. I understand that you--"

"I need you to activate my Hell-Fire Mode," Richard demanded.

She was staring at him with her half-smile. "I beg your pardon?"

"I'm not looking for lectures." He pulled out a pistol from his thigh. "Black Dog has gone into a rebel base. I intend on getting her out."

The half-smile didn't even flinch as she looked down the barrel of the gun. "Spare me the theatrics."

"Are you going to do it, or not?" He charged a round into the magazine. "I'm going in regardless, it's your decision if you're walking out of here."

"Fine." She knelt down to the ground, taking off her leather gloves and grabbed her thin, black briefcase. She was shaking her head. "You realize what you're doing?"

"Spare me the lectures. I don't have time."

The nails on both of her index fingers extended, and she slid both into the slits on top of the briefcase. The locks clicked open, and she opened it in a way Richard could not see into it. She grabbed a slender molecular multitool, closed the briefcase and stood back up.

"I can wire you my schematics for what you need to do."

"Don't worry," she said "I'm well acquainted with the War Devil Architecture." she grabbed his wrist and popped open the inner components, exposing his base system without a second thought. "You'll effectively be cutting your life down a couple decades the more energy you exert." She started setting the options on the multitool.

Richard stared towards the ceiling.

"If you drain yourself to low, you might not be able to get back to an Overman controlled location to recharge. In fact you could permanently shutdown in the middle of the engagement."

"I know."

The iris on her black eye expanded, engulfing her whole eye, as she focused the molecular electronic structure of Richards onboard computer. "With the amount of heat you'll be exerting, you also run the risk of permanently damaging your auto-repair systems, and sensors. You could melt down into a puddle of liquid metal."

Richard continued focusing on the ceiling, and felt a strange sense of deja-vu. He couldn't place why he felt that way, but the room, talking with Ada, and her applying modifications to his core systems felt too familiar in that moment.

Holding the multitool steady, she began to manipulate the necessary components. "You realize I could just shut your whole system down right now, have you shipped back to HQ to have your components reexamined."

"That would be a mistake."

"Why? The mistake would be letting the Rebels get their hands on Overman technology. We wouldn't be losing a man. You had a gun on me, and now you're trusting me to reconstruct your system on the fly." The iris shrunk back down, and she pulled the multitool way.

He turned his attention back towards her.

"I left a reserve battery in place. If you run everything else down, you'll have a month to live."

"Thanks." Richard turned away from her.

"One more thing." She caught his wrist. He turned back and was staring into her white eye now. It was almost glowing white like liquid metal, but she was still wearing a half smile. "I am Ada. The sole Spirit Tamer planet side." She said. "If you point a gun, and threaten me again, I will not hesitate to wipe your soul from the system."

Richard felt panic rise somewhere from his subsystems as he stared into her eye. "I'm sorry."

"Good," She said. Her expression hadn't changed in the slightest; she didn't even blink as she stared at him. She put a small chip into his wrist. "Here are your new orders. I expect you to be available tomorrow evening."

"Understood." He turned again.

She let his arm fall out of her grasp.

He started towards the door, before stopping short and turning back to her. "Has this been authorized by Ophilia?"

Ada paused as though thinking over the answer, before smiling and saying. "Everything I do is in service to our Lord, while working within the bounds of the laws of heaven."

Richard analyzed the words, before bowing his head, and walking out the door. He reached to put his pistol back into his thigh, but briefly remembered he never pulled it out. Leaving the five story hotel behind, he rushed down the street.

***

Zecona threw the bag across the room and sunk down onto the cot with his head in his hands. Gunfire echoed off the buildings. He stared out the window at a birch tree in the middle of the parking lot. The gunshots grew louder.

Grabbing another bag, he shoved more supplies into it. Clothe's, medical supplies, MRE's, and strapped it to his back. Foot steps echoed down the hallway. He smiled, scooping down and grabbing the last bag to hand to Richard. His smile faded at the realization that it was more than one pair of footsteps.

The barrel of a rifle rounded a corner. He saw his reflection in the visor of the rebel staring at him. The bag he had been packing hit the floor.

"Hands behind your head!" The rebel held his rifle up closer. Two more rebels rounded the corner.

Zecona shot his hands behind his head.

The rebel made his way to him. "On the ground now!"

Zecona dropped to his knees.

"Flat! On the ground!"

"Alright, alright!" Zecona fell prone as the rebel dug his boot into his back.

"Where are the others?" He pressed the rifle into the back of Zecona's head.

***

"Who are you working for?" The Major said, staring across the table at D.

"I don't know what you're talking about," she said, staring back at him.

He slapped the table with his palm and stood up walking over to her holding a folder. "You walked into a military compound carrying a bag full of explosives and an assault rifle. On top of that, we've been getting increasing reports about a woman with long dark hair being seen escorted by secure military personnel that were later found murdered." He was flipping through the papers in the folder.

"I don't know what you're talking about."

"We have a photo of you sitting in a holding cell at Skillimer's Mall before the checkpoint you were held at was assaulted by an unknown force." He laid the picture of her sitting in a cell. Coming to another sheet, he shook it and slammed it in front of her. "And this is you being impaled by one of our Spider Tanks."

D glanced down and saw the picture of her face, trying to pull the leg out of her abdomen. She sighed, unbuttoned her shirt, flashing him. "I don't exactly see a scar."

He smiled and gave her a swift backhand across the face. She took a quick breath grabbing her cheek, as he stood back up.

"You fucking pig."

"We heard from one of our scouting parties." He turned away from her. She was tucking her legs up to her chest. "They encountered a woman entering a manufacturing plant. Supposedly she was only passing through, but after sending a soldier out to escort her across the facility, she was later spotted without that escort. The squad leader made the call to terminate her due to that fact alone, and had the squad open fire on her. I believe there was a confirmed shot on her back, between her shoulder blades. The squad then proceeded to approach to confirm that the target was down."

He slapped the folder down on the table, and leaned against it staring at her. "In less than fifteen minutes, the majority of that squad was killed by that single woman. The last one killed even called over the radio, saying that he had shot a burst into the target's back, and had her pinned down to the ground. The squad leader reported shots fired. And after waiting, spotted a woman walking out of the compound without a scratch." He was smiling leaning towards her. "I don't think those were two separate women."

D was staring ahead at him, hugging her knees.

"A few days ago we had a scouting group fail to report back. Since we hadn't heard any radio reports we assumed that they were either jumped, or they came across a particular scenario we had started to warn against."

He was sitting down judging her reaction. "We sent out a group, to search and found he had left behind a bread trail for us. They also noted a Prowler strangely in the area. We decided to send out a Spider Tank with a squad on board to follow that path, and they identified two individuals at the end of the breadcrumbs. They cornered one." He opened the folder again and pulled out another photo looking at it. "The other attempted to fire at the tank." He placed it in front of her. It was a little more blurry, but she knew who it was. Zecona. "Then, we lost contact with that group." He snapped the folder shut. "Do you know what our second squad found when investigating that location early this morning?"

"I have no fucking idea," she barked at him.

"The husk of a burned out tank." He was sitting down now. "Our tank. Burned from the inside. The pilot was ripped in half, his torso was found a few feet away from the tank. The three support units sitting inside had what appeared to be gunshots. Gunshots! Less than five feet away from each other, along with the pilot. Gunshots, facing each other in the cabin. While they were still buckled into their harness. Now I'll ask again. Who do you work for? And what are you trying to accomplish here?"

"You're fucking insane," D said staring at him. "I don't know what the fuck you're talking about."

He smiled at her and reached down to his belt, pulling out a five-inch long knife. "Why don't we cut off a finger and see what happens in an hour or two?"

D's eyes grew wide at the blade. He was studying her reaction. D wasn't intimidated by the pain.

"You're insane," D whimpered. "I swear I don't know anything."

"We'll see," he said lowering his gaze.

They were stared each other down.

As he stood, she kicked the table into his stomach. The table caught him as her chair flipped over. He was already making his way around the table. She scrambled up, slamming herself into the corner of the room.

"No," D let out a whimper. As she watched him eclipse the light, she shielded her hands in the corner. He reached down grabbing her. She wailed, frantically trying to remember what a cut felt like. She twisted her arm to get out of his grip. Grabbing hold of her wrist, he slammed it against the wall. Clawing at his wrist, she tried to pull it off.

"Please," she cried out.

He pried out her index finger. She felt the cold blade resting against her skin.

"Please!" D screamed.

He raised the knife above his head. Her eyes opened wider just as the door swung open.

"Sir," a soldier called from the doorway.

He glanced away from D for a second.

"Delta team picked up an Abot from the location you wanted."

D positioned herself and landed a solid punch to the Majors ball's. The Major gasped for breath turning back to her, as he lost his grip on her finger. Jumping up, she reaching for the knife. He slammed her back against the wall. The soldier at the door aimed the rifle at her. She tried to push him away, but he slammed the knife into her wrist.

"Fuck!" D felt her hand go limp. The knife had cut a tendon in her hand, and had embedded itself into the wall three inches deep.

"What were you saying?" the Major said, turning to the soldier.

"Delta team picked up an Abot from the location you suspected the War Devil was set up in," the soldier continued.

D's mouth was hanging ajar from the visualized pain. Tears were streaming down her face. The Major looked at her, grabbed his knife back, and said to the soldier, "Good, I have some matters to discuss with him."

D was clutching her wrist sinking to the floor. "You fucking pig." She forced out.

"Keep an eye on her." He said to the soldier as he walked out the door.

"You fucking pig!" She yelled after him as he closed it. The solder stood straight with his hand resting on the rifle.

***

Richard was listening to the convoy heading up the highway and ducked behind a burned-out car on the side of the road. Judging by the remaining details from Seawood's intel, this convoy would most likely be passing through the Central Division. He disintegrated down into his spider form and waited for the first truck to drive by. Watching the gunner seated pass by him, he sprinted out as the bumper from the second truck rode by and jumped onto the undercarriage of the truck; he wrapped his legs around the fuel line.

***

Zecona was sitting handcuffed with his hands behind his back behind a table. Two armed guards stood in the corners of the tent. Their names were embroidered on their pockets. Marcus Corbbin, and Kurt Seawood. The Major threw the flap open and tossed a folder onto the table. He glared at Zecona.

"Well, this is a shock."

"You're telling me," Zecona said, shaking his head.

As the Major opened the folder and began flipping through pictures, Zecona's left hand began to creep towards the tiny hole in his jacket where the hairpin was.

"Mind telling me what you were doing in that building this morning?"

"I don't know. What was I doing?" His tongue rubbed through his dry mouth.

"Don't be a smartass."

"I wasn't trying to be," Zecona shot back, as he felt the cold metal and began to slide it out.

The Major produced a picture and laid it face down. "We have dedicated scouts who not only spotted you leaving and entering that building but also spotted you along the rooftops for some particularly hot areas the other day. Now tell me. What were you doing there?"

"I was waiting on a friend," he said as he rubbed the hairpin around, feeling for the handcuff's mechanical lock.

"A friend?"

"Yes."

"On the roof of a building?"

The hairpin slipped into the keyhole, and he began to spin the internal tumbler by instinct.

"Yes."

"I see. And would you care to describe this friend of yours?"

"I'd rather not."

The Major reached down into his belt. "I don't think you fully understand the situation." He drew out a still-bloodied knife and stabbed it into the table.

Zecona's eyes widened at the sight of the blood on the blade. His hands froze as his heartbeat picked up and he fought to keep his breathing steady, shifting in his seat.

"Why were you waiting on your <u>friend</u>?"

"I-I..." Zecona coughed, "I don't know. That is, we didn't discuss it. He wanted t-t-o..." Zecona stared off for a second. "Well, you see. Let me start over, I'd been s-s-scouting out the area, and I was --"

"Shut up."

Zecona took a double take at him.

He grabbed the knife and pointed it at him. "You're lying through your goddamn teeth. If you keep it up, I'll cut them out of your fucking head."

"I wasn't --"

The Major flung the picture over at him. "You were waiting for her!"

Zecona glanced down and saw the photo of D getting impaled by the leg of the spider tank. He glanced back up and shouted. "No!"

"She came here to attack this base, with a bag of explosives, and you were waiting for her to return."

"You've got it all wrong! I don't even know who this is!"

"This isn't you?" He flung the other photo at him. Zecona could see him standing down the street aiming the rifle.

He lowered his head, sinking forward. "I'm in way over my head, " he said, lowering his eyes to the floor.

"Just talk, and this'll be over."

"What do you want to know?"

An alarm started sounding off in the distance.

The Major raised an eyebrow, grabbing the radio on his shoulder. "Central do you read me?"

Zecona returned his focus to the lock again and continued shifting the internal tumblers again.

There was no response. "Radio dead?" He said looking at the other two. He looked over his shoulder at the open flap. "Shit. Marcus, go figure out what's going on."

"On it," Marcus said, exiting the tent.

The Major turned his attention back to Zecona. "Who are you working for?"

Zecona glazed over for a second. "I thought that would have been obvious. The Federation?"

"Who else is a part of your squad?"

"If there was anyone else, do you think we would have been caught?"

He stared at him for a moment. "You're lying."

"No, I'm not." He felt the final tumbler fall into place, and the lock popped open.

"Then who the fuck blew up the tank?"

Zecona was frozen staring at him.

"You know what I think."

Zecona tensed up.

"I think you're an android." The Major scooped up the knife and glided his finger along the edge. Seawood flipped off the safety on his rifle when the knife was drawn.

"Why would you think a thing like that?" Zecona said, wide-eyed.

The Major plopped down a notebook. "I'm sure you know what this is?"

Zecona stared at D's notebook, his chest tightened before he locked eyes with the Major and said, "Yes."

"It's a fascinating read," he said. "It marks all the convoy routes, all the names of our maintainers, bases, and personnel. I have to admit, it's an impressive little book."

The Major dug into his jacket pocket. "We also found this in the bottom of one of your bags." He pulled out a solid smooth metal cylinder and placed it in front of him. "Seems like kind of a weird thing for a Federation soldier to be carrying around? I was hoping you knew what was inside."

Zecona's eyes bulged as he stared at the KILROX. "I have no idea."

He stood up and started to walk around Zecona. "I don't think there's going to be any way to get a straight answer from you."

Zecona didn't say a word. He yanked the hairpin out of the keyhole as The Major walked behind him.

"So why don't we test a little theory of mine?"

Zecona felt the blood draining from his face as he gripped the hairpin. "What did you have in mind?"

He was looking at Zecona's closed hands. "Which do you prefer? Just the tip? Or to the knuckle?"

Zecona's mouth hung open, as he processed the question.

"To the knuckle then!" he said dropping to the floor.

The flash of the blade snapped him to his senses, as he shouted. "It's a transmitter!" He ripped his finger from the Major's grasp.

The Major stopped and walked back around, embedding the knife back into the table, and locked eyes with him.

"We gathered information on paper, then use the War Devil to store and transmit the data through it!" Zecona admitted.

The Major stayed stoned faced. "Transmitted it to whom?"

"I assume the Federation," Zecona said. "B-But for all I know it could have been leaking information to the Overman Corporation. I wouldn't really know!"

"You're saying there's information stored on here?"

Zecona nodded. "Yep! Loads more than we could put on paper."

The Major stared at the smooth cylinder before smiling. "Thanks, you've been a big help."

An explosion sounded off outside, followed by a loud screeching sound cutting through the air. Instinct kicked in, and Zecona rolled to the floor, knocking the table over with the knife still firmly in place.

The Major bolted up. The guards instinctively raised their weapons.

"Shit!" The Major grabbed a hand radio. "Douglas, what the hell is going on out there."

He pointed to Seawood in the corner. "Get him to the underground."

Zecona grabbed the knife out of the table with his freed hands. The Major had already bolted out the opening. Seawood leaned down and said,

"Giovanni." As he gripped Zecona by the shoulder.

The knife flashed slicing through Seawood's hand, Zecona lunged at him knocking him back, hugging the barrel of the rifle beside him.

The rifle fired.

The recoil knocked the wind out of Zecona and he caught the look of terror in Seawood's eyes. They crashed through the side of the tent. He took another flash of the knife across his throat. Blood sprayed into his eyes.

Zecona fought through the stinging pain in his eyes, as his side went numb from the continued recoil of the barrel firing. He smashed the knife back onto the hand gripping the rifle, the bone crunched beneath the blade. Smashing it again, his mind could just make out the gunshots still sounding out. Slashing the knife again, they both hit the ground.

Seawood was coughing for air. Zecona pulled the rifle out of his grip. He tugged on it a couple of times before realizing the strap was still around the soldier and cut it. Holding the rifle, he stood over the motionless soldier. A blast of air tore through the camp.

"I'm sorry." His eyes still stung, as he tried to wipe the blood out of them. It didn't help. His knuckles where white as he gripped the rifle. He locked eyes on a group of soldiers taking cover behind a stack of creates, and raising their weapons towards him. Standing to run, he fired the first burst.

***

D was still gripping her wrist. Her hand and forearm were drenched in blood. The soldier was avoiding eye contact with her. She could feel movement coming back to her hand.

"I need to stop the bleeding," D said, looking up at the soldier.

He stole a quick glance at her, shifted his weight and continued looking at the door.

"Please, could you just rip a bit of my shirt off? I'd do it, but I need to keep applying pressure."

He glanced back at her, before walking towards her, kneeling down, and moved the rifle to his back.

"Could you just rip along the bottom so I'm not exposing myself to everyone?"

"Sure." He gripped it in his hands and started to rip. She was watching the rifle from the corner of her eye.

"He got you clean through didn't he?"

D smiled, rolled her eyes and muttered. "Yeah." He draped the cloth over her wrist.

"If you would," she said, "could you pull it tight? I can probably tie it by myself, but I need to get my hand out first."

He smiled and nodded. "I'll tie it for you." He pulled the fabric tight around her wrist with both hands.

"Thank you," she said moving her hand out of the way. He wrapped it a couple of times. Blood soaked through the cloth.

"Sometimes I think we forget who the enemy is in this war," he said

She shook her head, stealing a glance at the service pistol in his belt behind her wrist getting bandaged up. "Tell me about it."

He was tying up the bandage. "We're not all bad, but we do need to be careful." He smiled.

"Let me ask you something."

He glanced up at her as he finished, her arm fell to her side.

"When did fighting a war mean giving up your humanity?"

The smile faded as he stared off. His eyes glazed over looking past her for a moment. Her bandaged hand snapped forward before he could react, she had the service pistol in her hand, cocked and pointed at his chest.

"Hands up," she said. He threw his hands up. Pressing the barrel close to his temple, she took his knife strapped to his shoulder and maneuvered the strap of the rifle off his back. She leaned back nodding across the room and ordered, "To the door."

***

Richard scanned the inside of the compound. Picking his targets. The convoy bumped along. He primed his battery, feeling the surge of energy course through him. In a blue flash of light, he transformed still clinging to the fuel line of the truck. Hell Fire mode was active, and he felt his life slipping away from him as the metal he was clinging to began to glow orange.

The fuel line burst and the truck exploded around him. The rebel soldiers surrounding the road jumped out of the way for cover and drew their weapons, scanning the area. Blue light began to erupt from the burning wreckage, as the air began to scream in pain. The War Devil stood in the middle of roaring inferno. His sensors began calculating the most efficient means of eliminating over five-hundred targets.

CHAPTER SEVENTEEN
DEATH

Zecona fired off another burst of shots as he ducked between a pair of tents. A blast of blue light shot out over the tents. Followed by a sudden shockwave of hot air. The air cried out again behind him. Popping back towards the tall metal wall surrounding the compound, he searched for a gate, or a solid building, but found tents. Another blast rippled through the air, as he sprinted down a dirt road. Gunshots whistled above him, and he ducked between two more tents.

He skidded to a stop and searched the roads. Soldiers shouting around him echoed over the tops of the tents. Boots crunched along the road behind him. Sprinting again down another pair of tents, he opted to avoid whatever was exploding in the middle of the compound, while making his way to the skyscraper.

***

D pushed the soldier forward down the corridors with the assault rifle.

"You can't keep this up you know," he said.

She smiled. "I'm aware." She glanced over her shoulder. "Just watch the hall."

They were outside the Central mass storage for the Rebellion.

"You can't get in there you know," he said, staring at the door. "And I don't have access."

"Just keep watching the hall," D said.

"You can't hack it." He stared down the hall. "Computers somewhere else."

D wasn't paying attention.

He glanced back at her. She was sitting down on the floor. "What are you doing?"

"Just thinking of what I need to do next." She had the knife beside her in one hand with the rifle in the other.

"You could give yourself up now." He stared at her.

"Yeah. That's not going to help." She nudged the rifle back towards the hallway. "Eyes front."

He shook his head, staring back down the corridor.

Still aiming the gun at the soldier, she cut the knife along the side of her abdomen. Taking a deep breath feeling the familiar steel. She reached her hand inside feeling around for a second, then pulled out a black rectangular device.

She stood up. "Ok. I want you to walk down the hallway." She pressed the rifle to his back.

"Fine. Where are we going now?"

"Just walk," D said, shaking her head.

She let him walk forwards as she walked backwards, and put the MC into the key slot. It instantly recognized Marcus Greeves as one of the owners registered to the device. The door shot open and produced an audible ding. T

"No!" he yelled, out running towards her.

D fired the gun before the door closed. She knew she'd missed when she heard him beating on the door from the other side.

She spun the MC in her hand as she made her way to the central compositor. Holding it closer to her face, she scrolled through the choices, smiling as she made her selections. Hooking it up, she punched in multiple combinations. The machine whined, and gave a loud clunk in the offloading compartment.

D opened the hatch and took out her new gun. A long and slender gun, carrying a massive magazine, and a narrow barrel. It specialized in firing micro-grenades. Even though they were smaller than normal. They packed a much stronger punch.

She could carry more of them due to the size. The gun came with various modes. Single shot, burst shot, and assault. She generated five extra clips. Strapping everything to her coat, she also generated light Kevlar and ballistic armor for her torso and legs, as well as a helmet equipped with a scanner.

Suiting up, she put the extra grenades into a tactical bag she generated as well. D turned on the sensor and spotted a group of soldiers just outside her door. Turning towards the compositor, she generated one last thing. She didn't bother taking it from the hatch but activated it where it was. Grabbing the MC, she turned loading a round of armor-piercing explosives, and fired through the door.

The bullets didn't kill them, but the explosions did. Forcing the door open, she had to move fast. An alarm was sounding off. Turning down another corner, she saw another squad coming, and she fired another burst of micro grenades.

The timer on the bomb she'd left in the compositor finished. A wall of flames scorched the hallway behind her. The lights went out, and then sprinklers kicked on along with the red emergency lights. Another alarm replaced the old one. D sprinted through the downpour of blood-red water.

***

The soldier erupted into a burst of mist as the War Devil punched through the armored helmet. Evaporated blood and molten steel flew out in front of him. 237. The Fabric tents around him continued to erupt into a crazed fire as he rushed past them. Grabbing a revolver he fired 4 shots. 238, 239, and 239 fell.

He spotted a group running between a pair of tents. Liquid lead was splashing against him from all directions. As he ran towards them, he left a trail of molten earth with each footstep.

Cutting through a tent, it erupted into flames. A group turned and sprinted towards the road. The War Devil punched a metal pole, sending molten metal flying towards them to slow them. Everything was fading into a blinding mix of white figures running in a red fog as his sensors degraded. Half of a Spider Tank appeared less than a hundred feet away. He shot the group. 239-243. And turned his attention to the Tank. The ground shook around him from where it was firing, but the bullets did nothing to slow him down.

Jumping up, he smashed into the cockpit, and the armored glass shattered, melted, and exploded all at once. The Spider Tank bled liquid metal to the ground as it slumped over. The War Devil lost track of the pilot but assumed he was dead, and continued running over the top of the tank, jumping off the back.

More targets than he remembered were popping up around him. He punched the ground with his palm and generated another KRISER. His sensors had begun reaching their final limit, as he began to shoot at the ghost rising from the bodies around him.

***

The explosions and gunfire intensified around Zecona. There was much more movement taking place around him as soldiers were screaming and yelling orders as they scrambled down the roads. Vehicles tore past him, packed with armed soldiers. The fires in the compound were growing, and it was getting harder to avoid getting spotted. The blue light grew in size amongst the orange glows, but Zecona was running towards the skyscraper regardless. He wasn't even sure if he was even being chased anymore. That was when he caught a glimpse of the white glowing figure amongst a blue bubble.

He hesitated, staring at the figure, before sprinting in his general direction. If he could get Richard, maybe he'd have a shot at getting out of the compound alive. At that moment, something passed by the sun, but he was too busy popping between another pair of tents too look up at it.

***

A single trumpet was playing over the elevator speaker, it was a dull jazz number D didn't much care for given the situation. She had retraced her steps back to this elevator blowing everything up in between.

Her sensors on her helmet picked up multiple armed figures on the other side of the door along with multiple movements across multiple floors of the garage. She hugged the grenade launcher to her side.

The elevator doors opened.

A soldier stood staring straight at her, then turned pale when he saw the gun. She opened fire, and killed him. Running forward from the elevator, she focused firing at a line of vehicles.

D spotted the letter C painted red on the wall. Her Prowler was on Level B. Pulling the trigger, she shot at another group of guards, until she heard the round click. She tossed the empty magazine, grabbed another one out of her bag, and slammed it into place. Opening fire at another row of trucks in the garage, she sprinted up an incline towards Level B.

***

She spotted section 21, with her Prowler still parked. A gun popped up from behind another line of trucks and fired at her. It nicked her leg, she fired back, sending the truck flying back pinning the soldiers to the ground. Hobbling over to the Prowler, she slung her grenade launcher over her shoulder. D Jumped on the back and cranked it up, before whipping it backwards and peeling up the ramps to Level A.

D could see the light of the opening, but stopped before the final turn. A massive line of soldiers were lined up against the way out. Trucks blocked the entrance. The Prowler grabbed the ground, and she whipped it back towards the ramp to Level B as the line of soldiers started firing towards her. She sped back down the ramp. Another straggler on the lower levels had gotten into a truck, and was driving straight towards her. Jerking the controls, she turned away from crashing into him. A gunshot nicked the back of her hand.

She spotted the elevator, and aimed the Prowler towards it. More trucks from the top level barreled down the ramp behind her. D skidded to a stop in front of the elevator. Pressing the call button, she grabbed the grenade launcher from her back and started firing a long stream of grenades at the approaching trucks.

A spread of bullets ripped into her arm and abdomen. Bullets pelted at the Kevlar ripping holes, and cutting her skin, a bullet ripped through and bounced off the top of the helmet. D continued firing at the onslaught. The door dinged open, and she kicked the neutral Prowler into the elevator.

***

Covering her flank with micro grenades. Punching the close door button, she hugged the wall as another stream of bullets ripped past. A stray bullet punctured the paneling, and ripped through her throat.

The door closed, and was traveling up. She was coughing uncontrollably as blood dripped down into her lungs. Ripping apart the shirt under her Kevlar, she wrapped it around her neck. While she couldn't breath normally, she was well aware this didn't matter. Taking off the Kevlar, she suddenly realized how many shots had been fired at her. Parts of the Kevlar vest were embedded into her skin. Dropping the splintered armor beside her, she sunk to the floor holding her head. Looking up at the floor indicator, she watched the numbers climb up, before turning her sensors back on. Watching the people running amongst the floors above.

Floor 23 glowed on the damaged control panel. The elevator dinged signifying floor nine. Getting up, she turned the Prowler around, which turned out great deal more difficult than what she was expecting. Facing the door now, she hopped on, and leaned down low watching the people move. She kept an eye on the numbers as they continued to climb up.

Floor 18.

She armed another bomb, and threw it to the floor beside her beside her.

Floor 19.

She backed up the Prowler so it was touching the back wall.

Floor 20.

She revved the engine up.

Floor 21. She sunk her head low behind the glass.

Floor 22. She flipped it into neutral, and pressed hard on the gas.

Floor 23 floated into eye level. Multiple armed targets had taken aim at the doors. The elevator <u>dinged</u>. She switched the gear back to drive.

***

The doors opened as she sped out under a hail of bullets. She blew past them, with the explosion catching them off guard. A wall of fire rocketed behind her with the elevator falling back down the shaft. D crashed into a computer console on the other side of the room, jumped off, and pulled her grenade launcher off. Charred remains surrounded her.

The elevator across the room was dinging. Her eyes rose up to it. The one beside the one she had blown up was at 13.

D reached into her bag to grab another magazine, but froze. She was spent. Dropping the bag and the gun, she felt her neck, the hole was gone. Leaning back, she sank to the ground, untying the knot, and took a deep breath, then instantly hacked up more blood.

A flash of blue light lit up the room. She was staring at the elevator still intact. The number was going down. Another blue flash. Standing up, she moved towards the window, and recognized an energy storm outside. Climbing up on top of the console her heart sank as she saw the white glowing figure in the middle of it. A line of torn vehicles and bodies surrounded ground zero below.

The room was cast into a shadow. She glanced over towards the window and saw her way out. The Rasvelg was eclipsing the sun outside of window.

D kicked the Prowler from the wrecked equipment. The Rasvelg was still on level with her. Revving the engine, she stared across the bare floor at it. The number on the elevator flashed 20. She could hear the cables clattering behind the doors.

She revved the engine again. The Rasvelg still hadn't moved. It fired a missile at the ground. Her wheels were lined up perfectly to the window.

The elevator stopped at her floor. She flipped the engine to drive as the elevator dinged one last time. The doors flew opened. D raced across the floor, rifles shots at her, they cut across her back, hand and legs, her eyes were to focused on the Rasvelg. It moved forward firing another barrage of missiles as she smashed through the glass.

It felt as though a cord had snapped her off her Prowler, and then she was twisting through the air. Falling towards the world below, she watched the Rasvelg fall with her. Her head jerked to where the silver beacon was. The blast of heat caught her, but the bubble was gone. She couldn't see Richard anymore.

"Shit," she muttered. watching chunks of the building fall with the Rasvelg. The ground was racing to catch her. As she twisted, she stared up at the sky.

"Funny." D muttered.

She came to a halt as a pole tore through her abdomen.

***

The War Devil was surrounded by a bubble of super heated air, radiating air blasted from the epicenter. Hot blue flashes kicked out. Licking the carbon out of the air, he stripped the air of its oxygen. Igniting it in his wake. Liquid lead splashed against his armor like rain. He could sense the rebels, but could no longer see. His sensors engulfed in a blinding white of pure heat.

The War Devil could feel the air sucking into him. He was breathing. Breathing in a deep unending breath of carbon around him straight into his gun and sub systems, while firing a nonstop spread of bullets. The numbers or details didn't matter anymore.

His focus was in sustaining the gun, repairing the chamber, and resupplying the ammo chain.

A rocket blasted from behind, it hit near him, but the heat only cooled him. His mind couldn't react. Hearing another missile whistling through the air, he felt it tear him in half, and explode.

***

Zecona could see the War Devil glowing as he ran closer to him.

"Richard!"

The War Devil continued shooting the surrounding tents in front of him. Zecona had to stop a few hundred feet away. The heat was getting too intense for him to stand.

"Richard!" he cried out.

That's when the missile screamed through the air above him. He ducked behind a metal bin, and felt the heat ripple past him. Richard hadn't even reacted to the explosion. Zecona opened his mouth to shout something, but it was lost amongst the explosion of the second missile.

Richard was gone.

Zecona's mouth hung open as he stared ahead.

A sharp crash pierced the air as the blades hit the side of the building. He jerked his head up and watched the Rasvelg rip down the skyscraper. Hot air rushed past him from the explosion, as he stood their coughing for breath, with his hands covering his mouth. Then he registered a quick series of high-pitched clicks behind him.

With the force of a sledge hammer hitting his back, a cold sting rippled across his body. He was tired, and gasped for breath like he had a blanket wrapped over his face. Pain from the force shot through his lower body. Feeling warm and cold, he tried to focus on the smoke floating up as he closed his eyes.

He wanted to sleep, but he fought against it. He forced his eyes open. Coughing echoed around him. Something warm washed over his lips. Zecona griped the rifle, and felt warmth pouring down his arm. His stomach was numb. Zecona tried to stand, but stopped as the pain spread to his legs. He heard the coughing sputter with his breath. He was breathing liquid lead. His head hit the ground. Focusing on the column of smoke, he knew he was going to die.

He shook his head into the ground to keep his eyes open, but they grew heavier. It was growing colder. Pain shot up his arm. Sleep was winning the battle. Gripping the rifle tighter, he fought his eyes from closing, but it was a losing fight.

Then there was only darkness.

CHAPTER EIGHTEEN
DUST

D pulled herself off the pole she was impaled on, and fell to the ground. Brushing the dust off, she ran towards the fallen Rasvelg. Walking towards the burning wreckage, she stopped at the mountain of steel embedded into the building. The Prowler was gone.

Hanging her head low, her eyes widened, as she glanced back, scanning the area. The battlefield was partially melted and barren. Her eyes lingered over the mouth parking garage. It laid empty as well, and she almost wanted to move towards it. She kept scanning the field she spotted a familiar face lying on the ground. Cocking an eyebrow, she jogged over to his body. Zecona was cut open along the gut, the arm and wrist. Kneeling down beside him, she felt a weak pulse.

D scanned the ground below. Richard was gone. A new idea began to grip her. Spotting the red cross painted on the flap of a tent, she bolted towards it. Gunfire sounded off in the distance as she threw open the flap.

No one in sight.

She grabbed hold of some scrubs, threw them over her clothes, and snapped a medical mask over her face. Taking an empty stretcher, she ran back across the empty space back to Zecona's body.

Lowering it, she dropped beside Zecona with stretched out hands and paused. A fear itched at the back of her mind. Jerking him by herself could cause more internal damage. She shook the thought away, and grabbed hold of him under his shoulders, pulling him.

He let out a cry as his eyes shot open. Ignoring him, she pulled his torso onto the stretcher. D scrambled around him as he passed out, and moved his legs onto the stretcher. She slung the rifle over her shoulder as she lifted the stretcher back up, and ran back towards the medical tent.

D had him in an open area in the back of the tent, savaging through cabinets and boxes searching for anything. Needles, thread, gauze, tape, staplers.

She studied Zecona's bullet ridden body as she laid out the instruments. The golden hour was ticking by. D only had twelve Abot patients during her career. Three required surgery due to complications from fractured bones.

D snapped a respirator over his mouth to make sure he was getting enough oxygen. Racing over the fact she had to keep the pressure on the area, she started with the gut and cleaned the area to see where the source of blood was coming from. Her mind barked out to nurses not standing beside her.

"Keep the pressure on that artery."

"Watch the arm, he'll bleed out."

"Ok. Hold it. Right there."

D placed clamps over the blood vessels to stop the bleeding, then stitched them up. Time ticked along. Despite blood soaking her latex glove, she wiped her head, and smeared his blood across her forehead. She stitched and stapled him back together.

She hooked him up to a blood generator, and after a quick analysis, it began generating a pint for him. Securing the gauze over the trouble area's, she taped it down.

Everything she could have done, was done.

Scanning the vials beside her, she grabbed a vial of morphine and a spare needle. D gripped the syringe at eye level and after pushing out the access air, she injected his arm with the pain killer.

Throwing the gloves away, she washed her face and hands at the wash station. She grabbed a chair, and pulled it up to Zecona. The clock ticked by, and she listened to him breathe.

Two minutes had passed and grabbed him by the collar of his shirt and said,

"Can you hear me?"

Zecona blinked his eyes, trying to focus. She snapped her fingers next to his ear, then patted his cheek. "Hey. Can you hear me?"

Zecona nodded.

"Where's Richard?"

Zecona shrugged, "I don't know."

D's eyes widened. "What was the last thing you remember? What happened?"

Zecona waved his hand at her, she backed away as he sat up. "Richard went to meet with his informant. Squad picked me up at Delta."

D was still staring at him. "He was with you right?"

"No, like I said, he was meeting his informant. He was out there. Got blown up."

It hit her then. She held her head in the palms of her hand and was muttering under her breath with her back to him, pacing back and forth.

She sat down on the edge of the chair.

"Thanks," Zecona said,

D wasn't looking at him. Her eyes glazed over. She was covering her mouth. Standing up, she shoved a medical trolley over and yelled out, "Shit!" She paced the row of beds with her head darting around, before her eyes locked onto his, "Any ideas?"

Zecona didn't say anything.

"Didn't think so." D sat back down on the Cot. "Didn't fucking think so."

She stared back out the tent again. "I-I," she said sitting up, then slumped back down, shaking her head. "It doesn't matter anymore." Glancing around one last time, she locked eyes with Zecona.

"What's the plan?" he said.

She stared past him. "Race into the face of death. See who blinks." D took a deep shallow breath. "There's a garage near here. We won't be able to make it out on foot. If we can get a hold of a truck, we can drive out of here," she said, nodding. "If there's anything in there, it'll be full of soldiers." She stared out of the tent. "Full of em"

D stood. "Sit tight. I'll be back."

He stared at her, "I'm not coming with you?"

"I did the best I could, but you're not ready for anything extreme." She stared at the rifle. "I'm going to try and find Richard, then I'll try to get a truck from the garage, and then come back for you."

Zecona shook his head. "What am I suppose to do in the mean time?"

"I don't know. Just sit tight." She grabbed the rifle.

"You're taking the gun too?"

She nodded. "What the hell are you going to shoot? There's no one around."

Zecona shook his head. "Take Richard's gun. I'm a sitting duck in here."

D handed him the rifle. "Don't make me regret this."

***

D ran through the burnt and mangled bodies of rebel soldiers. A flash of sun reflected by a piece of metal sticking up caught her attention. A silver arm was sticking out from beneath a pile of ash. Running towards it, she grabbed hold of it and dragged out Richard's torso and head from the rubble. The entire lower body was missing.

She slapped the helmet. "Hey!" D called out, "Can you hear me?"

Electric screeches and pops came out from behind the crescent moon eyes. Richards hand twitched. Shaking her head, she turned and spotted a silver boot heel sticking up. Running towards it, she dug through the ash, and dragged the lower portion of his body out. She pulled the two portions of the body together and knelt down beside him. Popping open Richard wrist revealed a distorted screen.

Before she could select anything, there was a sudden snap of metal as the metallic spine clipped together, and a quick jet of steam that shot out. Richard was moving his arms. He tried to stand, but tripped over.

"Hold it there buddy." She caught him, sitting him down.

"Ra-Ra-Rasvvvelg?" Richard shot out.

"It's destroyed."

"Wh-Wh-Where. G-o."

"Garage," she said. "We're going to the garage, it's the only way we can get out of here fast enough. Are you good to walk?"

"I-I-I can-n-n walk." Richard sat up.

D was scanning the ground around them again, but she couldn't find his rifle. "Right," she said, "time to leave." She scooped down and grabbed Richard by the shoulder, supporting him as they stood.

***

They inched towards the garage. Nobody was stationed at the front of it. D was dragging Richard along. There was only a single row of military trucks along the back. The sound of the alarms echoed in the garage.

Richard tripped in her arms and fell, dragging her with him.

"Hey!" She slapped his helmet. "Kick in your auto-repair system." A speaker squirked somewhere in him.

"He can't," a deep voice said behind her. She spun around, but a hand caught her by the jaw and tossed her to the ground. The Major was standing there.

"Stand up."

She kept her eyes on the Major, watching him tower over her.

"I said stand up," he boomed again.

She got up from the ground.

***

315

The soldier pressed the gun to her temple. There were five of them. Two had rifles aimed at Richard. The Major nodded over his shoulder. "Toletto. Go pick up the Abot."

Toletto nodded, and ran towards the road.

The Major jerked his head towards Richard. "Bring that along." He grabbed D's arm twisting it behind her and pushed her deeper into the garage. They walked towards a support beam, and the Major threw her against it. D caught herself, and turned back towards him smiling.

"I want chains," he said into the radio on his shoulder still glaring at her. "Chains, gasoline, and a couple of flame throwers." An inaudible buzz screeched over the radio. "I'm south of camp. In position 64, 53." Another buzz. "Then tell them to call it back!" he shouted. "There's no sense in nuking the base over a broken robot."

D was still smiling at him, leaning her back against the column. A distant gun shot pierced the air outside the garage.

"Is it on?" He turned towards Richard.

"We believe so sir," one of the soldiers said.

"Good." He stared down at Richard. "Perhaps, you could help me understand." He started, pausing as he glared at him.

Richard stayed quiet, covering the gaping hole in it's abdomen.

He smiled and chuckled. "I've talked to your comrades, to try and get a straight answer, but honestly they haven't been exactly helpful."

D lowered her head.

"Perhaps you could explain exactly why Overman is here?"

D laughed, still staring at the ground.

The Majors face shot to boiling red, as he spun towards her. She was still laughing as he grabbed her against the shoulders and slammed her head against the beam.

"Shut up!" he screamed.

She was laughing harder staring into his face. He slapped her. As D grabbed her cheek, the laughter faded away. She stared back into his eyes, smiling. "Since you asked nicely."

He slammed her back into the column. The Major spun back towards Richard, and shouted, "Why the fuck is Overman here?"

Richard could just make out the hazy gray figures against a gray muddy background. Every sensor in his head was busted, leaving him with a hollow windy noise to accompany the sharp shrill sounds of voices.

"Why wouldn't we?" a crackle popped out from the helmet. From his sensors, he could make out a gun pointed at him, but it didn't much matter to him in the long run. He could just pick up D. That much mattered to him.

"Why wouldn't you." The Major said wit a smirk. "I have--"

Richard cut him off. "Why is this such a shock? Wasn't Overman's involvement the cause of this war to begin with? Wasn't that the point of this bullshit? Federation dealings with the Overman Corporation? Wasn't that the f-f-fucking issue?"

He aimed his gun at Richard. "Are you working with the Federation then, or is this a part of an Overman operation?"

Cackly static started ringing through his helmet. "Are you trying to threaten me with death?" Richard said, tilting his helmet at him.

He paused aiming his gun at D.

Richard said, "Both." He couldn't see the Major's facial expression, but he had been quiet for too long.

"We're aiding in the goals of the Federation, while pursuing our own."

"And what would that be."

"Control. Our strategy is a diversion on multiple fronts. We've gathered individuals displaced, and picked up by the Federation. We develop clones, and enlist them as Mercenaries, augment them with our current tech, and grant them access to our Database. We send them back here to the area's they predominantly resided to weaken the Rebellion. But that's not where the real power of the Overman is, these are the foot soldiers. The real damage comes from the Silver Gecko's. They've been present within the Rebellion since first contact with the Federation. It was predicted that our presence would instantly ignite a rebellion. We've had the analytical capability of pinpointing who would construct the plans for rebellions, who the major players would be, and who would be the most influential towards them. But then again, we also know that Overman's arrival were merely an excuse for the Rebellion. Our Agents were well in position once the Rebellion began executing it's plan. They've been feeding information directly to the Mercenary groups we have been forming to widdle away the interior of the resistance, while the Federation pushes with it's own forces."

The Major smiled, "If Overman was so capable of pinpointing our forces before the war even broke out. Why didn't they stop it before it began?"

"Because that wasn't our goal."

"And what was your goal?"

"I don't know," Richard said.

An image of Ada popped into his head, she wasn't wearing a smile, and her mouth was moving at a fast pace, but he couldn't make out what she was saying.

A vein was popping out of his neck. "You honestly think I'm going to buy the fact, that Overman was capable of analyzing an entire civilization, in a matter of days, seamlessly replace people without that even begin noticed? Especially when we were capable of subduing a walking hulk of twisted metal? I'll blow her fucking head off if you don't tell me what I want."

"Then we're at a crossroads."

"I don't buy that," the Major said, shaking his head. He reached into his pocket and pulled out the KILROX. "And I think it has to do with this." He held it up close enough to where Richard could make out exactly what it was. "Now you can save me a lot of time, if you could just open this for me."

"N-not a good id-idea." Richard said, as he started kickstarting his auto-repair systems.

"And why's that?"

"Be-ecause of the hi-voltag-ge fusion batter-ry built insidde. It's set up too break car-carbon bonds in a quarter meter radius."

The Major shook his head. "Then I'll tell my boys to be real careful when they pop it open."

Three more soldiers came into the building, one clanged forward with chains wrapped around his shoulder caring a gas canister. Another had the flamethrower strapped to his shoulders.

The Major eased the gun to his side, and nodded to the soldiers towards D. She kept smiling as sweat rolled down her cheek.

"Fine," the Major said, lowering his head. The soldiers grabbed hold of D, wrapping the chains around her.

D started to laugh again.

"That's just..." he brushed the hair away from his face, "fucking fine with me." He grabbed the knife from his belt, spun towards D, and impaled the knife into her left side.

She laughed harder, straining to keep her eyes on him, and not to look past him to the front of the parking garage.

One of the soldier's eyes widened and he turned his head to look away and closed them tight. A sickening thud of bloody ground meat hit the ground. He gagged, and swallowed back the vomit. Her laughter was shallower. The Major held the knife firmly in his hand.

D was leaning against the chains tied against her chest, laughing in his face. He took the knife, and impaled a lung. She coughed, but continued to laugh, coughing harder, blood was running out of her mouth. Grabbing the gas canister, he poured it over her head. Gasoline, blood, sweat and tears were running down her face, but she kept laughing in his face.

The Major's face flared up as he glared at her. "Give me the flamethrower," he whispered under his breath. When nobody reacted fast enough, he yelled out, "Now!"

A soldier to his left jumped and unstrapped it from around him, slinging it around the major's shoulders. D's eyes were closed, she was laughing low under her breath, her chin was pointed right at his face. The Major struck a match against the hilt of the knife.

Flames spread across her clothes. Her laughter grew as she felt the flames dancing over her skin. Opening her eyes again, she stared right at him. The laughter grew with the flames.

The Major kicked on the flamethrower, sending a jet of flame over her body. It wrapped around her like wings, as her skin bubbled, popped, and melted down. The flames were roaring in her ears, and she roared with laughter along with it. She could feel the chains sinking into her skin. A patch of skin fell off her.

Richard struggled to get his auto-repair systems functional. All of the soldiers around him were all gawking around the light that was D. Motor functions were coming back to his hands, and arms. Transmitting signals had a way to go.

D arched her back and pushed against the chains as the heat tore into her. Her eyes melted away from her face. The laughter morphed into a blood curdling inhuman scream as the flames began to dance inside her mouth, and melted away her vocal cords.

"David!" The Major nodded to a soldier. "Get one of those trucks started up. We need to move that thing to a secure area before its repair systems are fully repaired." He tossed the flamethrower.

The truck started up, and the Major lit up a cigarette glancing at the group. He blew out a stream of smoke furrowing his eyebrows as he counted the people around him. Richard felt his radio controls kick in. David slammed the truck door close, and walked towards Richard.

The Major double checked the faces around him. "Hey. Has anyone seen Toletto?"

Gunfire rippled across the parking garage. Two soldiers of the group fell. Richard shot out a wireless signal.

The Major yelled out, "Shit. Get Be--" The KILROX cut him off as it ripped him in half.

Richard popped open the compartment in his leg, grabbed a pistol, and pointed at David who was pinned down behind the truck. David snapped the barrel of his shotgun as he watched the pistol fly out. His speakers barked as the shotgun blast tore through him, he fired back blowing a quarter of David's head off. A liquid began shooting out of the hole blown through him. More bullets flew around Richard.

The two remaining soldiers spun around. Richard fired off another shot from the pistol, nicking one in the shin. Another spread of gunfire ripped through the parking garage striking the other across the chest.

The last soldier dove across the ground, attempting to scramble behind cover, but Richard shot him in the head. Richard slumped forward, overriding the repair system away from his gears to focus on his sight. His trigger finger continued firing at the soldiers on the ground.

Zecona was still crouched behind the half concrete wall outside the garage. Watching and listening for any signs of movement from the bodies scattered along the ground. The gun was clicking from the empty magazine, but Richard kept trying to fire. Besides that and the painful whining from Richard's gears, nothing else was making a sound.

Zecona hobbled across the garage, keeping an eye on the mangled bodies, before grabbing hold of the Richard's gun. The radio kicked on. "Sir, they won't turn the bird around until they hear verification from you that the War Devil is contained."

Zecona's eyes shot open.

"Sir, can you hear me?" Dead air.

"Richard," Zecona said standing over him.

"Major, please respond. The bird is in the air to deliver the package. Please verify the War Devil is still contained."

Richard was collecting himself off the floor.

Zecona snapped his head to him. "Richard, if you can tap into that line, and, I don't know, mimic his voice, or whatever, just call off the nuke!"

"Can anyone please respond?" the voice cried.

As Richard stood up, he kicked onto the radio signal. His voice was still staticy, and was still blipping with digital artifacts. But Zecona, and everyone on the radio frequency could hear the message. "I am death. Destroyer of worlds."

"The fuck is wrong with you?" Zecona blurted.

"Change to Frequency HABO 2!" Someone yelled.

Richard scanned the area and spotted a cloth cover over a box of crates on a truck. He hobbled over to it, clutching his abdomen, and ripped the cover off.

"What are you doing?" Zecona said gasping for breath. "We have to go. Now!"

Richard gave up holding back the liquid spilling out of him, and focused on breaking D's chains.

Zecona was still gripping the rifle to his side. "Did you hear what I said? Come on, let's go!"

D was a hollowed blackened corpse dangling amongst the chains. Most of her skin and muscle had melted off, and had slid over the metal links.

Richard was holding D's body in both arms. The white liquid was running down his legs. He didn't say anything. His vision was fading to static, everything sounded hollower. Zecona was looking around the garage. He spotted the long military truck parked still running, ready to roll.

"Richard!" he yelled back at him.

Richard was still hobbling forward holding D's body close to his.

"There's a truck," Zecona said between breaths. "Move it!"

Richard stopped walking.

Zecona ran over towards him. He noticed the cracks in the helmet. Grabbing hold of his arm, he lead him over to the truck. The motors in the war devils body whined with each step.

Zecona stopped guiding him as he opened the passenger door. Richard turned towards the back of the truck with D's body.

"She's dead," Zecona said, staring after him. "Leave her behind. We need to go."

The War Devil kept limping towards the back. Zecona followed and opened the back for him. Richard put a foot up, but felt it slip with a jolt when he applied pressure.

Zecona glanced up, then held up his hand, under his arm. "Come on."

He took Richard' weight, feeling the shooting pain from the busted stitches. Blood was soaking his bandage. Richard laid D's body across multiple seats in the back, and made his way to the passenger seat. Zecona slammed the door shut, and ran up to the driver side.

"G-g-ive" Richard choked out. "Me- the- Ri-i-i-fle"

Zecona climbed up and closed the door. "What the hell are you going to shoot? You can't fucking see."

"J-j-j-st, d-d-d-drve," Richard motioned for the rifle.

Zecona glanced over at him. "Fine." he handed him the rifle. Richard leaned against the door holding the barrel of the assault rifle out the window.

Zecona slammed it into reverse hitting a Humvee behind him. He kicked it back into drive and sped out of the garage. Pushing the petal to the floor, he rammed the 150 ton truck 40 miles an hour through the chain linked gate. They smashed through the concrete barricades blocking the road at 70 miles an hour.

Zecona didn't let up on the gas pedal. Looking back in the mirror, he saw the silhouette of the plane flying behind them.

The speedometer climbed past 100 as buildings and intersections flew past them. The shimmer of the bombs silver shell hit the sun as it made its descent.

Zecona's body flew up as the truck jumped over a crater in the road. Richard sat motionless beside him.

The bomb was halfway to the ground. 200 MPH. He saw the T-bone intersection ahead, along with the guardrail. His knuckles turned white.

A bright blue flash of light engulfed the mirrors. The tower they had been at twist in the wind like a paper bag.

Zecona sat weightless as the truck ripped through the guardrail. Knuckles locked, the wheels spun helplessly in the air. The ground slam into them. His mouth slammed into the steering wheel. Richard was thrown beneath the dashboard. He heard the explosions of a couple of tires.

He locked his arms back sitting straight up, and held his foot to the gas. The onboard AI components corrected and maintained controls of the remaining wheels. 300 MPH on another stretch of road. Zecona was met with the black ash of the mushroom cloud behind him, as blue light faded from the mirrors. Easing up, he coasted along watching the bloated black mass grow and climb higher into the sky.

After being on the road for thirty minutes, Zecona straightened up in his seat, glancing over at Richard. The auto-repair systems were fast at work. His armor had eaten away part of the door beside him, and the chair was dissolving below him. He shuddered at the sound of D's body bouncing around in the cabin every time they hit a bump.

It was late when Zecona pulled in front of Delta Base.

"Why are you stopping here?" Richard said, turning to him. "This area's been compromised."

"It's all we have left," Zecona said opening the cabin door. Richard stood up, He was still hunching over, and hobbling, but Zecona didn't notice the gears winding. Zecona walked to the front door of the building, Richard opened the back, carrying D's body with him.

"What's the point?" Zecona said staring at him.

"We head out in the morning," Richard said, carrying her body through the front door.

Zecona sat there for a moment looking up the street, before getting up, closing the back door to the truck, and heading up the stairs. D's body was lying on a cot. He sat down on his cot and glanced at Richard standing at the window. They didn't say anything. Zecona's head was spinning.

Richard looked back and saw the blood soaked bandage. He reached out his hand to a wall and materialized a first aid kit from it, before kneeling down beside him. Zecona could hear a ringing in his head, as Richard was taking off the bandage D had put on.

"What now?"

He opened up the kit and pulled out a syringe. "We've received our next assignment. We'll move out in the morning." He inserted the needle and pushed down the plunger.

"That's it? We just move on?"

"Mission accomplished," Richard said. He was stitching up his arm.

It didn't feel like it. Richard wrapped a new bandage on the arm. He collapsed onto the cot. It didn't matter anymore.

"What was that back there?" Zecona said turning his head towards Richard.

"What?"

"You are death?" Zecona said.

"That was the best option."

Zecona just stared at him.

"If I had mimicked the Major's voice, we'd have an extraction team on us, and maybe even soldiers swarming the city to look for us. If I said nothing, it's possible that they would have still nuked us anyways, but I had to be sure they knew we were still there, and that the squad was dead. They're going to avoid the fallout for at least a short while, before they even attempt any sort of search through the area."

Zecona just shook his head. "And what if I didn't get us out of there in time?"

Richard shrugged. "My vital components can survive a small nuclear blast."

"Oh." Zecona nodded his head. "Great. I was worried." Zecona closed his eyes and rested his head on the pillow.

"Don't fall asleep just yet." Richard grabbed a cup of liquid from his kit. "Drink this."

Zecona took a sip and coughed.

"Drink all of it."

Zecona downed all of it, holding his head, staring at the ceiling. He was sweating, but was asleep in minutes. Richard was sitting beside him watching his vitals. He stood up, patting Zecona on the shoulder saying, "You did good."

***

Zecona woke up. The morning sun was diminished by the smart windows lining the halls. Staring up at the ceiling, he soaked in the silence around him, and the stiffness of the cot underneath him. He glanced over to D, and sprang up. Her pale skin clung to the bones intact, and didn't have a trace of hair anywhere. She glanced over.

"What the fuck are you staring at?"

"You're alive!"

"No shit."

"Are you alright?"

She sighed and stared back towards the ceiling.

Richard walked in the room, and tossed some cloths on D's cot. She glared at him.

"Is that any way to treat a friend?" Richard said,

"Couldn't just leave me."

"What do you mean?" Richard said, holding out a cup of coffee. "You're effectively dead. Regardless what happens with the contract, I have no intention of informing my contacts you made it. You're effectively free."

"But a renegade."

"But alive."

"Why would you do that?"

"I had a change of heart." He turned to Zecona, "As long as you're willing to keep this detail from the Federation."

Zecona shrugged. "I can keep a secret."

She tried to read his hollow eyes, before she took the cup. "Thanks." she strained a smile.

Richard opened his thighs and pulled out her lighter. "Thought you might still need this." He set it on the ground. She draped the shirt over her shoulders. Hesitating, she scooped and grabbed the lighter. "What, no cigarettes?"

"I didn't have enough room to carry everything."

She shrugged, feeling her finger along the engraved <u>D</u>. "Thanks."

He didn't say anything.

"When are you leaving?" She smiled.

"Immediately."

The smile fell. "That's a damn shame. Things were just getting interesting." She crossed her arms. "What will you two be doing?"

Richard looked over at Zecona, "I believe I need to get him back into contact with the Federation. I've been given orders to simply be present at a location this evening."

Zecona stared out the window, then glanced at her. "What'll you do?"

She gave out a short laugh "I haven't a fucking clue." she said, shaking her head, "No fucking clue." Her eyes fell to the ground. Richard stared at the wall Zecona stared outside.

"I think I'm going to grab a set of wheels, and head west."

"What's west?" Zecona said glancing over at her.

"I don't know. Nothing is?" She was flicking her lighter open and close. "I'll just travel around for a bit. Might get back into practicing."

Zecona blinked. "Practice what?"

She looked up at him, flipped the lighter close, and shook her head at him.

Zecona was still staring at her. "Mind if I ask you one more question?"

She cocked an eyebrow with her eyes still locked on the lighter. "Depends."

"What's your name?"

D shifted her eyes and met his.

"I mean before the war?"

She sunk her eyes back down. "It's D." She felt along the engraving. "It's always been D."

Richard was still analyzing the memory of Ada. The memory didn't line up with any other memory. No associated time stamp. It simply existed. Her white eyes burned into him as her mouth sped along between the words without a smile.

Ada's disembodied voice broke through the silent memory. "I don't care what your interpretation of the situation was. When I sign off on a contract, I expect you to fulfill that contract to the best of your ability."

Richard had turned his crescent moon eyes to D.

Zecona smiled, "Let's take a picture!"

"What?" D glanced up, Richard snapped his attention him.

"To remember this."

"Why the fuck would I want to remember you?" she said

Zecona smiled at her. He glanced at Richard "You have a spy camera, right?"

"I do."

"Great." He jumped off his cot, and grabbed D.

"The fuck?" She stared at him. Richard stuck the camera to the wall.

"Be sure to give a great big smile!" Zecona said.

"I never smile," D said.

"You smile all the time." Richard said getting beside Zecona

"You aren't smiling," D said to Richard.

"I don't have a face."

"I don't have any hair. That's no excuse."

The camera beeped. Zecona gave a big smile. D smirked. Richard crossed his arms. The flash went off.

"What the hell kind of spy camera beeps and flashes when it goes off?"

"You didn't smile," Zecona said.

She scowled at him. Richard grabbed the camera off the wall, and started forming blue light. Three separate pictures formed. "Here, one for each of us."

D looked at her picture, "See. I smiled. Happy?"

"That's not a smile, that's a smile!"

"Ya know what? Maybe I shouldn't have brought you back."

"Admit it," Zecona said "You'll miss us when we're gone."

"No. I won't. I'll burn this picture when you're not looking."

"See. The fact that you'll do it when I'm not looking shows you care."

"It's time to go," Richard said.

"Already?" Zecona turned to him.

"We need to head north a ways to the extraction point. It'll take a while."

"Ok." He turned towards D and stretched his arms out. She put her arm out. "Whoa?"

"I want a hug?"

"You ain't getting a damn hug!"

"But this'll probably be the last time we see each other."

"Fine. You get a handshake." She grabbed his hand and shook it firmly. "You whiny ass little shit."

Zecona smiled, and walked out the door. Richard went to follow him. D stepped in front of him and threw her arms around him, ignoring the spikes covering his armor.

"Thank you," she said.

They were motionless for a moment. He patted her on the shoulder. "Don't get yourself killed."

She smiled. "I won't." She put the lighter in her pocket, and they both walked towards the lobby. Zecona was staring at them from the top of the stairs.

"Were you crying?" Zecona said, staring at D

"Mind your own damn business," D said.

He smiled and walked down the stairs.

"I fucking hate him." She looked straight at him.

As they walked through the front lobby she turned to Richard and said. "Do you know who you'll be working for?"

"Yes. Ada Coronis."

D froze, wide-eyed in the doorway watching him walk down the small set of stairs out the front of the building. Her mouth was dry as she felt the words slip away from her. "I'm so sorry."

Richard glanced back at her. "Why's that?"

She shifted her attention across the road. "You know, they'll keep fighting," D said, studying the far row of shattered buildings. "You can't tame the human spirit."

Richard studied her expression, before saying, "I think we already have." He followed her gaze across the horizon.

D remained silent, watching the wind whip across the overgrown trees taking up the parking lot. Nodding, she gave a short salute. "Later, boys." They waved back.

She walked back inside. Richard turned into his spider form and clung to Zecona's wrist. Zecona walked under the rising sun.

www.ingramcontent.com/pod-product-compliance
Lightning Source LLC
Chambersburg PA
CBHW070211260626
47160CB00002B/522